Murder
Served Cold

Paula Williams

www.darkstroke.com

Discover us online:
www.darkstroke.com

Find us on instagram:
www.instagram.com/darkstrokebooks

Include **#darkstroke** in a photo of yourself
holding his book on Instagram and
something nice will happen.

To my Mum, who was responsible for my lifelong love of crime fiction by introducing me to Agatha Christie when I was 12.

This one's for you, Mum.
Wish you were here to read it.

Acknowledgements

My thanks are due to my family for listening to my ideas and supplying some of their own. In particular to my husband for being on this journey with me and trying not to look too worried when I come up with new and exciting murder methods. Thanks, too, to the readers of my blog at paulawilliamswriter.wordpress.com for sharing my journey towards publication.

A big 'cheers!' to the landlord and regulars at my local pub for providing me with such a rich source of material (much of which has found its way into this book!) and who bear no resemblance whatsoever to the landlord and regulars of the Winchmoor Arms. (The beer's a lot better for a start!)

Thanks too, to my fellow authors at Crooked Cat Books/ darkstroke who have been so generous in sharing their knowledge with this newbie and to my lovely editor Alice and her patience with All Those Capital Letters that I used with Such Abandon!.

You have all played a big part in making my dream come true. But the biggest thank you of all has to go to Steph and Laurence at Crooked Cat Books/darkstroke for believing in me and without whom none of this would have happened.

About the Author

Paula Williams has been writing since she was old enough to hold a pencil but she's been making up stories since she was old enough to speak, although her early attempts were more of the "It wasn't me, Mum, honest. It was him" genre.

Her first 'serious' effort was a pageant she wrote at the age of nine to celebrate St George's Day. Not only was she the writer, but producer, set designer and casting director, which was how she came to have the title role. She also bullied and blackmailed her three younger brothers into taking the supporting roles, something they still claim to be traumatised by.

Many years later, this pageant became the inspiration for her first publishable short story, *Angels on Oil Drums*, which she sold to the UK magazine *Woman's Weekly*. Since then she's had over four hundred short stories and serials published in the UK and overseas. She also has a number of novels in large print which are available in libraries.

With the changing face of the magazine market, Paula now focuses her attention on her first love, crime fiction and is busy planning and writing a whole series of Much Winchmoor mysteries. She is a proud member of both the Crime Writers' Association and the Romantic Novelists' Association. She also writes a monthly column, *Ideas Store*, for the UK writers' magazine, *Writers' Forum* and for the last five years has written the pantomime for her local village Theatre Group. She still hasn't run out of things to write about and is waiting for someone to invent the thirty hour day.

She has two grown up sons, two beautiful daughters-in-law and three gorgeous grandchildren. She lives in Somerset with her husband and a handsome rescue Dalmatian called Duke who is completely bonkers and appears frequently on her blog. (The dog, not the husband!)

Murder Served Cold

Chapter One

It's not quite true to say that nothing ever happens in the small Somerset village of Much Winchmoor. Back in 1685, the notorious Judge Jeffreys hanged a couple of villagers from the large oak tree that used to stand by the pond, for their part in the Monmouth Rebellion. Their sorry remains were left there as a grim warning to anyone who might be tempted to take up arms against the King.

It must have worked because no one in the village has taken up arms against the King or anyone else since then. Although, in recent memory, the vicar came pretty close when John Manning's cows got into the vicarage garden and trampled his prize begonias a week before the village Flower and Produce Show.

Apart from that, Much Winchmoor was as quiet – and some would say, as dull – as the grave.

But all that was about to change. Because someone in Much Winchmoor had murder on their mind. One carefully planned, undetectable murder. They spent most of their waking moments thinking about it, planning it, imagining what life would be like before, during and after. Especially after.

It was a shining beacon of light in a life made dark by constant frustrations and disappointments.

Murder was easy. Once you'd worked out how to do it. And, more to the point, how to get away with it.

***

You know, once you start thinking about committing murder, it's kind of hard to stop. And then again, why stop at just the one? I'd start with Ratface, of course. After all, if it wasn't for him I wouldn't be in this position. Off men for life and up to my ears in hair spray and perm lotion, with my jaw so firmly clenched, my teeth were in danger of fusing together.

But Ratface could wait. Elsie Flintlock had just worked her way to the top of my hit list.

For the last hour and a half, I'd put up with the members of the Much Winchmoor Grumble and Gossip Group picking over my love life (or lack of), my job prospects (or lack of) and my humiliation at being forced to return to live with my parents at the age of twenty-three. But Elsie Flintlock was the straw that had just broken this camel-cum-would-be-serial-killer's back.

I stared down at the thin, crêpey neck, stretched invitingly across the basin in front of me. It was so tempting. Just one quick movement. That was all it would take. Of course, I'd have to be careful to make it look like an accident. It was a risk but, I reckoned, one worth taking.

"Come on, Katie. Stop day dreaming," Mum called sharply, as if reading my mind. "You haven't been away so long you've forgotten how to shampoo, have you?"

"And you watch what you're doing with that water, young lady," Elsie Flintlock glared up at me, her beady little eyes sharp and challenging, her wet head looking like a gone-to-seed dandelion that had got caught in the rain. "I don't want water shooting down my neck. Not at my age. I could end up with them new-monials again, and Dr James said they nearly did for me last winter."

I shook my head and gave up on my daydreams of an Elsie-free world. "Sorry? You have a new what?"

"Elsie had a bad bout of pneumonia last winter," Mum explained.

"*New what?*" Elsie cackled, her small, thin body shaking under the protective cape that covered not only her tiny frame but most of the chair as well. "You were miles away then, girlie. Where were you?"

Would that I were miles away, I wanted to say, but didn't dare. Not with Mum listening. Would that I were somewhere where people called me Kat, not Katie. Where they treated me like an adult, not a little kid. Where they got the way I dressed and thought it was cool, instead of asking me if I'd taken to wearing my grandad's cast offs, and what had I been doing to rip my jeans like that? Or wondering what on earth had I been thinking of when I dyed my hair purple, and had I been cutting it with a pair of nail scissors?

In short, I longed to be anywhere that was not here. In Chez Cheryl. That's my Mum's hairdressing salon. Much Winchmoor's 'top hairdressing establishment', according to the faded sign on the front gate. It was, in fact, Much Winchmoor's only hairdressing establishment, and was established in our front room, which caused a bit of a space issue. Which was why, a few years ago, Mum and Dad were as pleased as I was when I moved out – and just about as unpleased as I was when I had to move back in while I recovered from a temporary financial crisis that was none of my making.

Before I could think of a suitable reply to Elsie, the front door crashed open and another elderly lady came in. She was tall and thin with a slight stoop and always reminded me of a grey heron. At that moment, a windblown one.

"My life," she exclaimed as she closed the door firmly behind her. "It's blowing a hoo-hah out there. Mind you, if March comes in like a lion, it goes out like a, like a—" She paused, frowned as she trawled her memory banks then shook her head and gave up. The memory banks had obviously been fished dry. "Well, something along those lines," she muttered.

"I'll be right with you, Olive," Mum called out. "I'm a bit behind this morning. Sandra's off with her feet again. Take your coat off and sit down."

"You've got Katie to help you this morning, I see." Olive Shrewton beamed across at me. "I heard you were back, Katie. Oh dear, my lovely. What's happened to your hair? Has your mum been experimenting again? Because I have to say—"

"Katie's hair is none of my making," Mum said sharply.

"Well, never mind," Olive patted me on the arm. "It will soon grow out. And it's good to see you back. You see?" She beamed around the room. "You can take the girl out of Much Winchmoor, but you can't take Much Winchmoor out of the girl."

You reckon? I wanted to say. I'd shaken the dust of Much Winchmoor (or Not-Much Winchmoor as I thought of it) off my shoes the day I moved out. Which, as it happened, had been the day John Manning's cows went on their freedom march down the High Street, so there'd been a bit more than dust on them.

"Have you seen Will yet?" Olive asked.

"No. I only got back yesterday." As if you didn't know, I could have added, but didn't. Instead, I focused on testing the temperature of the water.

"Well, don't bother going up to see him today," Olive said. "I've just seen him drive off with a trailer full of sheep. On his way to market, I dare say."

I had no intention of seeing Will. Today or any other day, if I could avoid it. But I wasn't going to tell her that.

"Come on now, Katie, you still haven't answered my question," Elsie persisted. "Some folk are saying that fancy boyfriend of yours, the one with the sandy eyelashes and the phoney posh accent, gave you the heave-ho. Is that right? Mind you, I always say, never trust a man with sandy eyelashes."

"Let me know if this is too hot, Mrs Flintlock," If my voice sounded strangled, it was because it was difficult to speak normally through rigidly clenched jaws. "But no, he did not kick me out. I walked out."

I could have said I'd walked out because he went off with my best friend, who also happened to be my flatmate, on Valentine's Day, of all days, just to rub salt into the wound. And I could have added that I'd then been unable to pay the rent, hence the temporary financial crisis that was none of my making. Not only that, but the lowlife took my car, my stash of two pound coins, and my signed photo of David Tennant as Dr Who.

I could have said that – but I wouldn't, not in a million years. And certainly not to Much Winchmoor's gossipmonger-in-chief.

If spreading gossip was an Olympic sport, Elsie Flintlock would be a quadruple gold medallist. They had no need of super-fast broadband in this village. Elsie and her cronies were quicker than the speed of light.

"I dare say Will Manning will be pleased to hear that," Elsie cackled. "Poor lad. I reckon he— ow! That's really cold. What are you trying to do? I'll end up with double new-monials at this rate. Here, Cheryl, that daughter of yours is trying to kill me, she is. I'm freezing to death, here."

"It's all right, Elsie. I'll take over now." Mum elbowed me away from the basin. She gave me one of her looks. The sort that said, *'you and I will be having words about this later, young lady,'* and hissed in a low voice, that had Elsie's ears wiggling like bats' wings as she strained to hear, "Go and see to Marjorie Hampton. Just take the perm rollers out and rinse off. Do you think you can manage that without drowning the poor soul?"

"If you'll come with me, Mrs Hampton," I said. "I'll rinse you off. Mum will be with you soon."

Marjorie Hampton was a big-boned, awkward woman with a long horsey face and long horsey teeth. She towered above me as she trotted along behind. Her stout brown leather shoes, polished to a mirror shine, were more suited to traversing stony mountain paths than Mum's front room.

"It's *Miss* Hampton," she declared in a firm, no-nonsense voice as she took the seat at the other basin. "I was never foolish enough to marry."

"They saw her coming and ran a mile, more like it," Elsie muttered as Mum wrapped her head in a towel and led her away before she could do any more mischief. But, thankfully, Marjorie didn't hear. Like Elsie, she talked non-stop. But at least, in her case, she wasn't interested in my love life, or lack of it. In fact, the only thing Marjorie wanted to talk about was Marjorie. Which was fine by me. I was quite happy to let her words wash over me while I unwound the rollers.

Marjorie was an incomer. A person has to live in Much Winchmoor for at least twenty years before they're considered part of the village, and she'd moved into the Old Forge at the far end of the High Street less than two years ago. And a terrible mess the previous owners had left it in, apparently. As for what they'd done to the bathroom, that, according to Marjorie, didn't bear thinking about.

But incomer or not, in a short time, she'd woven herself into the very fabric of village life. She was president of the Women's Institute and organiser of the church flower rota ("well, someone has to do it and goodness knows, the vicar's wife is about as useful as a paper parasol in a thunderstorm"). Not only that, she was chair of the Floral Arts Society ("standards had been allowed to wilt") and something to do with the Ramblers Association ("it was criminal, the shocking state of public footpaths in and around the village"). There was, it appeared, not a single pie in Much Winchmoor that didn't have one of Marjorie Hampton's long, bony fingers planted firmly in the middle of it.

Conversation with Marjorie was strictly a one-way process. She talked, I listened. Well, sort of. I relaxed a little as I heard, rather than paid attention to, her voice going on and on, while I unwound the rollers from her blue-rinsed hair. According to Mum's colour chart, the shade was Midnight Hyacinth, but I reckoned the poor woman looked more like a fancy new strain of blue cauliflower than a hyacinth.

"And so I said to him, *'I'll see you there,'*" Marjorie's booming voice droned on. And on. "*'And I'll want an explanation.'* It's about time someone around here found the courage to stand up to him. And stand up to him I will. He'll find, once I've got my dander up, I'm not that easy to shake off. The trouble with people in this village, they're too ready to stand back and let somebody else do the work, don't you think?"

"Yes, I suppose," I replied automatically, while my mind concentrated on what I was going to put on my CV. It was important I got it absolutely right. A job, a decent job, was my ticket out of this madhouse. And I needed that ticket badly, before the people in this village drove me completely bonkers. Or I ended up murdering one of them.

But how to word it, so it wouldn't sound as if I'd been fired from my last job? It's not like I had been, of course. More that I was a victim of the recession, of greedy bankers, of the radio station's falling ratings. All those things and more, according to Brad, the station manager. And, he'd added, it was hurting him more than it hurt me and someone with my undoubted talent would find another job, no trouble.

Which just went to show what he knew. After trying for four weeks to find another post in Bristol, and sinking further and further into debt trying to find two lots of rent on the flat, I'd finally had to admit defeat and come home to Much Winchmoor, where jobs were rarer than hens' teeth – and just about as appealing. In short, I needed a job, any job, that would earn me some money so that I could stop the bank sending me rude letters and charging me for the privilege, not to mention the exorbitant rate of interest on my overdraft which meant I'd still be paying it off when I was ninety-two.

"So he said that he was doing his best, and that he'd be advertising for staff as soon as he could get around to it…"

This time, it was Elsie Flintlock's voice that caught my attention. I cut across Marjorie's full-on rant about the disgraceful state of the bridle path up by John Manning's farm.

"Excuse me, Elsie," I called across. "Who—?"

"It's Mrs Flintlock, to you."

"Sorry. *Mrs Flintlock.* But did you say someone was looking for staff?" I asked. "Only, as it happens, I'm looking for a job."

"You've got a job," Elsie sniffed. "Not that you're making a very good fist of it."

"Oh, I don't know, Elsie," Olive said. "Katie's trying hard. She always does."

I flashed Olive a grateful smile. "Thanks. But, Mrs Flintlock, who were you talking about? Who's looking for staff?"

"Donald Wilson, at the pub. He needs a new barmaid. His wife's away on a cruise. With her mother. So they say," Elsie added darkly. "But if you ask me, I reckon she's left him, and who could blame her? He's got all the charisma of a wet week in Wigan, has that one. They had the most terrible row, the week before she went, and she called him a useless parasite—"

"Said she should have listened to her mother and never

married him in the first place," Olive chimed in.

"Course, she's the one with the money, you know," Elsie said. "And he—"

"And you think he's looking for a new barmaid?" I cut in. "Brilliant. I'll give him a call. Or better still, go and see him as soon as I've finished here."

"Well, I hope you make a better barmaid than hairdresser," sniffed Elsie, who always had to have the last word.

But I didn't care. Any job, any job at all, had to be better than being up to my ears in perm lotion and gossip all day. Not to mention wall-to-wall Radio 2.

Chapter Two

The Winchmoor Arms hadn't changed a lot since the last time I was there, just over a year ago. In fact, it would be safe to say, it hadn't changed a lot since the Queen's Jubilee Celebrations – Queen Victoria's, that is. The same faded prints of Cheddar Gorge on the walls, the same tarnished horse brasses above the fireplace. Even the same forlorn spider plant, which the landlady, for reasons best known to herself, had christened Sparky, still drooped unloved and undusted on the far end of the bar.

Then there was Donald Wilson, the landlord. Dippy Donald, a lot of the locals called him. He was one of those men who'd be hard to describe if you were giving the police a witness statement. Average height, average build, average hair colour. The sort of man who crept through life unnoticed and unremarked.

"I understand you're looking for someone to work in the bar," I said.

He smoothed back his thinning grey hair with long nervous fingers and looked around furtively, as if checking no-one was listening. Even though the bar was completely empty.

"Well, yes. I suppose I do need someone to help out," he said hesitantly. "But it's only temporary. Joyce is away on a cruise with her mother. She'll be back in another two months."

"Oh, that's fine by me," I assured him. I was banking on getting another job – a 'proper' job, as I thought of it – long before Joyce Wilson returned from her cruise. Although I wasn't going to tell him that. "And I can start immediately. Tonight, if you like?"

"Really?" His pale grey eyes looked slightly less anxious. "Do you have any experience?"

"Loads. Mostly the students' union bar, when I was at

college." It was almost true, although most of that experience had been gained on the other side of the bar. "Do you want to see my CV? Only I don't have it with me, but I can let you have it later."

To my relief, he shook his head. "That won't be necessary," he said with a quick glance at his watch. "Not for a temporary job. Ok then. Let's see how you get on, shall we? On a trial basis. Although I heard you were working for your mum."

"That was only while Sandra was off with her feet. When would you want me to start? Tonight?"

"Well, yes, I suppose." He looked at his watch again and moved towards the door. "Now, if you'll excuse me, I'm supposed to be meeting Councillor Crabshaw at the site of some proposed new playing fields they're considering out on the Dinstcombe Bypass. He's keen for residents from the nearby villages to get involved right from the start, so he roped me in. I said I'd be there by 3 o'clock. So, if you don't mind," he herded me towards the door. "I'll see you tonight."

"Brilliant. Thank you." I gave him the full force of my most glittering smile, determined to show him what an asset I would be to his bar.

He took a step backwards, the worried look reappearing in his eyes. "If you can be here by about quarter to six, I'll run through things with you before the early evening crowd comes in."

"No problem. I'll see you then." But, as I reached out to open the door, he called me back.

"Katie? There is one thing..." A flush of red crept up his pale cheeks. "If – if you don't mind. What I mean is, could – could you wear something more appropriate this evening?"

"Appropriate?" I blinked at him. "What? Do you mean, low cut tops? Things like that?"

"Good Lord, no. No. *No*. No. Nothing like that." His pale grey eyes bulged with horror. "I meant – I meant the torn jeans. The customers, you know, they wouldn't – I mean, I couldn't – the thing is—"

I grinned and put him out of his misery. "That's ok. I get it. No ripped jeans. I'll see you tonight then, appropriately dressed. I'm a hard worker, Donald. You won't regret taking me on, honest."

***

He might not regret it, I thought later that evening as I stifled a yawn, but I was beginning to. My feet ached, my back ached, my heart ached for the good old days when I had a 'proper' job. I had the sinking feeling I'd jumped out of the frying pan of tedious local gossip in Chez Cheryl into the fire of even more tedious local gossip in the Winchmoor Arms. But the smell of beer didn't make my eyes water, the way the perm lotion did, and at least there was no Radio 2 doing my head in. All this enforced smiling was making my jaw ache, though.

"Just keep smiling at the customers, Katie," Donald told me. "That's the thing you need to remember."

"I prefer to be known as Kat, if it's all the same to you."

He shrugged and gave a weak smile. "Yes, well, I prefer to be known as Don, but nobody ever calls me that. Everybody knows you as Katie, same as they all know me as Donald, and that's the way it is, I'm afraid. Just look cheerful, even if some of them aren't exactly—" He pulled a face and shrugged. "Well, just remember, the customer is always right. Oh, and don't stand around chatting while there are people waiting to be served. They don't like that either."

But smiling and being nice while pulling pints of Ferret's Kneecaps Best Bitter was easier said than done, when you're listening to a load of grumpy old men – and some of them not so old – moaning on about the weather, England's chances in the third Test and the date of the next recycling collection, while at the same time fielding yet more questions about my non-existent career prospects and even more non-existent love life.

"Hey, Katie, I hear you and your fancy boyfriend have split up. If you ever want to see life in the fast lane, sweetheart, you're welcome to a ride in my cab any time you like." This particular witticism came from Shane Freeman, a regular with more tattoos than brain cells, who always wore the same scruffy old leather jacket whatever the weather. He'd been a couple of years above me in school and had always been a big guy, but since becoming a lorry driver, too many years of greasy spoon breakfasts had collected around his middle and he was now almost as wide as he was high. I wondered how he managed to clamber in and out of his cab. I also worried for the bar stool he was perched on as he waited for his pint.

"I'll pass on that, thanks, Shane," I handed him his pint.

"Well, if you change your mind…" He took a long drink, called the dog dozing at his feet, then shambled off to take up the space of two people on the settle by the window.

"Same again, please, my sweet." My heart sank as Gerald Crabshaw, the man who put the sleaze into sleazeball, oozed up to the bar. "Hey, Katie, you know what they say, don't you? You can take the girl out of Much Winchmoor but you can't take Much Winchmoor out of the girl."

Didn't they just say that? Again and again and again. I glanced down at the pint in my hand, then across at Donald watching me, and wondered if it would be worth going for the quickest sacking on record, if only to see the leery grin wiped off Gerald Crabshaw's mottled red face by a well-aimed pint of Ferret's. He'd been the ninth person that evening to make the *'couldn't keep away, then?'* comment and the joke, such as it was, was wearing thin. Besides which, when he came to the bar, he'd lean across the counter and leer down my top every time I bent over.

Tomorrow night, I vowed, I'd wear a blouse buttoned to the neck. Preferably one with the words, "yes, I am back and no, I didn't choose to be," emblazoned across it.

This wasn't the future I'd planned for myself when I'd left Much Winchmoor four years ago. I'd honestly believed I would never be back here again. Except to visit.

"So, what happened to that fancy job you had with that radio station?" asked Gerald Crabshaw, or Councillor Crabshaw as he preferred to be known, picking up the pint I'd just poured him and taking a sip. "From the way your dad talked, you were indispensable. Practically running the place, he said you were."

14

I glared at Dad, who was perched on his usual stool at the far end of the bar near the dartboard. "Well, you know how things are," I said, trying to sound like it didn't still hurt. "The recession's hit everyone."

No way was I going to admit to him, or anyone else in the village, that my so-called top job had in fact been a minimum wage general dogsbody role (or radio broadcast assistant, to give it its full title). And, far from being indispensable, I'd been dispensed with faster than Alan Sugar could say, 'you're fired'.

"Do you know what, Councillor? Me and Cheryl, we're victims of the boomerang generation, that's what we are," Dad called across the bar. "This is what it's like these days. You think your kids have left home for good and you just start making a nice bit of room for yourself when boom, back they come, like a flipping boomerang. She's got more bags and boxes than Parcelforce. And there goes my snooker table."

This earned him a burst of laughter from his cronies, a pint from Gerald Crabshaw and another glare from me. Even Donald, not known for his joviality, smirked as he came up behind me, soft-footed as a cat, and placed a pack of mixers on the floor.

Gerald Crabshaw had lived in the village all his life and was out of the Marjorie Hampton mould of fingers into everything – except he was there first. He was a district councillor, chairman of this, treasurer of that. He saw himself as Mr Much Winchmoor, or Sir Gerald of Winchmoor if he got his way. There wasn't a planning application submitted, a village hall booking made nor a complaint about the local bus service lodged that Councillor Crabshaw didn't have a hand in, or an opinion about.

"And what do you think the lovely Joyce is going to say about her Donald employing pretty young barmaids while she's away?" Gerald asked the group around the bar, who sniggered like a gaggle of ten-year-old boys who've just heard a rude word. Gerald gave me what he obviously imagined was a long suggestive wink. Instead, it merely made him look as if he had a severe tic on one side of his face.

15

"Here, Donald, how's Joyce getting on with her cruise? Have you heard?" asked a man with close cropped hair and a fatuous grin.

Donald jumped, as he always did when someone spoke to him directly, seeming surprised someone had noticed him. He was, after all, a very easy man to overlook and seemed to appear and disappear like a small grey shadow. "Joyce? Oh, right, Dave. No, I haven't heard from her. I don't expect to, really."

"Still, make the most of the quiet, eh?"

Donald turned away and forced a smile at Gerald Crabshaw. "Good meeting this afternoon, Gerald. Worth doing, wouldn't you say?"

"What?" Gerald looked startled for a moment.

"The meeting about the playing fields," Donald said quietly. "It went well, I thought. Considering. I should think that will bring about a very satisfactory outcome for all."

"Oh yes. Yes, of course. Excuse me, my companions over there are dying of thirst."

"Donald!" someone shouted, in a shrill tone that Basil Fawlty would have jumped to. Everyone in the bar laughed. Except Donald, who gave a tight-lipped smile, like it was something he'd heard many times before. I gave him a sympathetic grin but it was not returned.

The Winchmoor Arms regulars were not known for the originality of their repartee, as I could testify. That evening, as well as the 'couldn't keep away, then, Katie?' question, there was the 'does Will Manning know you're back?' query. Not to mention the 'what have you done to your hair? Is that courtesy of rent-a-nest?' one.

On the other hand, over on Gerald Crabshaw's table, the conversation suddenly sounded a lot more interesting.

Gerald's red mottled face was even redder, even more mottled. His shrill, angry voice cut through the tedious chorus clustered around the bar.

"For heaven's sake, man," he bellowed at the browbeaten man sitting opposite him. "What are you blathering on about? Everyone knows it was that wretched Marjorie Hampton who

16

killed—"

"Here, Katie, don't stand there like a spare part," Donald pointed to the crate of mixers. "Unpack these and put them on that bottom shelf, will you? And we're running low on crisps."

If that wasn't typical. The first time this evening there was a remotely interesting conversation and what happened? I missed it. Who was Marjorie Hampton supposed to have killed? She was a bit of a busybody. Correction: a lot of a busybody. And it was common knowledge that she and Gerald Crabshaw were at daggers drawn. But a murderer? Here in Much Winchmoor, where the main topic of the evening, after my love life and job prospects, had been the muddle over the date of the recycling collection? Surely not.

By the time I'd put out the mixers and replenished the cheese and onion, the conversation on Gerald's table had moved on to the riveting topic of the closure of rural post offices and an upcoming planning appeal. The browbeaten man's brow was looking more beaten than ever.

"What were you saying just now, about Marjorie Hampton?" My curiosity got the better of me when Gerald came up to the bar for a refill and another eyeful.

"Get me another packet of pistachios and I'll tell you, sweet Katie," he smarmed, knowing I'd have to bend down to get them.

"So who's she supposed to have killed?" I asked as, with a move that would have impressed a limbo dancer, I managed to grab a packet of nuts without having to bend over.

"Interfering old baggage," he growled as he reached into the inside pocket of his tweed jacket for his wallet. "That wretched woman has been nothing but trouble since she moved in to the village. Sticking her nose into things that don't concern her."

"But you said she'd killed somebody," I handed him his change.

Gerald laughed. "Not someone, my dear, but something." He took a long pull at his beer and looked round to make sure he was the centre of attention. He straightened his regimental tie and puffed out his chest like he was practicing for Prime

17

Minister's Question Time.

"Marjorie Hampton," he declaimed, "killed the farm shop."

A farm shop? Talk about a let down. I thought he was talking about a nice juicy murder that would liven up the place a bit and give everyone something to talk about other than last night's Corrie and how things used to be back when men were men, women knew their place and the railway still went through the village.

"You've done it now," Shane Freeman muttered. "Once you get old Gerald started on that, there's no stopping him. He'll be banging on for the next half hour about how this townie government is ruining rural life and all that rubbish. Isn't that right, Gerald?"

Gerald ignored him. "If poor Sally Manning was still alive it would break her heart to see what a sorry state her precious farm shop is in now, thanks to Marjorie nose-into-everything Hampton." He scowled and there was no sign of the smiling, genial man he'd been a few moments earlier. His too-close-together eyes were hard and cold, his small mouth taut with barely suppressed anger. "I tell you, that woman is going to poke her sticky beak into one pie too many one of these days, and she's going to come to a very unpleasant end, you mark my words. A very nasty end indeed."

Before he could come out with any more words for anyone to mark, the front door crashed open and a large unkempt man stood swaying in the doorway. Conversation in the pub stopped as abruptly as if someone had thrown a switch.

"Evening, John," Donald said warily as the man zig-zagged to the bar.

"Pint of Ferret's and a whisky chaser," he slurred, and the fumes on his breath suddenly made this morning's perm lotion seem a lot less noxious.

"That'll be £6, please." As I handed him his drinks, I looked at him closely for the first time. I almost spilt the whisky as I recognised the wreck of a man who half stood, half leant at the bar, his eyes red-rimmed and bloodshot, his face dark with several days' stubble, his hair tousled and matted. His clothes looked like he'd slept in them for weeks.

It was John Manning, husband (or, rather, widower, I reminded myself with a twinge of sadness) of Sally and father of Will, the guy I'd always thought of as my brother and best mate when we were growing up.

It was over a year since I'd last seen John Manning. I'd been home for the weekend and had looked in on the farm to collect a pie from Sally and to tell Will what a prize idiot he'd been the night before. John was a big bear of a man, gentle, strong and softly spoken, who often teased me about my aversion to mud and farmyard smells. At least, that was how he used to be.

"How – how are you, Mr Manning?" It was a stupid question because I could see how he was. And it wasn't good. But he didn't answer. Gave no sign he'd even heard me, least of all recognised me. Instead, he tossed back the whisky, picked up his pint and shuffled off to a table in the far corner where he stayed, speaking only to order more drinks, until staggering out at about half past nine, ricocheting off the door frame as he did so.

Mum had told me how, after Sally's death from cancer four months ago, John had fallen apart. But I'd thought that must have been a bit of exaggeration on her part. Sadly, it wasn't. Poor John. And poor, poor Will.

Tomorrow, I promised myself, I'd go up and see Will. Even though he probably wouldn't want to see me. Not after the awful things I'd said to him that last time we'd met.

Chapter Three

Next morning, Mum was in the kitchen when I got back from my early morning run. She looked up as I came in, her eyes sparking with annoyance.

"Look at this, Katie," she said, stabbing at our local paper, *The Dintscombe Chronicle*, spread out on the table in front of her. "It's a disgrace."

"What?" I peered over her shoulder. "'Thieves stole washing from launderette'? I agree. As headlines go, it's not the snappiest. I think I'd have gone for *Phantom knicker nicker strikes again*. Much more impact."

"I don't mean that. It's this. Look." She pointed at a small paragraph in the final column. "It's a report on a planning committee meeting that was held last week. They're only talking about building another hundred and fifty houses on the edge of Dintscombe. It's bad enough trying to find somewhere to park on market day as it is."

Dintscombe was the nearest town to Much Winchmoor and even that was a thirty-minute drive away. But that could easily extend to an hour, if you were foolish enough to try and go there on a Wednesday, market day, ever since a celebrity chef opened a gastro pub a couple of miles away and had praised the quality of the fresh, local produce to be found at Dintscombe Market. It brought people flooding in from miles around, many of whom were only there in the hope of catching a glimpse of Sleb Chef poking the potatoes or prodding the parsnips. Except, of course, he had minions to do that for him. Not that the stallholders ever told anyone that. Instead, they'd say things like: "Do you know, you've just missed him. You'll have to get here earlier next week." Which, naturally, the punters did.

All this, while good news for the charity shops and coffee

houses which was all that had survived the opening of the new retail park a couple of years earlier, was not so good if you were in town for a visit to the doctor or dentist and had forgotten it was market day. Parking was a nightmare in the town, and was a constant source of grumpy letters to the editor of *The Chronicle*.

Mum had got up a head of steam now and there was no stopping her. "Honestly, what's the Council thinking of?" she muttered as she went across to the stove and stirred whatever was in the saucepan so vigorously, she was in danger of wearing a hole in it. "They're destroying our towns and villages with all these ill-considered developments. If you ask me, they're all on the take, the whole sorry lot of them."

"Even our own Councillor Crabshaw?" I raised my eyebrows in mock horror. "Surely not."

"Especially our own Councillor Crabshaw," she growled.

I poured myself a glass of apple juice. "Well, at least they're not building those houses in Much Winchmoor."

"Not for want of trying. There was an application for outline planning permission for a development of sixty houses made a while back."

"Sixty? But where?"

"On a field off the lane that comes out at the back of the village hall. Drove Lane, the old boys in the village call it."

"The field with the old stone barn, that belonged to Jules's grandad?" My friend Jules and I used to spend hours in there, when we were kids. It had been everything from a haunted castle, to an indoor arena for imaginary horses. As we got older, it progressed to our favourite place away from adult eyes, where we experimented with illicitly acquired cigarettes and cider. Both experiments were spectacularly unsuccessful and I, for one, had been unable to so much as smell a glass of cider without wanting to throw up ever since. A bit of a downside to my new, but hopefully temporary, career as a barmaid.

"Not that field. The one next to it. Anyway, it's not going to happen because, to give Gerald Crabshaw his due, he spoke up against it and the whole thing was rejected on account of the poor access."

"Thank goodness for that." The population of Much Winchmoor was a mere nine hundred (or nine hundred and one if you counted me) and an extra sixty homes would have a significant effect on the character of the place, not to mention the increase in traffic on the narrow, single track lane that was the only way in and out of the village. "Although, having said that, at least it would probably have ensured that the village school stays open," I added.

Mum frowned as she peered into the saucepan. I looked over her shoulder, didn't much care for what I saw and hunted in the cupboard for a packet of biscuits.

"Do you want some of this?" she asked as she spooned globules of grey, gloopy sludge into a bowl. "It's highly nutritious."

"No thanks," I said quickly. Frogspawn was probably highly nutritious as well. But that didn't mean I wanted to eat any for breakfast. "Do you need me in the salon this morning?"

She shook her head. "No, love. Why don't you go and see Will instead?"

"I would, but the thing is—" I bent my head and wrestled with the wrapping on the biscuits. "I thought I'd work on my CV this morning. And check through the situations vacant in *The Chronicle*. You never know. Then I've got a load of washing to do and—"

"It won't get any easier," she said quietly. "You can't keep putting it off."

"Putting what off?" I asked, although I knew full well what she was getting at.

"Going to see him." She leaned across and covered my hand with hers. "I don't understand, Katie. You used to be such good friends. What happened?"

"People change. That's all. We've changed. Will and I, we —" I broke off, as I caught the look in her eye. Mum always knew what was in my mind, sometimes before I did. "The truth is, Mum, I don't know what to say to him. Not just that silly row, but not going to his mum's funeral. I feel really bad

22

about that."

"Well, don't. You and Nick were away skiing. Even if you could have afforded to fly back early, there was no way you'd have got there in time. Will understands that." She took a spoonful of the grey gloopy sludge and chewed it slowly. "You're surely not going to have nothing but a couple of chocolate biscuits for your breakfast, are you? Eat some real food, for pity's sake."

"Real food? Is that what you're eating? What is it?" I pointed at the mixture that looked more like wallpaper paste – or frogspawn. "You're not on another diet, are you?"

"It's barley risotto with chia seeds. And it's not a diet. It's a change of lifestyle." Her eyes shone with that fanatical gleam she always got at the start of a new diet. It was a look that Dad and I knew and dreaded.

"You remember Janet Thornton, don't you?" she went on. "Well, she came in to the salon a few weeks ago and I didn't recognise her. She's lost three stone on this. It's brilliant. All you have to do is eat a couple of bowls of this highly nutritious mixture every day, and the rest of the time you can eat normally."

"Eat normally?" I laughed. "In all the time I've known you, you've never eaten normally. There was the grapefruit diet, the baked beans diet – and what about the one where you ate all that disgusting cabbage soup?"

Mum gave the contents of her bowl a stir. "It's all right for you. You can eat whatever you like and still be like a stick insect."

"Hardly. Don't you remember how Gran Latcham used to tell me it was just puppy fat? That I'd grow out of it?"

"And, for once, she was quite right, wasn't she?" Mum said grudgingly. Mum had shared a very uneasy relationship with her mother-in-law and even now, after all these years, still blamed Gran Latcham for encouraging me to do a Media Studies degree at college instead of the hairdressing and beauty therapy course Mum had earmarked for me.

"Do you know, I still can't get used to going past her old cottage and not seeing her, pottering around in her garden," I said as I took another biscuit. Gran Latcham died just a couple of months before my eighteenth birthday and, even though that had been five years ago, I still missed her.

"It's a holiday cottage now." Mum pulled a face as she took another spoonful of sludge. "Half the houses in the village are."

"Sure you don't want one of these?" I held the packet towards her.

She shook her head. "No. I mustn't. And neither should you."

"As for me losing my puppy fat, as Gran called it, that was nothing to do with diet and everything to do with taking up judo when I was at college." In judo, I'd discovered a sport that I was not only good at, but actually enjoyed. And although I could no longer afford to go to a gym now that I was unemployed, I still kept myself fit by going for a run two or three times a week. "You should forget all those daft diets and come running with me instead," I said.

"Oh yes, that's exactly what I need, after a day on my feet in the salon," she said. "And don't lecture me on healthy living, young lady. How can breakfasting on chocolate biscuits be healthy, for goodness sake? At least have a banana."

"I'm sorry, Mum, but I'm not that hungry. And, by the look of it, you're not either."

She sighed as she put the spoon down and pushed the dish to one side. "It's no good. I can't eat this. Maybe I made a mistake in the recipe. Here, pass me one of those." She took a biscuit. "I'll start tomorrow. I've got a busy day ahead of me. I need to keep my strength up. Thank goodness Sandra will be back today."

Sandra had been working for Mum for as long as I could remember. The years of standing up all day had taken a toll on Sandra and she was, she always said, a martyr to her feet. She'd spent the previous day travelling all the way to Bath to try some wonderful new chiropodist somebody had told her about. Which was why I'd been co-opted into working in the salon.

"Sure you won't need me?" I asked. "I'm due at the pub for

the lunchtime shift. But I can work until half past eleven, in case Sandra's feet are still playing her up."

"Absolutely sure. Sandra and I will manage. So you've got no excuse not to go and see Will, have you? Just say you're sorry about his mum. That's all you have to do. For goodness sake, Katie, how hard can it be?"

How hard? She had no idea. For a start, the last time I'd seen Will had been when Ratface and I were still an item (before I found out what a cheating lowlife he was) and I'd brought him home for the weekend. He and Will had met in the pub and it had been a case of mutual loathing at first sight. And now, I knew, Will would be unbearably smug about how he'd known it wouldn't last and how I must have been pretty desperate to have been taken in by such a poser. He wouldn't be able to resist it.

But the other reason, The Big One, was that I didn't know what to say to him. Not after that terrible row. It was going to be pretty difficult to say how truly sorry I was about his mum (which I was – Sally was a really, really nice person and used to make the best meat and potato pies on the planet) while trying to forget that the last time we'd met, Will had called me – among other things – a stuck-up, selfish little cow. And I'd called him – among other things – a pig-headed, carrot-crunching oik.

When his mum died, I tried to call him but he didn't answer his phone. I tried texting him but he never looked at his messages, least of all replied. In the end I sent him a card, but I didn't know what to say so just wrote something banal. And the longer I left it, the harder it got. I hated being bad friends with him – and he had been right about Ratface. So I'd just have to put up with his I-told-you-so. I guess I owed him that one.

Mum was quite right. I couldn't put it off any longer. I left her working her way through the chocolate biscuits, fished my bike out of the garden shed and set off to cycle up the steep, narrow lane that led up to Pendle Knoll and the Manning farm.

***

Before I moved to Bristol, I could cycle right up to the top of the hill without breaking into a sweat. Now I told myself I must have pushed myself a bit too hard on my early morning run, as I was gasping for breath before I'd even reached the village primary school, which was only about one third of the way up. As I struggled past, the children were obviously all in the main hall for morning assembly as I could just about make out the sound of their shouty singing above the rasping of my breath.

To add to my discomfort, the rain, which had been threatening ever since I left the house, arrived at the farm the same time as I did. It was blown in on the ever-present wind that rampaged around Pendle Knoll. A light breeze in Much Winchmoor always morphed into a full-on gale by the time it reached the farm. Pendle Knoll Farmhouse was, I reckoned, built in the windiest place in the county and Will always said he was going to install a wind turbine at the back of the house, even though it would probably bring howls of protest from the village, spearheaded no doubt by Marjorie Hampton.

I leaned my bike against the gate and headed across the thankfully empty farmyard. I was not terribly fond of cows since the day one of them head-butted me into a ditch and Will had laughed himself silly as he pulled me out.

Half way across the yard I stopped and looked around me. Something was weird. Out of place. Different. Like that feeling you get when you go back to a place you haven't been to in years, and you find that nothing's quite as you remembered it.

When I was young I'd spent every spare moment up at the farm. It was my second home and I would follow Will around like a little duckling. We were both only children and he was the brother I'd never had. And like any other siblings, we squabbled and fought all the time (it was always his fault, of course) but we usually made it up pretty quickly.

But when we fell out, the last time we met, it was for keeps. His refusal to answer my calls or texts made it pretty clear he didn't want any more to do with me.

All the time I'd been struggling up the hill on my bike, in

between fighting for air, I'd been practicing what I was going to say to him. But I needn't have bothered, because the place was so deserted I half expected to see tumbleweed bowling across the yard towards me.

No tumbleweed. No humans either. And the only animals I could see were a load of black and white kittens skittering in and out of the barn doors like leaves in the wind, and one of those crazy, wild-eyed collies that always lurked about the place.

It took a few minutes to work out what it was that was so different. Then I saw it. Mud. Or, to be strictly accurate, the absence of mud. I'd put on my oldest shoes in the certain knowledge I'd be wading ankle deep in goodness-knew-what just to get to the back door of the farm house. Instead the concrete yard looked as if it had been bleached, the raindrops leaving big fat splodges on its unnaturally clean surface The door of the milking parlour, its once shiny blue paint now faded, lurched half-open on broken hinges. The windows, that used to be clean and sparkling, would now let in precious little light through the thick grime that coated each surface.

The whole farm had a down-at-heel air, so different from the bright, well ordered place it had been when Sally was around.

Mum said John Manning had let himself go, and I'd seen it for myself last night. But Will? Had he let himself – and the farm – go as well? I'd had no idea things had got so bad. Poor, poor Will. My heart contracted with pity for him and I felt worse than ever for leaving it so long.

"Hello? Will? Anyone around?" I called, but the only answer came from a dog inside the house who started barking and sent the other one in the yard into a frenzy, running around me like I was a stroppy old ewe she was determined to return to the flock.

"Tam. Enough." My heart lurched as I recognised Will's voice. I turned round to see him emerge from one of the barns on the far side of the yard. He looked bigger than I remembered, his shoulders broader, his hair a little longer. But his eyes were the same deep blue with the long, sweeping eyelashes that I'd always told him were completely wasted on a bloke.

He stopped dead when he saw me and, instead of the welcoming grin I'd been sort of hoping for, he scowled.

"Oh, it's you. I heard you were back. What do you want?" he said, while the dog sidled up to him and pushed against his leg, ready to pin me down at the first nod from her master.

"Well, not to be bowled over by the warmth of your welcome," I retorted. "Which, as it turns out, is just as well, isn't it?"

He scowled again, looked as if he was about to say something equally snippy, then changed his mind. He raked his fingers through his hair and gave a half smile. "Jeez, I'm sorry, Katie. I didn't mean—"

"My name's Kat now as you very well know –" I began, but might as well have saved my breath.

"I'm sorry, Katie." This time he emphasised my name deliberately. He was doing it to annoy me. Like he always did. Although I had the feeling it was more out of habit than conviction. But at least it was a bit of normality between us, so I let it go.

"I'm a bit distracted, to be honest," he went on, his hair sticking up all over the place, like a small boy who's just been dragged out of bed. His eyes were as blue as ever, but now I was closer to him, I could see they were underscored by deep shadows, as if he'd not slept properly in weeks.

"What's wrong?" I asked.

"It's Dad. The old fool didn't come home last night."

"But I saw him last night," I said. "He was in the pub."

"I know he was. But I've already phoned the pub. It was the first place I checked. Donald said he left about half past nine."

"Yes, that would be about right."

"Was he with anyone? More to the point, did he leave with anyone? Donald was his usual vague self when I asked him."

I thought how John had sat, alone, in the furthest, darkest corner of the bar. How each time he'd shambled up to the bar everyone else had done this kind of side-stepping shuffle, as they'd tried to edge away from him without making it too

28

obvious. It was like some weird slow motion dance and all a bit sad. But John had been too far gone to notice.

"He was on his own all night," I said. "Donald was chatting to him for a bit at one time, but that was all. I don't think he even recognised me. And I'm pretty sure there was no one with him when he left."

If there had been, I thought, they might have stopped him ricocheting off the door frame. But I kept that thought to myself.

Will rubbed his face, his fingers rasping across several days' growth of stubble. There was a bleak, hopeless look in his eyes, as though he was lost and a bit scared. I'd never seen him look like that before.

In all the years I'd known him, he'd always been so strong and in control. So sure of himself. A bit too much, sometimes, I thought grimly as I remembered that last terrible row we'd had. But now, he looked like he didn't know who or where he was. He looked, too, like a man who'd completely run out of options.

"Will, I'm – I'm so sorry I haven't been to see you sooner." My tongue seemed to have fused to the roof of my mouth as I stumbled over the inadequate words. "And – and I'm so very sorry about your mum."

"I got your card." His words were clipped.

"I'm sorry I couldn't get back for the funeral. It must have been tough for you."

"Tough?" He looked up, his eyes meeting mine for the first time. He looked so angry I backed away.

"Look, I'm sorry. That was a stupid thing to say," I murmured, my words falling over themselves as I floundered about, not knowing what to say next – but not knowing how to stop talking either. "I knew I'd say the wrong thing. I shouldn't have come. I can see that now. I'm just making things worse, idiot that I am. I just wanted to say I'm sorry. About your mum. And everything. And your dad, too, of course. It's really sad. I – that's all. I'll go now. Sorry."

The rain had begun in earnest as I turned from him and hurried away. But he called after me.

"Katie?"

I kept walking.

"Oh, all right then, Kat. Wait." He caught up with me before I reached the gate and put his hand on my arm to stop me. "Come back, please. I'm sorry. I shouldn't have barked at you like that. As for you not being at the funeral, your mum explained. To be honest, I didn't even notice who was there and who wasn't. Look, we're both getting soaked out here. Come in and have coffee and we'll catch up. I've got ten minutes before I have to go and take some feed up to the stock in Top Meadow."

Without waiting for me to say yes, he strode across the yard where the fat splodges of rain had now all joined up into one large puddle that was getting bigger by the minute. I half ran, as I always did, when I tried to keep up with his long legs.

"But what about your dad?" I said, as I tried not very successfully to dodge the puddle. "I thought you were on your way out to look for him?" I stopped dead as a horrible thought occurred to me. "Oh, my God, Will. Do you think he's had an accident? Have you spoken to the police? You don't think he's —?"

He turned back and frowned at me. "I think he's sleeping it off somewhere. He's done it before. I've already checked the obvious places. The only question is – where? Come on. You're standing in the middle of a puddle; in case you hadn't noticed."

'What's happened to him, Will?' I asked and could have bitten my tongue off for asking such a stupid question. It wasn't like I needed a degree in psychology to work out the answer to that particular question myself.

He opened the back door and, with a sharp command, quietened both dogs.

"You must have seen the state of him, last night," he said, bleakly.

I bent down to take off my wet shoes, saw the mud-streaked state of the floor, and decided not to bother.

"He – was a bit, er…" I paused for a moment as I wondered if I was about to break some barmaid code of conduct, but what the heck? Will was, or at least used to be, a mate. "He was already in a bit of a state when he came in, reeking of whisky. He stayed for about an hour, downed several pints with whisky chasers, then left. And you're saying he never made it home?"

Will shook his head. "I don't know where else to try. I've been from here to the pub and all round the village and back, expecting to find him sleeping it off under a hedge somewhere, like he was the last time. I've also been down to the pond and walked as far as I could up the river. Shouting. Calling. Nothing. He seems to be on one permanent bender at the moment. He could be lying dead in a ditch for all I know – except I've looked in all the ditches."

Chapter Four

"Are you sure you shouldn't contact the police?" I asked, my voice crackling with panic. "I mean, anything could have happened to him. And if you're that worried—"

"Nothing will have happened to him." Will sounded as worn out as he looked. "Hey, I'm sorry. I didn't mean to freak you out. I'm just tired, that's all. Didn't get much sleep last night and then up at dawn this morning. Dad will turn up. He always does. When he sobers up. Which he'll do for a couple of days, then something will set him off and it starts all over again."

"Was there something in particular that 'set him off' as you put it, this time?"

"Damn right there was," Will growled and kicked the door shut. "I had to take some lambs to market yesterday so I was out for best part of the day, more's the pity. Like I don't have enough to do around here without the market run on top. Dad always used to do it and I was pretty damn mad at him by the time I got home. Ready to have it out with him about not pulling his weight."

"Your dad doesn't do the market run any more?" I was surprised. John always used to love going to the livestock market. It gave him chance to catch up with all the other farmers and have a good old moan about everything, the way farmers do when they get together. "You always used to whinge about how he'd never give you the chance to do it."

"Yeah, well. That was then. This is now and it's one job I can well do without. He hasn't done it since Mum died. Don't suppose he wants his old mates to see what a mess he's become."

"That's so sad. Poor guy."

"Like I said, I was going to have it out with him yesterday,"

Will went on. "Tell him straight. He was in the kitchen but as soon as I saw him, I could tell he'd been drinking. And before I could say anything, he'd launched into this mostly incoherent tirade about Marjorie Hampton. He didn't make a lot of sense but the gist of it was she'd come up to see him, something about a footpath."

"She was saying something like that to me yesterday morning in the salon when I was rinsing off her hair. But I'm afraid I wasn't really listening."

"Best way to deal with her. That's what I do. I told Dad to take no notice of her, that she's nothing but an interfering busybody. But I'm not sure he heard me. He just grabbed the whisky bottle, which by that time was almost empty, and stomped off to his room with it. Then, about half an hour later, I heard the front door slam and realised he'd gone out. I reckoned he'd gone to the pub. I don't get it. There's hardly enough money to pay the animal feed bill, not to mention put food on our own table, and yet he always seems to find money for booze from somewhere. I had a word, quiet like, with Donald the other day about whether Dad was running up a massive bar tab, but he said no."

"It's true. Donald keeps account of the tabs on a chalk board behind the bar and I certainly don't remember seeing your dad's name there."

Will shrugged. "Who knows? Anyway, when I tackled him about it, he said it was none of my damn business. Or words to that effect."

I shook my head and sighed. "It's hard to believe, isn't it? He was always such a careful, together man. In all the years I've known him, I've never seen him the worse for drink, not even that time at the harvest supper when someone was a bit heavy-handed with the fruit punch and we all ended up tipsy, even your mum and my gran. But not your dad. He was the only sober one in the village. And that included the vicar."

Will gave a little half-smile at the memory. Then his smile faded abruptly. "Not any more, he's not," he said bleakly.

"How long's he been like this?"

"Ever since the funeral. He started that night, after everyone

33

had gone home, and has been drinking steadily ever since. It's like he's got a flipping death wish, the stupid old fool."

"He's grieving, Will," I said gently.

"And I'm not?" Those three quietly-spoken words told me, more plainly than anything else could have done, the depths of his grief. That and the bleakness of his eyes. Once again I felt guilty that I hadn't been there for him, my oldest friend.

"Of course you are." My voice was husky as I squeezed his hand. "Now, what about that coffee you promised me?"

I followed him down the long dark hall and into the kitchen where I'd spent so much of my childhood, bottle-feeding orphan lambs in front of the range or sitting at the big scrubbed table, trying to talk Will into doing my maths homework for me. Mum used to grumble I spent more time at Will's house than my own. But then, Will's house didn't smell of perm lotion or hum with the constant buzz of gossip. And Sally baked proper cakes and wasn't forever on some daft diet, the way Mum was.

The outside of the farmhouse was more or less the same, even down to the Victoria plum tree that Sally had trained up the front, one branch as tantalisingly close as ever to the upstairs landing window where Will and I would risk life, limb and Sally's anger every autumn as we reached for the luscious purple-red fruits.

Nothing had changed at the farm. Except, of course, for the unnaturally clean yard. And the broken door. And the grimy windows. But it was still essentially the same cluster of honey-coloured stone buildings, perched on the top of Pendle Knoll, with its spectacular views down across the valley to the Mendip hills in the distance. A view that hadn't changed significantly for hundreds of years, since the days when the infamous Judge Jeffreys had roamed the West Country, looking for rebels to hang.

Inside the farmhouse, however, was something else. In Sally's time, the kitchen had been warm and welcoming, always smelling of furniture polish and baking. Now it was freezing and I didn't want to think about what it smelt of. Even the big cream range that Sally always polished until it gleamed had given up and gone out. She'd have been heartbroken.

At the sight of us, a black and white cat shot off the table, where it had been eating the remains of what I imagined was a microwave curry of some sort, judging by the lurid colour. But even the cat, it seemed, had wisely decided to pass on the unappetising lump of sweaty cheese and the grey-blue slices of mouldy bread that spilled across the cluttered table.

"Jeez, what a tip." The words were out before I could stop them. "Oh Will, I'm so sorry. I didn't mean—"

"Forget it." Will switched on the electric kettle, then rummaged among the teetering pile of crockery in the sink for mugs. "Dad's as much use as a chocolate teapot these days so I'm running the farm single-handed. It's all I can do to look after the livestock. There's precious little time left for housework at the end of my day."

Nor for eating properly, either, I thought, as pity wrenched my insides. But this time I kept my thoughts to myself. Instead, more from a desire to change the subject than anything else, I asked, "Where are the cows? I've never seen the yard so clean."

"I'm so glad something meets with your approval." A hint of the teasing smile I remembered so well tugged the corner of his mouth as he rinsed out two mugs. "We got out of dairy. There's no money in milk production any more so we sold the herd a while ago now. Just as well, as things turned out. If I was having to cope with twice-daily milking on my own, on top of everything else, I'd have given up. We've only got beef cattle now – and the sheep, of course. They're the reason Mum started the farm shop in the first place."

It was more than a year since I'd been in Sally's farm shop, back before Sally became ill with the cancer that had overwhelmed her with such sudden, shocking swiftness. Ratface and I had been on a rare visit home and Mum had more or less insisted I go up to the shop to collect some pies that Sally had put by for us.

I wasn't keen. The last thing I wanted to do that morning was bump into Will again. We'd done so in the Winchmoor Arms the previous night and to say that Ratface and Will hadn't hit it off would be like saying Tom and Jerry weren't exactly best buddies. It wasn't helped, of course, by the way Ratface kept saying 'ooh arr' in a poor and extremely annoying imitation of a Somerset accent and making jokes about local yokels that were about as funny as a party political broadcast.

But I needn't have worried. Will wasn't around. Just Sally, as pleased as ever to see me.

The farm shop was in a small stone building that used to be the cheese store, back in the days when cheese was made on farms and not in factories. Sally had stocked the shop with chest freezers full of home-reared lamb, chiller cabinets stuffed with home-made pies and cakes, and shelves that groaned under the weight of jars of her pickles and jams.

She was a small, compact woman with enough energy to power the National Grid. Always busy, always with some new project on the go, always full of life and laughter. It hurt to think of all that brightness snuffed out. Sally Manning, I thought, as a lump in my throat the size of a hen's egg made swallowing difficult, was one of the good guys. It was so unfair.

I blinked away the tears that were making my eyes sting, accepted the mug of coffee Will handed me, and pulled a face. "No milk?" I asked.

He picked up a carton from among the debris on the table, sniffed it and tossed it into the overflowing bin. "Not unless you fancy taking a bucket to one of them up in Top Meadow," he grinned, knowing how jumpy I got anywhere near the rear end of a cow. Or, to be strictly accurate, either end of a cow, ever since the head-butting incident.

"Your dad wasn't the only one wound up about Marjorie Hampton." I changed the subject quickly. "Gerald Crabshaw was in full rant in the pub last night. I thought at first he'd said she'd killed someone and that we had a nice juicy murder on our hands in Much Winchmoor, which would have livened the place up a bit. But he was talking about the farm shop. He shut up quickly enough when your dad came in, though."

Will put a third spoonful of sugar into his coffee and stirred it vigorously. "That's just Gerald, trying to put one over on Marjorie as usual. He's had a down on her ever since he lost his license for drink driving after one of Donald's late night lock-ins. Gerald's convinced she was the one who tipped the police off. Apparently, she'd had a go at him only a couple of days before about driving his Porsche when he'd had one too many. So, chances are, he was right. It's the sort of thing she would do."

"But in what way could she have been responsible for the..." I shied away from Gerald Crabshaw's melodramatic turn of phrase. "The difficulties of the farm shop? I assume it does have difficulties?"

"It's all but closed. Which is a shame because things were going really well until Mum..." He paused, and I reached across and squeezed his hand. "Until Mum got ill. Remember old Mr Taylor who had the Post Office?"

I nodded, took a sip of coffee, then wished I hadn't. It tasted like the inside of a hen house. "Dad told me he'd retired," I said as I tried to suppress a shudder. "That he sold the shop to a developer who promptly turned it into a holiday cottage."

"Couldn't blame the poor old chap for selling up, although there were lots around here who did. He tried to sell it as a going concern but nobody wanted to know and he was getting desperate to move up north, closer to his daughter, which is what he did. But Mum worried about how the old folk were going to collect their pensions and wanted to save them the hassle of having to catch the bus into Dintscombe and back every week. So she persuaded the Post Office to set up what they call an outreach service in the farm shop."

"And that worked, didn't it? I remember Mum telling me about it."

"It certainly did. Worked really well to start with. Mum used to love chatting with them all and started buying in a few bits and pieces of groceries. Tea, coffee, baked beans, that sort of stuff, which seemed to go down really well. But then, Marjorie Hampton decided it was too far for the old folk to come all the way up here to collect their pensions and that Mum's prices were too high. Do you want some more coffee, by the way? See? I remembered how you drink it by the gallon."

"No, I'm fine," I said quickly, wishing there was a convenient house plant I could tip it into. But Sally's lovely collection of pot plants had, judging by the desiccated remains on the window sill, died with her. "I'm trying to cut down on caffeine. Go on with what you were saying. What did Marjorie Hampton do?"

"She took it upon herself to organise a minibus to take them all into Dintscombe, to the main Post Office and then on to the supermarket. She even got some local bigwig to sponsor it as well, so it didn't cost them a penny in fares. And, of course, they jumped at it. Why wouldn't they? Then the Post Office had one of their regular culls of rural outposts and the one at the farm shop had to go."

"So that's what Gerald Crabshaw was on about. How awful. It must have been a desperate blow after all your Mum's hard work."

"Not really." Will took a sip of coffee, pulled a face and added yet another spoonful of sugar. "She'd become ill by then and it was all Dad and I could do to keep the farm ticking over, without taking on the shop as well. And when she died, neither of us had the inclination to do anything about it. Dad because he can't see his way out of a bottle at the moment and me because – well, the truth is, I can't bear to go in there, knowing Mum's not going to come bustling in any moment. I've tried a couple of times but only got as far as the door. I'm a right wimp, I know. But I just couldn't…"

His voice trailed away and there was such unbearable sadness in his eyes that I forgot about the stupid row and remembered we were mates. I put my mug down and moved across to take the chair next to his.

"It's ok." I put my arm around his shoulders and hugged him hard. "Your Mum would understand. She wouldn't want you to beat yourself up about it. That wasn't her way."

Will sat there for ages, saying nothing, staring straight ahead. I sat there too, and for once, didn't say a word. Just held him. Gradually I became aware of the silence, the sort I hadn't heard for years. It was broken only by the ticking of the clock on the old dresser, the dog snoring at Will's feet and the distant bleating of sheep. To my surprise, I found I kind of liked it. Even though I always said I preferred the hum of city traffic to the unnatural silence of the middle of nowhere.

"I've heard Gerald and his nonsense," Will said eventually. "But, you know, it wasn't Marjorie Hampton who killed the farm shop. More the fact that we're only a thirty-minute drive from the nearest supermarket."

"You might not blame her. But perhaps your dad does? Do you think that's what they rowed about yesterday? As well as the footpath thing?"

"I shouldn't think so. He doesn't seem to give a toss about anything on the farm. Now," he went on with a false brightness that didn't fool me for a nanosecond. "There's bound to be a nice leg of lamb in one of the shop freezers. Do you think your mum and dad would like it?"

"No, that's all right. I don't want you going in there on my account."

"I've got to do it sometime. In fact, I thought, well, now you're here, you might…"

He gripped my hand. His hand felt work-roughened and cool on mine. "Will you come with me, Katie? Please?"

My heart went out to him and, once again, I cursed myself for staying away from him for so long. "Of course I will. But only if you promise that you and your dad will come and eat it with us," I said as I followed him out of the house, across the yard and towards the old farm shop.

He paused at the entrance, took a long steadying breath and pulled a bunch of keys out of his pocket.

"Yeah, right. You're on." He put the key in the lock. "I haven't had a roast dinner since I don't know when and I think even Dad might be persuaded. He likes nothing better than a nice roast leg of lamb. It might – hello, what's been going on here?"

"What's the matter?"

"The door's already unlocked." He swore softly. "I didn't think to check in here. That's probably as far as the old fool

39

could stagger last night. What's the betting we find him stretched out in here?"

We did, indeed, find John Manning stretched out across a couple of chairs just inside the entrance. Sally had put them there for the old folks to have a sit down if the Post Office counter was busy.

We also found a nice leg or two. But they didn't belong to any lamb.

Instead, they were sticking out of one of the freezers, clad in thick grey tights and wearing what my mum would have called a good, sensible pair of brown leather, lace up shoes.

Chapter Five

"Wh-what's-the-matter?" John Manning struggled to his feet and shambled towards us, his eyes bloodshot, his breath more toxic than anything that ever wafted out of his farmyard. "Can't a fellow have a kip in peace now?"

"Is this your idea of a sick joke, Dad?" Will asked, pointing across the room to the open freezer.

"A joke?" I let go Will's hand, which until then I'd been holding so tightly it had probably left nail imprints. A joke. Of course. It was a joke. Stupid of me to have been so freaked out. It was just a sick joke.

"Look, Mr Manning," I laughed, light-headed with relief as I walked towards the open freezer. "Someone's stuck a pair of dummy's legs in here and for a moment, I thought—"

"Katie. No." Will pulled me back but it was too late.

I'd got close enough to see that the legs in the sensible, but surprisingly muddy, shoes didn't belong to a dummy, but to a woman with a good, tight, perm and a Midnight Hyacinth rinse. Only there wasn't much left of Mum's handiwork. Just this sickening mess where the back of poor Marjorie Hampton's head should have been. But wasn't.

Will's arm was around my shoulders, pressing me into his chest and holding me so tight I could hardly breathe. Somewhere, someone was making a low, moaning noise. It took me several seconds to realise it was me.

I looked up at Will. His face was the colour of Mum's gloopy grey breakfast as he stared at his dad. "Dad," he said, his voice urgent. "Dad."

John Manning didn't move. He stood rigid, staring at the freezer. Jaw slack. Eyes wild. Uncomprehending.

"What the hell have you done, Dad?" Will asked in a hoarse whisper.

John Manning dragged his horrified gaze away from the freezer. He looked at Will, then back at the body. Bewilderment changed to fury. "Hell's teeth, boy! You think I did that?"

"Then what's she doing here? I know she came to see you yesterday afternoon. You told me the two of you had had a blazing row. Something about footpaths?"

"Interfering old baggage," John snapped, the colour coming back into his face. "Going on about what a terrible state it was in. Said it was a disgrace, and, and so was I. Told me I should pull myself together. That Sally would be ashamed of me."

"She's not wrong there," Will growled.

John grunted and kicked at the floor with the toe of his scuffed boot. "That's as maybe. But it's not her place to go sticking her oar in. So I told her to clear off and mind her own damn business. And, furthermore, I said when she made as if to start on at me again, if I caught her on my land again, I'd get my shotgun—"

"Dad." There was a warning note in Will's voice. "Look, let's get out of here. We need to call the police."

John moved as if he was sleepwalking and blundered into the wall. Will took his arm and guided him out of the building. As we reached the door, I looked back, my attention caught by something behind the chairs where John had been sleeping.

It was a shotgun.

"Will?" I said softly. "I think you should see this."

But he was concentrating on steering his father through the door and didn't hear me.

"Come on, Katie," he called. "I need to get this door locked. Right now."

It couldn't mean anything, could it? Just a coincidence. Probably where John kept his gun. That was all. Without looking back, I followed Will and John into the yard where the steady rain came as a welcome sign of normality.

"Come on. Let's go in to the house. I'm going to ring the police," Will said. "And when they get here, Dad, don't you dare say anything about threatening her with a shotgun, otherwise they'll think you did it."

Especially as it's one of the first things they'll find. I thought. *After the body, that is.*

I should have told Will about the shotgun. Of course I should. But I couldn't bear the thought of going back in there again. Besides, it meant nothing.

John and I watched in silence as Will locked the farm shop door. He went into the house but John made no attempt to follow him. He stood in the middle of the wet yard, as the rain trickled, unheeded, down his face.

"Come on, Mr Manning," I said quietly. "Let's get out of the rain, shall we?"

But he didn't appear to have heard me. Least of all registered the fact that it was raining.

"Of course I didn't do it," he suddenly roared after Will, who was by then already in the house and couldn't possibly have heard him. Then he turned to me, his anger spent, his voice heavy with despair. "How do you like that, Katie? My own son, thinking I could do something like that."

"Of course he doesn't." My voice was soothing, as if I was talking to a fretful child. "He's just telling you to be careful what you say to the police. Well, to anyone. That's all. Now, come on. Let's go in, shall we? We're both getting soaked."

But he was beyond caring about the weather. "But it's the truth. Marjorie Hampton and I had words. I've just said that, didn't I? And I was angry with her. As I had every right to be. But I didn't," he shook his head, as if, like me, he too had that horrific image indelibly printed on his mind and couldn't shut it out. "I didn't do that terrible thing to her. I swear to God I didn't. I told her to get the hell off my land and she did just that."

"What time was that?" I asked.

"What?" He looked at me as if I'd just asked him to prove Einstein's theory of relativity.

"Do you happen to know what time she left here?" I said. "Only it might be important. And the police are sure to ask you."

"No, of course I don't know what the bloody time was," he said sharply, then checked himself. "Hey, yes, wait a minute. I do, as it happens. While we were stood there, we heard the kids coming out of the school. You know what a noise they make. In fact, the old baggage had a grumble about that too. You know how she goes on. 'Young people today,' and all that. So that must have been half past three, or so. Isn't that the time they come out?"

"The police are on the way," Will said, coming back into the yard. "They say not to touch anything or talk to anyone until they get here. Come on, let's go indoors and wait. We'll have a cup of coffee and you can get out of those wet clothes, Dad."

"Will, your dad says Marjorie left here about half past three because she commented on the noise the children made when they came out of school," I said as John and I followed him into the house and back into the cheerless kitchen. John shooed a cat off a chair and sat down heavily.

"And you're sure about that, Dad, are you?" Will asked. "You're sure you stood there at half past three and watched her walk away?"

"Well, no. I didn't exactly stand and watch her. I—" John smoothed a hand across his head, his wet, thinning hair sticking to his skull like a sleek grey cap. "To be honest, I don't rightly recall. It's all a bit of a blur after that. I'm pretty sure I went into the house. Yes, I must have done because I was there when you came in, Will, wasn't I? I had this bottle of whisky, you see, and..."

"And everything else is a blur, as you said." Will finished as John's voice trailed away. "Well, the police are going to really love that story, aren't they? Are you sure you didn't go in the farm shop yesterday afternoon?"

"What about that, Katie? My own son, thinking I could do something like that." John shook his head. His anger died abruptly and he sort of shrivelled, like a leaking balloon. With a pleading look in his eyes, he added, "I suppose she is dead, isn't she? I mean, shouldn't we have tried the kiss of life or something?"

"No. No. There was nothing we could have done." I closed my eyes in a futile attempt to shut out the image that would surely haunt me for the rest of my life. I was no first aider but I didn't need to be, to know that Marjorie Hampton was dead. Very dead.

"We should have covered her up." John took a grubby towel from the rail on the range cooker and made for the door.

"Where are you going?" Will asked.

"To put this over her," John said in a dazed voice. "She wouldn't want people to see her like that, would she?"

I touched his arm and took the towel from him. "I don't think it makes any difference to her now, Mr Manning," I said gently. "Now, come and sit down while Will and I get this coffee sorted. Ok?"

But, of course, it wasn't ok. And, just at that moment, I had the feeling that things would never be ok ever again.

Chapter Six

The last time I'd seen so many police together at any one time had been the Glastonbury Festival. Only this was no noisy, fun-filled, up to your knees in mud weekend. No 'nice juicy murder' either, I thought with a stab of guilt as I remembered what I'd so stupidly wished for earlier. Murder wasn't nice. Or juicy. Nor some entertaining, intellectual puzzle to while away a couple of hours in front of the television.

Murder was shocking. Disorientating. Messy. It was sordid, degrading and deeply, deeply scary. It took your lovely joined-up world and shattered it into millions of tiny, disconnected fragments. And nothing would ever be the same again.

I was alone as I sat in the wreckage of Sally's once-lovely kitchen, no longer noticing the messy table or the mountain of unwashed crockery in the sink. John and Will had gone outside when the first of the police cars arrived but I'd chosen to stay inside. To be honest, I couldn't bear the thought of being asked to show them exactly where we'd found poor Marjorie. My stomach churned at the thought of ever stepping into the old farm shop again.

I wish I could say I spent the time clearing up the kitchen, not wanting anyone else to see the sorry state Will and his dad were living in. But I didn't. Instead, I sat at the table, surrounded by mouldy cheese and the remains of last night's curry, and tried to get my head around it all. What was I going to say when they asked me for a statement? I'd always thought I would make a good witness. But my mind had gone blank. Everything was all jumbled up and nothing made sense any more.

I jumped, startled by a tap on the door. My heart lurched as a policeman walked in. I got up, wanting to turn around and run. Only he stood between me and the door.

"Katie? It is Katie Latcham, isn't it? I heard you were back. When Will said you were in here, I offered to take a preliminary statement from you. Thought a friendly face might help."

"Sorry?" A friendly face? That was the last thing I was expecting to hear. He looked kind of familiar, but I couldn't place him.

"You don't remember me, do you?" he said with a smile as he removed his cap. "Ben."

"Ben Newton!" We were in the same year at school and there was a very good reason I hadn't recognised him. Apart from the obvious one, of course, of my brain being totally frazzled.

When Ben Newton was at school, he was a tall, weedy-looking kid with heavy framed glasses. He had a severe crush on my friend Jules which, unfortunately for Ben, was not reciprocated. She used to call him Nerdy Newton. But, holy moley, he was anything but nerdy now. He had filled out in all the right places. And then some. Even in my current state I could register that fact.

"This is a bad business," he said. "I understand you found the body, is that right?"

"Marjorie." My stomach did its usual backward flip at the memory. "Her name is Marjorie Hampton. She lived in the village. The Old Forge. It's at the end of the High Street, just opposite the pond. I – I only saw her yesterday morning. She – she was having her hair done."

"What time was that?" He sat down at the table opposite me. Although his face was expressionless as he moved the mouldy cheese and other detritus to one side to make room for his notebook, it seemed to me that there was an element of criticism in the movement. I'm sure it was all in my head but I glared at him, as defensive as a tigress with cubs. So the place was a tip, but that wasn't Will's fault. And I was furious with myself for having sat there like a piece of wood for the last ten minutes or so, when I could at least have cleared the table.

'How can the time of her hair appointment have a bearing on anything?' I snapped as I jumped up and threw the mouldy

47

bread into the bulging bin.

'Leave that for a moment, Katie, will you?" he said. "I meant, what time did you find the body?"

"How on earth would I know?" I was flustered, upset and, in my anxiety to hide the wobble, my voice was sharper than I'd intended. "I had other things on my mind, rather than doing a time check." Like trying to keep the contents of my stomach in place, for a start.

"I'm sorry but I have to ask these questions," he said quietly as he stood up. "But if it would be easier for you to be interviewed by a stranger, I understand."

"No. No. Of course it wouldn't. Sit down. Please, Ben?" I gave him an apologetic smile. "I'm sorry I barked at you like that. I'm – it's all a bit of a shock. That's all. I've been sitting here trying to get my head around it. What did you want to know? Ask away."

"I asked what time you discovered the body. Roughly."

"I suppose it must have been some time after nine. Not long after, though, because when I went past the school on my way up here, the children were still in morning assembly. Then Will and I had a coffee, so it was probably about 9.45. Any rate, you should be able to tell because Will phoned you within minutes of us finding the – finding poor Marjorie." I felt my stomach begin to heave again and clapped my hand to my mouth.

"Are you ok?' he asked.

I nodded. "Oh God, Ben. She was – she was stuffed half in, half out of a freezer. Will tried to stop me from seeing her. But it was too late. Her poor head. It was—"

"It's ok. I don't need you to describe what you saw."

That was a relief. Because I couldn't have. I gave a weak, grateful smile, then asked, "Who could have done such a terrible thing?"

"That's what we intend to find out."

"Where is Will?" I asked.

"Giving a statement to one of my colleagues."

"And Will's dad?"

"John Manning is talking to another colleague." He looked

48

closely at me, his eyes kind and concerned. "Are you ok to continue?"

"Yes. I'm fine." It was a complete lie. I was anything but fine. But, right then, I just wanted to get all the questions over and done with. So that I could get on and do something that didn't involve thinking. Something like clearing up the kitchen.

"You say you were with Will. What were you doing in the building?"

I didn't think he needed to know that Will had asked me to go with him, as he hadn't been able to bring himself to go in the old farm shop ever since his mum had died. Besides, that wasn't my story to tell.

"It's the old farm shop," I said. "Will said for me to go and choose a nice leg of lamb for my parents. He said that there were still some left in the freezers from when his mum ran the shop. She died, you know. About four months ago. And Will and his dad gave up on the shop."

He nodded, wrote something in his notebook and went on: "And what happened when you went into the building?"

"That was when we found – we found…"

He paused in his note taking. "When you discovered the body."

I nodded.

Then came the question I'd been dreading. "And Mr John Manning? Where was he? Did he come in to the building with you?"

"No. He – he was already there." I said slowly. Reluctantly. But knowing I'd probably make things even worse by lying.

"Close to the freezers?"

"No. No. Nowhere near the freezers. He was just inside the entrance. There are a couple of chairs that Sally put there, for people to sit and wait if the Post Office counter was busy. Mr Manning was in there, stretched across them. Asleep."

Ben made no comment. Just carried on writing in his notebook. "Did you notice anything else? Anything unusual?"

I shuddered. "Apart from Marjorie, stuffed head first into one of the freezers, you mean?"

I didn't mean it to sound so flippant. But the words were out before I could stop them.

"Apart from that." Suddenly he'd stopped being the old mate from school and had become very business-like.

"No. Nothing," I said quickly. Nothing, this is, apart from John's shotgun lying in the corner behind the chairs where he'd been 'sleeping'. But, old school mate or no, I wasn't going to volunteer that particular bit of information. I figured they'd have found it by now anyway. "I'm sorry, Ben. There's nothing more I can tell you. I wish there was. Because I really, really want you to find whoever did this."

I turned away, not wanting him to see the tears that had sprung to my eyes.

"We will, Katie. I promise you," he said as he stood up to go. "That's all for now. Apart from your contact details, of course. Are you still living with your mum and dad, at their place off the High Street?"

"Yes, and my name—" I stopped. I'd been going to tell him that I preferred to be called Kat these days. But suddenly all that rubbish about what I was or wasn't going to be called seemed trivial and childish.

I gave him my mobile number, and Mum and Dad's full address and number, then followed him back outside. I went across the yard to collect my bike, trying not to look at the entrance to the old farm shop. The rain had stopped now and the blue and white police tape that cordoned off the entrance fluttered like bunting in the chilly morning breeze.

I stepped back as a police car drove past, with John Manning, hunched, head down, in the far corner of the back seat, a grim-faced policeman by his side.

Will stood by the yard gate, ashen, gripping the top bar of the gate as he watched them drive away. The dog, Tam was, as always, by his side.

I walked up to him. Tam nuzzled my hand as I did so, her nose cold against my skin. "What's happening? Where are they taking your dad?"

"Yeovil Police Station." He sounded dazed, like he'd just been roughly woken from a deep sleep.

"But why? They're surely not going to charge him? He'll need a lift home once they realise they've made a mistake. Come on, Will. Get the car out and we'll go after him."

I was already half way across the yard towards Will's car, but he called me back. "There's no point. According to the sergeant over there, he's just 'helping them with their enquiries'. Not that he's in any fit state to help anyone, least of all himself, he's that hung over, the silly old fool."

"But that's ridiculous. Why can't he help them with their enquiries right here? Why drag him all the way to Yeovil?" I looked around to ask Ben Newton the same question, but he was nowhere to be seen.

Will shrugged. "Search me. He wasn't helping himself, that's for sure. I tried to get him to shut up but the moment the police got here, before they'd so much as asked him a single question, he went on and on about how he and Marjorie had had words and he'd told her to push off. Even called her an interfering old baggage, would you believe? Right there, in front of that stony-faced sergeant. He – he said—" He gripped the gate rail tighter than ever and turned to face me. "You know what they found in the shop, close to where Dad had been sitting, don't you?"

"His shotgun."

Will stared at me. "How the hell did you know that?" he asked.

"Because I saw it. Like you said, it was behind the chair where he'd been sleeping. Propped up in the corner."

"You saw it, and you didn't think to tell me?" He glared at me.

"I didn't know what to do." My anger, as always, flashed to meet his. "I was shocked, not thinking clearly. And no, I didn't tell the police. They asked me if I'd seen anything unusual – apart from Marjorie, of course – and I said no. After all, a shotgun's not exactly an unusual sight around a farm, is it?"

"That's something, I suppose," he muttered.

"Besides, even if I had told you, what would you have done? Removed it from the scene?"

He chewed his thumbnail. "I don't know."

"So they found his shotgun. But it hadn't been fired, had it?" I went on.

"They're taking it away for forensic examination. He said he'd been using it to shoot rabbits yesterday."

"Then that's what he'd been doing, isn't it?"

"Yes, I think so." He pushed his hand through his already tousled hair. "I can't swear to it but I'm pretty sure I heard him, up there in Top Meadow. But it's one of those sounds you hear so often that you don't take any notice. So even that didn't help him."

"So they think Marjorie was shot, do they?"

"How would I know?" His voice crackled with bitterness. "They don't tell you anything. Just ask the same damn questions over and over, like they're hoping to trip you up."

"They're only trying to find out what happened."

"Trouble was, Dad was getting more and more wound up, the more they asked." He turned his face away and looked down at his hand, still gripping the top of the gate, his knuckles white. "I was waiting for him to come out and say how he'd threatened her with his shotgun if she came back. For all I know, he's probably done so already. They're going to pin this on him, Katie. I know it." His voice was low, hopeless.

"Of course they won't. Because he didn't do it," I said with complete conviction.

"Yeah, right. And they never get things wrong, do they? Innocent people never get convicted. Because he is innocent, isn't he?" He wiped his hand down across his face and his eyes, when he looked up, were full of fear. And a hint of doubt. "You know, Marjorie Hampton really got under his skin the other day. Lecturing him about how he should pull himself together, how ashamed Mum would be of the way he's behaving. He was still beside himself with fury when I saw him. I've never seen him quite that bad before."

"Will, don't go there," I placed my hand over his and squeezed tightly. "Marjorie Hampton is – was – an interfering old busybody who had no right to speak to your dad, or anyone else, the way she did. Of course he got mad with her. Anyone would have done. That doesn't mean she deserved to be murdered, of course."

"Of course not. And yeah, I suppose you're right." Still the doubt – and the fear –shadowed his eyes. "He couldn't have done it, could he?"

"Now you listen to me, William Manning," I said fiercely. "Your dad's one of the gentlest, kindest people I know. Of course he couldn't have done it. Remember how he showed me how to take care of the orphan lambs? And taught me to ride that bad-tempered little pony of yours, when all you did was laugh at me and call me Scaredy Cat? And how he cried, along with us, when Blue died?"

"He loved that old dog, didn't he?" A smile flickered across Will's face as he reached down and fondled Tam, and the black and white collie whimpered and pressed closer into his legs.

"Like I say, he's a big softy. He could never—" I swallowed hard as that dreadful image filled my head again and my stomach gave yet another sickening lurch.

"And in the pub last night," he said harshly, his eyes bleak. "Was he a big softy then, do you reckon?"

"Well, no," I said slowly. "He was…"

"Morose. Drunk. Anti-social. Bitter and angry. Not exactly the man you remembered, I'll bet. Not the same man who cried over a dead dog."

I was forced to admit I hadn't even recognised John when he'd first stumbled into the bar last night. "Even so, underneath it all, he is the same man. He'd never do something like that. No matter how drunk, or angry, he was."

"I hope to God you're right. But if he didn't, then who did?"

"How would I know? I just know it's not your dad," I reached out a hand towards him. "Look, Will, come on down to our house. At least you'll get a decent cup of coffee there. Don't stay here on your own."

He shook his head. "No. I'm going to see if I can get hold of a solicitor. Then I've got to go up and sort out the animals. I was on my way up there before… before. Thanks for everything, Katie. For being there. I appreciate it. And I'm sorry for barking at you like that just now, about the gun. You were right not to tell me. Because I don't know what I'd have done if I'd known. I'll let you know, about Dad."

As he turned to go into the house, the dog and I both followed him.

"It's ok," he said as we reached the back door. "I'm fine. I don't need babysitting. Honest."

"You might be fine. Your kitchen, on the other hand, is disgusting." I glanced at my watch, surprised to see that it was still only ten past eleven. "I've got half an hour before I need to get away for my lunchtime shift at the pub. You go and do what you have to do and I'll clean up here. It's not going to help anyone if you go down with salmonella poisoning. Because I'll tell you now, I'm not looking after those vicious cows of yours."

"You, doing some housework? Now that's a first. This I must see." he said with a quick grin. And in that moment, in spite of the grimness of the day, my spirits gave a little lift. It was so good to feel back on the old easy terms with Will again. But it was a pity it had taken such a horrible tragedy to bring us back together.

I punched him on the shoulder. "Don't go getting the wrong idea, Will Manning. This is a one-off, you do realise that, don't you? It's just that I don't want to taste anything as foul as that coffee you made me before ever again. It was gross."

"You didn't complain at the time."

"That's because I was being polite, you idiot."

He laughed. "Now I know I've wandered into a parallel universe. Katie Call-Me-Kat Latcham, not only volunteering to do the washing up but being too polite to complain that the coffee doesn't meet her exacting townie standards? You'll be wearing a frilly apron and rubber gloves next."

"In your dreams, boy. And if you don't get out of here, I'll have you drying up." I started lifting the crockery out of the sink, but paused and turned to face him. "I've just had a thought. Someone's bound to have seen Marjorie Hampton yesterday after she'd been up to see your dad, because she'd have had to go back down past the school again. It's the only way to the village. I wouldn't have thought her confrontation with your dad would have taken more than five minutes. I should be finished in the pub in time to catch the school run this afternoon. Some of the young mums must have seen her. Damn it, I wish I'd thought to tell Ben that."

"Ben?" Will looked puzzled.

"You must remember Ben Newton? He was in your year at school. Nerdy kid with glasses."

Will shrugged. The only people he remembered from school were the lads in the rugby team. And my friend, Jules, of course. But then, everyone remembered Jules.

"What about him?" Will asked.

"He's a policeman now. He spoke to you. Said it was you who told him where to find me."

Will shrugged. "They all looked the same to me."

"Well, he was the one who interviewed me. And I wish I'd thought to tell him that Marjorie stopped to have a go at one of the mums on the way up here to the farm. If one of them remembers seeing her on the way back down, that would put your dad in the clear, wouldn't it?"

It was a long shot. But, like the washing up, it was good to be doing something. Or, at least, planning to do something. Anything to stop me thinking. And remembering.

Chapter Seven

There was no need for superfast broadband in Much Winchmoor, which was just as well because there was zero chance of getting it. The news of the murder went round the village faster than a rat down a drainpipe and reached the pub way before I did, particularly as I'd stopped off at home to shower and change.

"Are you sure you want to go to work, Katie, love?" Mum asked anxiously after I told her what had happened. "You've had a terrible shock. I'm sure Donald would understand."

"But, Mum, I want to do it," I said. "If I stay here, I'll just think about it. Over and over again. I'd much rather be busy."

Besides, I could have added but didn't, I wanted to see if anyone had seen or heard Marjorie Hampton after she'd left John Manning yesterday afternoon. Ok, so I wasn't going to wade in and solve the murder before the police did. That only happened in books, not in real life. But I needed to do something. And if I could find someone who saw Marjorie Hampton after she left the farm, that would go a little way to easing the feeling of utter helplessness that hung around me like a November fog.

So, as I often do when I'm feeling a bit shaken up, I dressed to impress. I chose my tightest jeans, my spikiest-heeled boots, my sparkliest, pinkest tiny little biker jacket. I even spiked my hair up, to match my boots. It was all a bit much for Not Much Winchmoor. But it made me feel better. At least for a while.

Donald did a double-take when he saw me and muttered something about how he thought we'd already had a chat about 'inappropriate clothing' and how I'd better watch out I didn't harpoon someone's foot with those heels.

But he couldn't go on at me for long because, as soon as the doors opened, the customers poured in on a tidal wave of ghoulish curiosity. In no time at all the bar was heaving – and nobody was interested in what I was wearing. The only thing on anyone's mind was the murder. The wildness of the speculation increased in direct proportion to the number of pints of Ferret's Kneecaps consumed. After a couple of hours of it, I found myself wishing (a) that we could turn the clock back to the night before when they were all talking about my love life, and (b) that I'd worn more sensible shoes.

The frantically busy lunchtime session had Donald breaking into a smile every time he went to the till, in spite of my 'inappropriate clothing.' He was one happy bunny.

But I was wishing I'd listened to my mum and stayed at home. I felt tired and shaky as the shock was beginning to kick in. I couldn't wait for my shift to end and glanced down at my watch for the tenth time in as many minutes.

"Are we holding you up?" Elsie Flintlock said sharply. "Only the way you're hopping about, you're giving me heartburn. Me and Olive have come in here for a quiet pensioner's lunch and we don't expect to be hurried out, like we're in the way. This isn't one of your fast food, eat all you can as quick as you can, places. Respect, young lady. That's what you need to learn. Respect for your elders. We fought a war for the likes of you. Just you remember that."

I was aware of Donald hovering in the background, so bit back a retort. Besides, there was no point in arguing with Elsie Flintlock. You could never win. Her keen blue eyes missed nothing and her acid tongue could have stripped varnish. Donald frequently grumbled that the pair of them always stayed longer if the weather was cold, to save on their heating bills at home.

She was the unelected leader of the Much Winchmoor Grumble and Gossip Group – or, to give it its correct title, the Much Winchmoor Young Wives' Group. Not that any of the members were under sixty-five. It was just that there hadn't been a vicar in the last thirty years with the courage to change the name.

But, if anyone knew who was doing what, where and to whom, Elsie Flintlock was that person. What she didn't know about the goings-on in the village probably hadn't happened.

"No, of course I'm not in a rush, Mrs Flintlock. You take all the time you need," I said, as I collected the empty glasses and put them on the bar, ready to stack in the glass washer. "I was just hoping to catch Jules, on her way to pick her daughter up from school. But it doesn't matter. I'll catch her later."

"Jules? What sort of name is that when it's at home?" Elsie snorted. "I suppose you mean Olive's granddaughter, Juliet. The girl you used to be really friendly with until you dropped her for your trendy new friends in Bristol."

"I didn't drop her," I protested. "She got married and I moved away, that's all. We've kept in touch."

Not strictly true. Jules had got pregnant with Kylie at about the same time I started college. Over the last five years, we'd exchanged the odd email and followed each other on Facebook, not much else. But Elsie didn't need to know that.

"I've heard she's in the family way again." Elsie said, with a shake of her head. "That useless husband of hers doesn't earn enough to keep himself in shoe leather, let alone a growing family. And they're already bursting at the seams in that little shoebox of theirs. Olive here was only saying just now, how are they going to fit another in…?"

"I want to ask her about John Manning. Or rather, if she or any of the other mums saw Marjorie Hampton on Tuesday afternoon after she'd been up to the farm to see him."

That diverted Elsie's attention away from Jules and Ed. Her sharp pale blue eyes glinted as she drained her glass and handed it to me. "I'll have another half of Ferret's, please, and Olive will have an orange juice. And you can tell that skinflint boss of yours, he can be done under the trade descriptions act for calling that soggy mess we've just eaten a steak and mushroom pie. Not a single mushroom, and if that was steak, then I'm Victoria Beckham."

I smothered a smile. Anyone less like Victoria Beckham than Elsie Flintlock was hard to imagine. The only thing they had in common was a pair of razor-sharp elbows, that Elsie used to good effect if she wanted to clear her way through a crowd.

"Do you want me to pass your complaint on to Donald?" I asked, handing them their drinks. "I'm sure he'll want to know if a customer isn't satisfied."

"No point," Elsie sniffed. "He takes no notice. Now, what were you saying about John Manning? I hear he's been charged with Marjorie Hampton's murder and that it was you who found her headless body."

"Not headless." I suppressed a shudder. "And John Manning hasn't been charged with anything."

"Not yet he hasn't, but it's only a matter of time. Not that he was the only one around here with a motive. Marjorie Hampton has got up more noses than grass pollen in the hay fever season. I'm surprised there wasn't a queue lining up to do for the nosy parker."

Settling down for a long, cosy chat with Elsie Flintlock was the last thing I wanted. On the other hand, the old gossip might be able to tell me something.

"Anyone in particular?" I asked.

"She's upset practically everyone in the village at some time or another," Elsie said. "Even told poor old Olive here that she shouldn't let her cat do his business in other people's gardens. Isn't that right, Olive?"

I didn't think Olive Shrewton was capable of killing a wasp, least of all Marjorie. But then, neither was John Manning.

"So when was the last time either of you saw Marjorie?" I asked.

"I saw her at your mum's," Elsie said, while Olive nodded in agreement. "Having her hair done. As you know, seeing as you were there at the time, trying to make me catch my death of cold, pouring freezing water down my neck. Even though I was good enough to tell you about the job going here." She looked at me critically. "You know, you're not a very good advert for Cheryl's salon and I've told your mother as much on several occasions. If you're going to work in there on a regular basis, you're going to have to smarten yourself up, young lady. Have you combed your hair this morning? And what sort of colour is that supposed to be? Purple? It isn't natural."

I was about to say that Blue Hyacinth wasn't natural either, but that brought back memories of Marjorie Hampton. So I let it go.

"Of course I've combed my hair. And it's supposed to be like this. It's the fashion. And I'm not going to be working in the salon any more. I was only covering for Sandra while she was away having her bunions done, or whatever it was." I cleared away the empty plates and resisted the urge to point out that the steak and mushroom pies couldn't have been that bad, seeing as both plates looked as if they'd been licked clean. "Did you happen to know where Marjorie was going, after she'd had her hair done?"

"How would I know?" Elsie picked up her glass and took a long drink. "You were the one she was talking to, not me. Weren't you listening?"

"Well, yes. Sort of. She was going on about footpaths and something about how she was going to stand up to someone once and for all. But it was quite noisy in the salon, and I didn't catch all she said."

"Did she now? Going to stand up to somebody, eh?" Elsie became fully alert, like a bloodhound picking up a scent. "Now, who do you reckon she was meaning?"

"I don't know. Except, I don't think she meant John Manning, because—"

"I think it's about time you were off home, Katie."

Damn it. I wished Donald wouldn't do that. He came up so quietly behind me, it made me jump. He did it all the time and it was starting to freak me out. It was as if he had a hidden camera that sent him an alert every time I stopped to talk to anyone.

But I didn't have to be told to go twice. Particularly as it was obvious that information gathering was strictly a one-way process as far as Elsie Flintlock was concerned.

I grabbed my sparkly pink biker jacket and hurried out, determined to catch Jules on her way to school.

The icy wind which had been screaming around Will's farm this morning had obviously decided to include the whole village in its rampaging bid to bring March in like a lion. The village's narrow High Street, with its higgledy-piggledy stone cottages, acted like a wind tunnel and I caught the full force the moment I stepped outside the pub.

I looked down the street and saw, with a jolt, a police car parked outside Marjorie's cottage. Would they find anything there that would tell them who she'd been planning to meet yesterday afternoon? Something that would put John Manning in the clear? I certainly hoped so.

The wind gave another furious blast that set the Winchmoor Arms sign swinging wildly and sent an empty drink can scudding down the road like a heat-seeking missile. I pulled my jacket closer to me and cursed myself for having chosen to wear something that looked and felt good on the streets of Bristol but here, in Not Much Winchmoor, was totally inadequate. I thought about stopping off at home to add another layer or two and to change from the spiky-heeled boots into the less glamorous but infinitely more comfortable shoes I'd been wearing earlier. Then I spotted Jules in the distance. She was with a gaggle of mums and buggies and they'd just turned up towards School Lane.

I decided against the ropey old shoes and baggy fleece. I hadn't seen Jules in ages and wanted to look cool. She'd always had a very critical eye (and tongue) when it came to matters of fashion and all through our schooldays and, before I discovered judo, had made me feel the plain and dumpy one.

I called her but my voice was snatched away by the wind so there was nothing for it but to break into a light trot in a bid to catch up the girl I'd been friendly with ever since primary school.

"Jules!" I called again.

This time, she turned round. A big beaming smile lit up her face as she recognised me. "Katie, I heard you were back. Hey, you're looking good, girl. I love your hair. It's really cool."

"Thanks." Praise from Jules warmed me where my sparkly pink biker jacket had spectacularly failed. "I was asked by Elsie Flintlock just now if I'd combed it this morning. And then she went on to say I was a pretty poor advert for Mum's salon."

Jules laughed. "I should think that's a good thing, wouldn't you? No disrespect to your mum intended."

"None taken," I assured her.

"And you've lost a shedload of weight. Given up the chocolate digestives for good now, have you?"

I laughed. "Never. It's a combination of judo and running."

"Whatever. You look brilliant. Hey, it's great to see you, Katie." Jules linked her arm through mine in the way she always used to. "One of the other mums was just telling me about Marjorie Hampton. And that it was you who found her body. Is that right?"

"Yes. It was pretty grim, actually."

"Of course. It must have been awful. But a murder? Right here in Much Winchmoor. It's just terrible, isn't it?"

She couldn't quite keep the excitement out of her voice and her eyes shone. But I couldn't really blame her. I'd probably have been just the same if I hadn't been the one to find the body.

"Yes. Terrible. And I prefer to be called Kat now, if you don't mind," I said automatically.

"Of course you do. Sorry. I keep forgetting. You told me the last time you were home. Look, it's too cold to stand around here chatting. I'm on my way to pick up our Kylie from school. Walk with me a little way?" Jules pulled up the collar of her thick padded coat as we set off in the direction of School Lane, arms still linked, like the old days.

"I'm not surprised you can't get anyone to remember your new name," she went on. "You know how folk around here hate change. In their eyes you're little Katie Latcham. And that's that. Always have been. Always will be. Even when you become a rich and famous radio presenter."

"In my dreams." With my spare hand I tugged my jacket closer, as the chill wind cut through the thin fabric. "You know I got made redundant from the radio station, don't you?'

"Yeah, I heard. That's tough. So, apart from that, how are things with you, Kat? I heard you and that guy – what was his name? – split."

"Nick." I said shortly. "Otherwise known as Ratface. And is there anyone in this village who doesn't know about my love life?"

"Shouldn't think so," Jules grinned. "Once Elsie Flintlock gets hold of a piece of goss, it's like taking out a front page advert in *The Chronicle* and announcing it to the world."

"Tell me about it," I sighed. "She told me at lunchtime you were in 'the family way' again, as she put it. Is that right?"

Jules stopped so suddenly I almost toppled off my spiky heels. The last time I'd seen that stricken expression on her face was the day she found out she'd failed GCSE maths for the second time.

"Jules, I'm sorry." I gave her arm an apologetic squeeze. I really hadn't meant to upset her and should have known better than to assume that just because Elsie Flintlock knew something, the information was in the public domain.

I looked at her closely and for the first time, noticed how tired and frazzled she looked, the dark circles under her eyes accentuated by the pallor of her skin. Her hair, which was usually as sleek and glossy as one of the adverts for hair products in Mum's salon, was scraped carelessly back into a lank ponytail. And her clothes looked as if she'd grabbed the nearest things to hand. It was so unlike her. Of the two of us, she'd always been the fashionista, the one to follow the latest trend. But the baggy tracksuit bottoms and scuffed trainers she was wearing didn't look that trendy to me. Although, I had to admit it, her outfit looked a damn sight warmer and more comfortable than mine.

"Old witch," Jules muttered, "How the hell did she know? I haven't even told Eddie yet. He's going to be over the moon – I don't think. Another baby was definitely not part of the plan. Not now things were just getting to be a bit easier, with our Kylie starting school. And then, I had this job, which I had to pack in because I've been getting the most terrible morning sickness that lasts morning, noon and night, and the boss wasn't prepared to give me any more time off. I've been feeling absolutely dreadful."

"God, I'm sorry, Jules. That's tough," I gave her arm another squeeze. "This place is the pits for knowing everyone's business, isn't it? I'd forgotten just how bad it can be."

Jules glanced at her watch. "Look, I can't just stand here, much as I'd like to. I must get on. Kylie goes mental if I'm not there when she comes out of school. She started in September and I thought she'd be over all that by now. It's been six months but she hasn't really settled yet. Her teacher says not to worry, that they all settle in at their own pace but you can't help worrying, can you? Why not walk up to school with me and and we'll talk as we go along? It'll be a trip down memory lane for you, seeing the old place again."

"Sure." After all, it was not like I had anything else to do that afternoon. Apart from take off my boots, that is.

"I hear Marjorie Hampton was decapitated," Jules said, the gleam of excitement lighting up her face again. "That her head was in one freezer and the rest of her in another. Is that true?"

"No." I said shortly. I preferred not to think about Marjorie's blue cauliflower head as it had been the last time I saw it. But, as far as I could tell, it had still been firmly attached to her body. "I saw her, you know. I mean, alive and well. It was yesterday morning. Just a few hours before the – before it happened, I suppose. I was helping Mum in the salon because Sandra had gone to Bath to see a chiropodist—"

"Sandra!" Jules gave a shriek of laughter. "God, is she still working for your Mum? I thought she'd been pensioned off years ago."

"Still there. Do you remember how we used to call her Mrs Overall, after that Julie Walters character?"

We giggled and, for the first time since coming back to Much Winchmoor, I felt a sense of connection with someone. Apart from Will, of course. It was so good to see Jules again and have a laugh over old times. Good, too, to forget, if only for a fleeting moment, Marjorie Hampton's brutal murder, which had filled my mind ever since the grim discovery. But there was no getting away from it for long. Not even with Jules. Especially not with Jules, who was, I reminded myself, Olive Shrewton's granddaughter and, although she moaned about it, shared her grandmother's love of a good gossip. Providing, of course, it wasn't about her.

"So, go on," Jules prompted. "You say you saw Marjorie in the salon yesterday morning?"

"She came in to have a perm. Said she was going up to see John Manning later. Something about a footpath closure. Said she was going to have it out with him, once and for all. But there was something else she said that made me think—"

But Jules wasn't interested in whatever it was that had made me think. Her eyes gleamed. "And you reckon that's when he murdered her?"

"No, of course I don't. John Manning didn't do it. No way. For pity's sake, Jules. You know the guy as well as I do. He couldn't possibly have done it."

"That's not what I heard. Not what the police think either, by all accounts."

"Then the police are wrong," I said with total conviction. "It has been known. Look at that time they thought your Eddie had been receiving stolen copper cables."

"That was a mistake. The dumbo bought them in good faith from a dodgy mate. I'm always telling him he should pick his friends more carefully."

"Exactly. A mistake. The police were wrong about Eddie, and they're wrong about John Manning."

She stopped and turned to me. "But then, if John didn't do it, who did?"

"That's the million-dollar question." An image of Will's shocked expression as he watched his dad being driven away in a police car filled my mind. Swiftly followed by one of John Manning's face, as white as his son's. How must he be feeling now, locked up in a police cell? He was a man of the outdoors, never comfortable in confined spaces at the best of times. It must surely be freaking him out. "I don't know who did it," I added. "But I intend to find out.'

"Hah!" Jules laughed. "Hark at you. Much Winchmoor's answer to Miss Marple."

I turned and looked back on the village, stretched out below us now. It looked so quiet. Dead, even. The sort of place where the most exciting thing to happen had been the vicar falling off his bike into the village pond after the Harvest Supper, when he'd foolishly mistaken Abe Compton's Headbender cider for apple juice.

Yet, somewhere down there in that tiny cluster of houses was someone who thought that he – or, of course, she – had just got away with murder.

I shivered and held Jules's arm more tightly as we walked on up the hill. "No, seriously, though," I said. "Did you see Marjorie up here yesterday afternoon?"

"No. But I was late picking Kylie up. I had to go into Dintscombe to see the doctor and the wretched bus was late coming back. It had to go all round the lanes as there'd been a nasty crash and the dual carriageway was closed most of the afternoon. That's why I don't want to be late today. She'd got in a terrible state, convinced herself that I was never coming back and Miss Davenport, her teacher, now has me marked down as a bad mother."

"What about any of the other mums?" I asked. "Did any of them see Marjorie?"

"I don't know. How would I? You'll have to ask them."

We'd arrived at the school by this time and I spent several minutes going from one group of mums to the next. But nobody, it seemed, had seen Marjorie Hampton coming back after John Manning had told her to get off his land, although a few had seen her when she was on the way up. One had even spoken to her. A red-haired girl called Amy.

"Interfering old cow," Amy said. "Only told me my little Skye shouldn't be eating a lolly. That it would rot her teeth. Like it was any of her business."

I smiled down at the child in the pushchair, who was bundled up in layers of furry blankets, which I envied. I went to say hello to her but her small red face puckered as I leaned towards her pushchair and I pulled back hastily.

"I'm sorry," Amy shrugged. "She's a bit shy with strangers."

"Very wise, too," I said. "So when Marjorie spoke to you, that would have been about half past three, would it? And was she on her way up to the farm or coming back?"

She shook her head. "On her way up. And it was more like

quarter past. I was early. I always am. First to arrive, last to go, that's me."

Quarter past three. That meant Marjorie would have reached the farm at about twenty past. How long does it take to have a row and be ordered off? One thing was sure, John wouldn't have invited her in for a cup of tea and a biscuit.

"I didn't see her come back down, though," Amy went on. "And I was here for ages, waiting for my Marlon who'd lost his reading book and had to stay behind until he found it. He'd lose his head if it wasn't screwed on, that one. Just like his dad. It must have been closer to four when we finally got away."

I frowned. That didn't make sense. The only way to and from the Manning farm was via the lane that led past the school. Once it reached the farm, it ended abruptly in a rough farm track that wound its way up to the top of Pendle Knoll itself. It was obvious from the deep muddy ruts that Will had been driving his tractor up and down. There was no way anyone else could have gone that way, unless they'd borrowed Will's tractor, and somehow I couldn't see Marjorie doing that.

But if she had left John at the time he said, then she'd have had to come back down the lane. And Amy would have seen her. The other mums, too, no doubt.

Which meant either John had got the time wrong, and she'd left much later, or she hadn't come back at all. That John had lost his temper, which he admitted he had and—

And nothing. I shook my head, cross with myself for letting my thoughts skitter off in that direction.

John Manning was innocent. Of course he was. And I was going to prove it. One way or another.

Chapter Eight

It had worked! Who'd have thought murder could be so easy? Of course, it was all down to meticulous planning. And, he was big enough to admit, a small bit of luck. Hearing her and John Manning arguing like that. Well, a fellow would have to be a complete fool not to have capitalised on that.

And he was no fool. Nobody would ever call him that again. Because if they did… Well, they always said the first one was the hardest, didn't they? But that had been a piece of cake. She went like a lamb to the slaughter. Which, when you think where the interfering old biddy ended up, was kind of appropriate.

A suitable place to die. He'd chosen well. It was a pity he couldn't have finished the job properly. If he'd had time to put her whole body in that freezer, she'd have been there for ages, undiscovered.

But still, the memory of that last view of her, legs up in the air, was priceless. Hilarious. And worth the risk.

He was safe now. That was all that mattered. Nobody, but nobody, could mess things up for him now.

His plan had worked.

Chapter Nine

The noise level around the school suddenly rocketed as the doors opened and a swarm of over-excited children surged into the playground. I had a certain sympathy with Marjorie's comment to John about the din from the school yesterday. I'm sure we were never allowed to be so noisy when we were that age.

I froze, horrified at my train of thought. I'd been back in Much Winchmoor – how long was it? Three days? Four days? It felt more like a month. And already I was beginning to sound like a fully paid up member of the Grumble and Gossip Group. What was happening to me?

There was no point hanging around in the school playground, asking any more questions. I turned away, disappointed that my first attempts to find someone who'd seen Marjorie after she left the farm yesterday afternoon had drawn a resounding blank. I'd been so sure somebody must have seen her.

As I walked away, I heard someone call my name and turned back, my hopes rising.

"Katie?" It was Amy, with a small boy I took to be Marlon pulling at her sleeve. "I just wanted to say I love your jacket. It's really cool. Where did you get it?"

Isn't that always the way? At any other time, I'd have been dead pleased by someone commenting on the way I looked. But right then I was so focused on Marjorie and her movements that I stared blankly at Amy while I tried to work out what she was on about.

"My jacket? Oh, yes. Thanks." I said, desperate not to spoil the effect by shivering as the mad March wind, which showed no sign of calming down any time soon, sliced through my 'cool' jacket like a knife through butter. I also didn't want to tell her that I'd bought it for a fiver in a charity shop in Bristol. I had my pride.

"Oh, you know," I said vaguely. "One of those small trendy shops in Clifton. Can't remember where exactly. You will let me know if you hear if anyone saw Marjorie Hampton yesterday afternoon, won't you?"

Amy nodded. "My mum lives just opposite her. I'll ask around and…"

At that moment, Marlon decided that the tatty one-eared toy rabbit his younger sister was clutching was in fact his and our conversation, such as it was, ended abruptly.

I moved out of ear splitting distance and took out my phone to call Will. But, as always, he wasn't answering. Not that I was looking forward to adding to his worries by telling him none of the mums had seen Marjorie, after his dad ordered her off the farm. And yet, if John was to be believed, which of course he was, then surely somebody must have seen her? This was Much Winchmoor, for pity's sake, where a person couldn't sneeze without the whole village speculating on what they'd been doing to catch a cold – and who they'd been doing it with.

But who had seen Marjorie? And when?

I hoped the fact that Will wasn't answering his phone meant he was on his way down to Yeovil to collect his dad. I was dying to go home, take my boots off and thaw out. But as I was so close to the farm, I reckoned I might as well go on up and see if he was around. Just in case.

I still couldn't get used to seeing the farmyard so clean and cattle-free. It was deserted, apart from the kittens who were playing with the blue and white police tape that still fluttered around the entrance to the old farm shop. They skittered back to the safety of the barn as I pushed open the yard gate.

I was relieved to see that, apart from the tape, there was no other sign of any police activity now. Will's mud-encrusted Land Rover was parked in its usual place. And the fact that there were no hysterical dogs rushing towards me as I crossed the yard told me that he must be out on the farm somewhere.

Pendle Knoll Farmhouse didn't run to such luxuries as a

door bell or knocker, so I banged on the farmhouse door long and hard, in the hope that John might be back and would open it. But all I got for my effort was a set of sore knuckles.

I got my phone out to try Will again but changed my mind. What was the point? His mobile was the most immobile phone on the planet, spending most of its time sitting among the detritus that littered the old oak dresser in the kitchen. I scribbled a note asking him to let me know what was happening and if there was anything I could do, pushed it through the letterbox, then went back home to spend what was left of the afternoon trawling the internet for jobs and sending out applications.

It was a soul-destroying task. I knew that most of my applications, if not all of them, wouldn't even get an acknowledgement, least of all be taken any further. It was almost a relief when it was time for my evening shift in the pub, even if it did mean another evening of mind-numbing boredom. But I figured that after the sort of day I'd had, a bit of boredom would come as a welcome relief.

But I'd reckoned without the power of a gruesome event like a murder to pull a community together. Or, as was more likely, to bring out the ghoul in everyone within a twenty-mile radius. Just as it had been at lunchtime, the Winchmoor Arms was heaving like it was Christmas Eve, as people flocked to the place in the hope of finding out what had really happened, rather than settle for the stark statement that had been on the early evening local news.

Talk about one man's tragedy being another man's good fortune. Donald had a smile on his face like he'd won the lottery. He'd even put roast lamb – a rare treat and something he usually reserved for high days, holidays and, for reasons best known to himself, Trafalgar Day – on the Specials Menu. The kitchen was working flat out all evening, while his beer sales went through the roof.

I was rushed off my feet, now thankfully clad in shoes which, while not in the Marjorie Hampton mould of 'sensible footwear,' were a lot more comfortable than my earlier choice. There was one tiny consolation, though. There was no sign of

71

Councillor Creepy Crabshaw who, together with his wife, my mum and Sandra, were probably the only Much Winchmoor residents not in the pub that night. The only downside was that, after his unsubtle attempts to look down my top the night before – and given that I'd frozen half to death that afternoon – I'd dressed in a warm, fleecy, high-necked sweatshirt which, before the evening was half over, felt like one of those sauna suits people wear to sweat the fat off.

When I'd first arrived at the start of my shift, Donald nodded his approval and muttered something about how glad he was to see me in more appropriate clothing, but as the pub filled, the temperature soared. My face went from tomato red to beetroot purple and glistened with sweat as I raced about like a hen on hurry-up pills, trying to keep pace with the seemingly endless demand for food and drink. Not to mention fielding as many demands for information about the murder.

Everyone, it seemed – except, of course, me and Will – was convinced of John Manning's guilt and had the poor guy tried and convicted. They came out with one story after another about his heavy drinking, and the unrelenting anger that had been eating him alive ever since Sally died. And, as the evening went on and the beer flowed, the stories and speculation grew more lurid and outrageous, until my jaw ached with the effort of controlling the urge to scream at them all to shut up.

I was asked so many times if it was really true that I'd been the one to find the body – always with that same, barely contained frisson of excitement – that by closing time I was wishing they'd go back to asking me about my love life, as they'd been doing the night before.

I was also wishing I'd worn the same scoop neck top as I had then, as sweat trickled down my back and pooled around the waistband of my jeans. It would certainly have been a lot cooler.

***

"Honestly, Mum," I said next morning as we sat down

together with a cup of tea at the kitchen table after I'd got back from my morning run. "Last night, the entire village had poor John Manning in prison for murder. It was awful. How can people be so horrible?"

Mum sighed. "Let's face it, love. John's not the man you knew anymore. Surely you could see that for yourself on Wednesday night, when he showed up at the pub? Your dad mentioned what a state he was in."

"Well, yes, he was. That's true. And all this heavy drinking and cursing he goes in for is so out of character, that's for sure. But nobody changes that much, Mum. Not underneath. There's no way he could do something as terrible as—" I broke off, as the image of Marjorie, never far from my mind, returned in all its gruesome, stomach-churning detail. I closed my eyes and wished I had a delete button that would remove the unwanted image from my mind permanently.

"Try not to think about it, sweetheart," Mum said gently.

"Easier said than done," I said. "Particularly as that's all anyone wanted to talk about."

"Well, I told you to take the night off, didn't I? In fact, why don't you pack the job in altogether? You can help me out in the salon. I told you poor Sandra's feet are playing her up again, didn't I? An infected bunion now. It's in a terrible state, she says, and—"

"Oh, right," I cut in before she could go into any more detail. "And, of course, your customers won't want to hear all the gory details about the murder, will they? I don't think."

Mum pulled a face. "Sadly, you're not wrong there, love," she sighed. "According to the talk in the salon today, the overwhelming majority of them think John's guilty, too, I'm afraid."

"But you don't, surely?"

"Well…" she shook her head as she got up to pour herself another cup of tea. "Ready for a top-up?"

"No thanks. But, Mum, this is John Manning we're talking about, remember? A gentle giant who wouldn't hurt a fly. The man who taught me to ride that bad-tempered little pony of Will's. And who fixed my bike so that Dad wouldn't know I'd ridden it into the village pond and buckled the wheel."

"Did you?" she looked up in surprise. "When was that? I didn't know."

"You weren't supposed to." I prised the lid off the biscuit tin and peered inside. "And where are my chocolate biscuits? There was half a packet left in here yesterday."

"Well, you know..." Mum looked as guilty as a Labrador caught with its head in the pedal bin.

"So what happened to this wonderful new diet of yours? The one that was supposed to end all diets."

"It was making me depressed," Mum said, then gave a coy smile and a little toss of her head. "Besides, your dad says he prefers me with a few curves. Says it gives him something to hang on to."

"Whoa! Way too much information," I cut in hastily and went for a much-needed change of subject. "Seriously, Mum, you don't really believe John could have done such a terrible thing, do you?"

Mum's smile disappeared and her voice softened. "Not the John we used to know, no," she placed a gentle hand on my arm. "You're quite right. He was a lovely, gentle and very kind man. But he's changed, love. It's as if when Sally died, that John died along with her and this bad-tempered, rude and aggressive stranger took his place. I'm not saying he meant to kill poor Marjorie. Goodness knows, she could be a bit trying when she got on one of her campaigns. It's more likely he struck out wildly in one of his drunken rages. You have to remember, grief can do terrible things to a person and John – well, like I said, he's not the man he used to be anymore."

"Well, I still don't believe it," I said. "And I don't believe you do either. I keep thinking of the poor guy, locked up in a police cell. He must be going through hell. I feel awful, not being able to do anything to help."

"But you are doing something, love. You've made it up with Will and that can only be a good thing. And didn't you say you had a bit of a clean-up in the kitchen for them? That would have helped, too. I'd no idea they'd let things get that bad. Sally would have been horrified to think of them living like that."

"Wouldn't she just?"

"I'll tell you what, I'll pop a casserole in the oven in a minute and you can take it up to them after you finish at the pub at lunchtime. And, no, before you ask, it's not one of my special diet recipes. It's a good old-fashioned lamb hotpot, the way Sally used to make it."

I thought it would take more than lamb hotpot to take the haunted look out of Will's eyes. But I didn't tell Mum that.

***

The lunchtime shift at the pub wasn't quite as manic as yesterday's had been. As soon as it was over I collected Mum's lamb hotpot and went straight up to the farm to see if Will had any news.

As I got there, he was crossing the yard, the deranged Tam pooling around his feet as always, like a mid-day shadow.

"Hey, Will?" I called. "Why didn't you answer my note?"

He turned at the sound of my voice. Tam came running across to me, ears flattened, hackles raised. I could tell from the look in her eyes, she was dying for me to make a run for it so she could have me by the ankles. She slunk away, disappointed, when Will called her back.

"What note?" He looked blank. He also looked as if he hadn't got much sleep last night.

"The one I put through your front door yesterday."

He shook his head. "Jeez, Katie. You have been away a long time, haven't you? You know we never use the front door. So what did your note say?"

"Nothing really. Just asking you to let me know if you've any news. About your dad."

"Get down, Tam," Will said, as the dog began to dance around my feet again.

"I expect she can smell this. It's a lamb hotpot. Mum made it for you – and your dad." I handed him the bag containing the casserole.

"Thanks. That was good of her. Tell her I appreciate it. But

75

it looks like I'll be the only one eating it."

"Your dad's not back then? Have you heard anything?"

"I've heard, all right." His voice was razor edged with bitterness. "And it's not good. He's still helping them with their enquiries, as they put it. Oh yes, and the stupid old fool is refusing a solicitor. Says he doesn't need one and is ready to confess to killing Marjorie."

Chapter Ten

For the first time since I'd returned to Much Winchmoor, the sun decided to put in an appearance. Talk about bad timing. A blanket of fog would be more appropriate, more in tune with the sense of grey, gloomy hopelessness that engulfed me at Will's news.

John, ready to confess to killing Marjorie? The news was as bad as it could be. But still I refused to believe it. Had he been pressured by the police into admitting it? Or been driven so crazy by being shut up that he'd say anything, to get out of there?

"Did he say why he killed her, Will? Or how? Or why he dumped her body half in, half out of the freezer? It certainly wasn't to hide it, was it? The whole thing makes no sense."

Will kicked at a dandelion that was pushing up through a crack in the concrete. "Murdering a harmless old biddy like Marjorie makes no sense, but someone did."

"Yes, but not your dad."

"He doesn't remember what happened after the row. He just said he supposed he must have done it when he was drunk."

"He supposed he must have done it? But that's not the same as confessing to murder," I said, clutching at the slenderest of straws.

"In their book it is. They haven't charged him yet, but it's only a matter of time. They've collected all the evidence they need from the farm shop, or the crime scene as they call it. Right now they're waiting for the results from the various forensic tests to come through."

"And what about your father's shotgun? Have they been able to prove that Marjorie was shot with it?"

"Apparently not, which is something, I suppose. It turns out she wasn't shot at all but hit over the back of the head with the proverbial blunt instrument. And before you ask, it wasn't the butt of the gun. They've ruled that out completely."

I gulped back the now all-too-familiar wave of nausea at the memory. "But, surely, that's good news for your dad?"

"Not if they find the blunt instrument with his fingerprints all over it. You know what a farm is like. Blunt instruments all over the place. They've taken away most of my tools for analysis. I only hope they're going to let me have them back soon."

"But, obviously they haven't found anything yet. Otherwise they'd still be crawling all over the place, which they're not. And your dad would have been charged with murder. Which he hasn't."

"Not yet, he hasn't. Although the farm shop is still sealed off, as you can see." He pointed to the blue and white tape across the entrance. "And they've been through the house with a fine tooth comb. Scenes of crime officers were crawling all over it until early this morning. Oh yes, and they were very suspicious at the sight of recent attempts to clean up the kitchen. Spent for ever testing that. Must have gone through every pot and pan in the place. Not to mention the overflowing rubbish bin. Bet that was fun."

"But I was the one who cleaned the kitchen," I said quickly. "Why didn't you tell them that?"

"I tried to. But they didn't take any notice."

"Then I'll tell them." Guilt washed over me. "Oh God, Will, I hope I haven't made things worse for him."

"I shouldn't think so," Will said heavily, giving the last of the dandelion a well aimed kick. "Face it, they could hardly be a lot worse, could they?"

"This is terrible. I was only trying to help. I didn't imagine for a moment they'd think…"

"For goodness sake, Katie, don't beat yourself up about it. I wish I hadn't told you now. I promise you, no one's making things any worse for Dad, other than himself. And he's doing a pretty good job at that, I can tell you."

"But Will, you surely don't think he could have done it?"

"Of course I don't. Even if he was blind, stinking drunk, he wouldn't have done that. That's what I tried to tell him. But he wouldn't listen. Just kept saying he must have and that he was going to confess and get it over with. And there's plenty around here who agree with him – and who won't hesitate to tell the police so. Dad's rubbed a fair few people up the wrong way in the last few months."

He wasn't wrong there, if the talk in the Winchmoor Arms was anything to go by. But I decided against telling him about some of the crazy stories that were flying around last night. He had more than enough to worry about without that.

"But he said Marjorie left when he told her to, remember?" I said. "That she was at the farm at half past three, because he heard the children coming out of school, which he said Marjorie commented on. And that would tie in with the fact that one of the mums was early and saw Marjorie go past the school not long after quarter past three. Somebody must have seen her after she left your dad. She couldn't have walked all the way down the hill and back to her house without being seen, could she?"

"You're forgetting something, Sherlock," Will said quietly. "Her body wasn't found in her house but here on the farm."

I thought for a moment. "Yes, but maybe she met someone after she left the farm, and he lured her back here and into the farm shop, where he killed her."

"But why would he do that? I mean, why here? Why the farm shop? It's taking one hell of a risk. Either Dad or I could have turned up at any moment."

"Well, not you," I said. "Everyone in Mum's salon knew you were away at the market on Wednesday, including Elsie Flintlock. And if she knew, then you can take it as read that everyone in the entire village would have done as well."

"True. But, even so, I was back at the farm by half past four. I think I would have noticed Marjorie and her murderer hanging about the place, don't you?"

"I would imagine by that time, the deed had been done and the poor soul was already in the freezer," I said. "As to why lure her here, well, to implicate your dad, of course. Or – or maybe the murderer intended to hide her body in the freezer, but was interrupted. After all, it's common knowledge that nobody goes in there, since your mum—" I broke off and wished I hadn't said that.

Will's fists clenched and his eyes darkened. "You mean, it's common knowledge that I've been such a pathetic wimp I haven't been able to set foot inside there since Mum died. And Dad can't find his way out of a bottle at the moment, least of all run a farm shop. Is that it?"

I squeezed his hand. "I'm sorry, Will. No way does anyone think you are a wimp. I shouldn't have said…"

"Forget it," Will said wearily.

"Of course, there's another possibility," I said quickly. "Maybe someone—"

"Jeez, Katie," he cut in. "You read too many detective novels, that's your problem. You're making my brain ache."

"Even so, tonight I'll make a point of asking everyone who comes in the pub if they saw Marjorie, or if they saw anyone else on their way to and from the farm. It was a bit difficult last night because we were really busy, and Donald was hanging around all the time."

"According to Dad, his 'discussion' with Marjorie lasted only a few minutes. If, as he says, she'd gone straight back home, she'd have been seen by at least half a dozen mums waiting by the school gate. Which, according to you, she wasn't."

"No. That's true, I'm afraid. But what about her neighbours? Surely they'd have seen her coming and going on Tuesday afternoon?"

Will shook his head. "It's all holiday cottages down that end of the village now, and at this time of year most of them are empty."

"Except for Amy's mum. She lives just opposite. I spoke to Amy at the school this afternoon, she said she'd check."

"I'm not holding my breath," he said. "Let's face it, if anyone had seen Marjorie, they'd have come forward by now."

I sighed. He was right, of course. "Nevertheless, it won't hurt to ask around, will it? Just in case."

"Go ahead, Sherlock. You're going to do so anyway. But,

Kat?"

"Yes?"

"We both know Dad didn't kill Marjorie. So that means, there's a murderer on the loose in this village. This isn't a game, you know. It's all too horribly real. Be careful."

I shivered as if today's gentle breeze with its promise of spring had suddenly morphed into yesterday's mad March wind and sliced through my clothing again.

Will was right, of course. It wasn't a game. His dad was still banged up in Yeovil Police Station. There was a murderer on the prowl. And nobody I had spoken to so far had seen Marjorie after she left the farm.

I chased the shadows away and forced a smile. "You called me Kat," I said.

He smiled back, then reached his hand out and touched my cheek. "So I did," he said softly.

There was this weird, jumpy silence between us, which thankfully was broken by Tam suddenly whining and pushing against Will's leg.

Will cleared his throat. "Look, Katie – Kat, I, I just want to say how much I appreciate – Dad and I really – well, it's good of you to…" He pushed his hand through his hair, something he did when he was stressed, even though I'd told him often enough that startled hedgehog was not a good look.

"You don't have to say anything, Will," I said, putting him out of his misery. He'd never been one for fancy speeches.

"And I'm sorry I didn't answer your calls or texts," he said.

"That's ok."

"And – and I was also sorry to hear you and that – I mean, your boyfriend, have split up," he said, his eyes never leaving my face. "Even though he was a—"

"You don't have to rub it in," I said quickly and stepped away. I didn't want him to start banging on about what a loser Ratface was, though it was the truth. "Look, I'm working this evening. Why don't you come down to the pub and have a drink? Get out for a bit? It'll do you good."

"And have everyone asking me about the murder? Or trying to hide the fact that they all think my dad did it?" He stepped away from me, his eyes hot and angry again. "I don't think so, do you?"

He was right, of course. But I didn't like the thought of him spending another night in that cold, bleak farmhouse. Alone.

***

As soon as I left Will, I took out the card Ben had given me and punched in the number. It was answered almost immediately.

"Ben?" I said. "It's Kat here."

"Kat?" he sounded uncertain.

"Kat. From Much Winchmoor. Oh, all right then. Katie. Katie Latcham."

"Katie? I'm sorry. Not really with it today. I caught a double shift yesterday, I'm afraid. What can I do for you?"

"You said to ring you if I thought of anything," I said.

"And have you?" Suddenly he sounded fully awake.

"Well, yes and no." There was no way I was going to tell him my attempts to find someone who'd seen Marjorie after she left the farm had drawn a blank.

"So, which is it to be?" he said, and I could tell from his voice he was smiling.

"It's just that – well, Will said your colleagues were very suspicious about the fact that there'd been an attempt to clean up the kitchen in the farmhouse. But, you see, Ben, that was me. After you took John away I – I had to do something to keep my mind off things. So I washed up and tidied the kitchen a bit. It wasn't John, I promise you. You've got to believe me."

"I do," he said.

Relief flooded through me. "Oh, thank goodness. I was so worried I may have made things worse for him."

He paused. "I shouldn't really be telling you this, Katie, but I can't see it will do any harm. I knew the attempt to clean up the kitchen was way after we'd arrived on the scene. If you remember, I had to move a pile of dirty crockery and mouldy food before I could find somewhere to put my notebook. And, as John Manning and his son were with my colleagues at the time, it couldn't have been them. I told the SIO that and he was ok with it. Said he didn't really think there was anything significant in the clean-up, but they had to go through the motions."

"SIO?"

"Senior Investigating Officer. He's the guy in overall charge of the investigation. Inspector Hardy. A good man."

"So, does that put John in the clear, then?"

"Hardly. There's still the small matter of the fact that he was found within a few feet of the body. And has admitted to having a row with the victim, not to mention threatening her."

"But surely, if he'd been the one to do it, the first thing he'd have done would be to get as far away from the crime scene as he could?"

"Not if he'd passed out. And judging from the blood sample we took from him, his blood alcohol level would suggest that is a distinct possibility."

"There's something else I've thought of, too," I went on. "When I saw Marjorie in the salon that morning, she was saying something about how she was going to have it out with someone, once and for all. It sounded pretty serious to me."

"Did she say who she was talking about?"

"If she had, I'd have told you," I said crisply. "All I remember is that she said it was about time someone stood up to him and that now she'd got her dander up, she was going to be the one to do it."

"You've already told me that, Katie," he said. "Is there anything else you'd like to add to your statement?"

"Not really. Except to say that I was pretty sure it wasn't John Manning she was talking about. She'd already been talking about him, you see, and had moved on to someone else."

"I see. Did she mention a name?"

"I'm sorry. I'm afraid I wasn't really listening. The salon was very busy at that time and there was a lot of chatter going on…" and I'd zoned out, I should have said, but didn't. It didn't matter how hard I tried, I could not bring to mind any more details of that conversation, as I'd rinsed the perm lotion off Marjorie's blue cauliflower head.

"I'm sorry," I said. "I've wasted your time, haven't I?"

"Not at all. If you think of it, just let me know, ok?"

"Of course."

"And Katie?"

"Yes?"

"I'm not always on duty," he said. "You can waste my time as much as you like then."

I frowned as he ended the call. Was PC Ben Newton coming on to me? I shook my head. No, of course he wasn't. What was I thinking of? That sort of thing didn't happen to me. While I might well come across as someone with bags of confidence who didn't give a toss what people thought, the truth was, it was all a bit of a front. That was why I loved the anonymity of city life where I could be whoever I wanted to be – though much good it had done me. Back here, everyone knew me as little Katie Latcham, with crooked teeth and glasses, though the glasses had been replaced by contacts and the teeth had been straightened.

But even the 'new me', the one I'd left behind in Bristol, hadn't been one of those girls with a string of guys all begging for my favours. Not like Jules used to be, before she and Ed got together. When we were still at school, she collected hoards of admiring boys the way other people collect bottle tops. Whereas I was the overweight, geeky friend who blushed scarlet if a boy so much as looked in my direction, which wasn't very often.

"Take your time, sweetheart," Gran Latcham used to say. "You don't have to sample all the chocolates in the box to find the one that's right for you. He'll come along soon enough."

Trouble is, Gran, I wanted to say, I didn't want all the chocolates in the box. Just one would do very nicely. In the meantime, my friend Jules was having a whole heap of a better time than me, with her pick 'n' mix.

I wondered what Gran would say, if she were still around now. If I told her how I'd thought I'd found that one special 'chocolate' she'd promised me – only to find he'd turned out to be more self-centred than soft centred, and had put me off chocolates for life?

**

The Winchmoor Arms was not as crowded as it had been the night before. The roast lamb was now shepherd's pie and the talk had gone back to potholes, recycling collection dates and England's poor showing in the rugby/football/tiddlywinks or whatever. Things felt a bit more normal and a little less frantic, for which I was thankful.

Nevertheless, I remembered my promise to Will and, whenever I got the chance, I asked almost every person I served that night if they'd seen Marjorie after half past three on Tuesday afternoon. Every time I got the same negative answer. Nobody, it appeared, had seen her after she'd stopped to lecture Amy about the state of her child's teeth.

Nobody except John Manning. And the murderer, of course.

"So, where were you on Tuesday afternoon, Shane?" I asked in desperation as Big Shane Freeman shambled up to the bar.

He stared at me blankly for a second. Then, "Pass," he said with a broad grin, like we were doing Mastermind.

"As in you don't remember, or as in you don't want to tell me?" I asked.

"Pass," he said again, this time accompanied by a snort of laughter. "Hey, my offer of a ride in my cab is still open, Katie."

"And I'll pass on that too, if you don't mind, Shane," I grinned back at him as I handed him his pint. "Seriously though, were you here in the village on Tuesday afternoon? I know you were here in the evening because I served you. If so, did you see Marjorie Hampton?"

"Tuesday? Let's see." His round, good-natured face creased in concentration. "I'd been doing local drops that day. Nothing further than Bristol. So, yes, I was in the village and no, I didn't see Marjorie Hampton, thank goodness. She was forever banging on at me for parking my lorry in the back lane. Here,

85

you're surely not putting me in the frame for doing her in, are you? Should I be sorting out my alibi?"

"You have an alibi?" I asked. But at that moment, Donald came up to the bar with some empty glasses and his glare, which he'd directed at me every time I'd stopped to chat to anyone, went from stormy to full-on hurricane.

"I pay you to work, not stand around gossiping all day," he hissed, his pale grey face looking quite animated for once. "If you want to do that, maybe you'd be better off working in your mother's salon."

Shane pulled a face behind Donald's back, winked at me and went off to take his customary two places on the settle in the corner, where his elderly black Labrador was waiting anxiously for the crisps that Shane had bought with his pint. I began loading the glass washer.

When Gerald Crabshaw came in a little later, I waited until Donald had gone down to the cellar to change a barrel, and beckoned Gerald to come closer.

He bounced across the bar towards me, looking like Shane Freeman's Labrador on the scent of another packet of crisps.

"You're looking stunning again tonight, sweet Katie. I have to say you brighten up the old place no end," Gerald said with his usual leery grin as he leaned across the bar towards me, moving in so close I could see each individual pore on his mottled red nose. "You're certainly easier on the eye than old Donald, and that's a pretty top you're almost wearing. What was it before? A handkerchief?"

I pulled back to a safe distance, yanked at the hem of my favourite stretchy blue top and wished I was wearing last night's zip-up-to-the neck sweatshirt instead. I'd chosen the top because (a) it was cooler than the sweatshirt and (b) it also had a high collar. I hadn't given a thought about how it flashed a bit of bare midriff every time I moved, something that had never bothered me until that moment. But the way Creepy Crabshaw looked at me, his piggy little eyes gleaming like he was famished and I was the main course, made my flesh crawl.

Still, I reminded herself, this was not the time for the snarky put down, tempting though it was. Instead, I forced myself to give a little giggle, as if he'd just said something incredibly witty, and handed him his pint. "There you are, Gerald. Enjoy. By the way, did you happen to see Marjorie Hampton any time after half past three on Tuesday afternoon?" I asked.

His smile vanished as abruptly as if I'd just spat in his beer. He went from smarmy to snarly in an instant, his fleshy upper lip curled in a sneer. "Me? Of course I didn't. Why on earth would I? Fancy yourself as an amateur sleuth, do you? With me as suspect number one? Here, Donald, I've just been interrogated by one of your staff," he called out as Donald appeared, soft-footed as ever, behind me.

"What's the problem?" Donald asked as he placed a glass under one of the beer pumps, pulled on the handle, then held up the contents of the glass to the light to test the new barrel.

"Young Katie here reckons it was me and not poor mad John Manning who did for Marjorie Hampton. Can you believe it? Me? The master criminal?"

Although he laughed as he said it, I could see from the spots of colour high on his already red cheeks that he didn't find it terribly funny. And Donald looked ready to blow a head gasket as he put the glass down and glared at me.

"Don't take it personally, Councillor Crabshaw, and have that one on the house," he said in a low voice that was not meant to be overheard, in case it started a stampede of people demanding free drinks because they too had been 'interrogated'. It was a clear indication of how rattled he was, as Donald was well known for his aversion to handing out anything, particularly drinks. "Our Miss Marple here has been asking everyone who comes in the same question. She even had the cheek to ask me if I had an alibi for Tuesday afternoon, and of course I told her that you and I had a site meeting about a possible new playing fields for the village out on that bit of waste ground on the by-pass, didn't we? And that it took the best part of the afternoon."

It wasn't true, of course. I'd asked him nothing of the sort. But I'd already annoyed him enough for one night so I figured, if I wanted to keep my job, it would be best to let it go unchallenged.

But I needn't have bothered. Because at the end of the shift, as I went to get my coat, Donald called me back into the bar.

"Don't come in tomorrow," he said.

"Oh? But I thought my day off was Monday? Tomorrow's Friday."

"I'm well aware of what day of the week it is," he said, his eyes looking anywhere but at me. I had a bad, bad feeling I wasn't going to like what was coming next.

I was not wrong.

"Look, I'm sorry. But it can't be helped. Here's what I owe you for the hours you've worked." He handed me an envelope, looking about as sorry as a fox in a henhouse, and added, "Less, of course, the cost of Gerald's pint."

"But it's not pay day, is it? I don't understand…" I began, but I should have saved my breath. I could tell from the way he pointed his finger at me that he was a fan of The Apprentice. This was his Alan Sugar moment and he was milking it for all he was worth.

"You're fired," he said.

Chapter Eleven

"You're firing me? But why?" Donald wasn't known for his sense of fun, but this was a joke, surely? I'd only had the job for two days. Dad was going to go ballistic. And Mum was going to insist I spent more time in the salon.

"Well, not exactly fired," he mumbled. His Alan Sugar moment over, he now reverted to type and refused to look at me. "It's – well, the thing is, it's more a case of being made redundant. After all, I warned you the job was only temporary, didn't I?"

"You did. But there's temporary and then there's downright unfair." I struggled to keep my cool. My second job loss in as many weeks. I could see a pattern forming, and it was not a pretty one. If it followed the path of the previous one, he'd soon be telling me it was hurting him more than it was hurting me.

Only he didn't. In fact, he said nothing at all. Just stood there and looked terribly embarrassed and so miserable I could almost have felt sorry for him, if I hadn't been so busy feeling sorry for myself.

"But – but you said your wife wasn't due back from her cruise for a couple of months," I said.

"Well, yes I did, I know. But the thing is, Katie," he picked up a beer mat from the counter and began pulling it apart. "The thing is, you weren't replacing my wife, but my other barmaid, who's been unwell but is now fit for work again. I – I thought I'd explained that."

"No, you most certainly didn't." My words came out as an indignant squawk. "You can't do that."

He flinched at my raised voice, placed the shredded remains of the beermat in a neat pile on the counter and cleared his throat. "I'm sorry, but I'm afraid you'll find I can," he said, his voice so low I had to bend my head to hear him. "And – and, well to be perfectly honest, you're not really what I'd call barmaid material, are you? People come in here for a quiet drink, you know, not to be given the third degree by some smarty-pants college kid playing Cluedo. And before you bite my head off, that's not my words but how one of my customers described you. And I'm sorry, Katie, I really am. But I've got to act on my customers' complaints. Otherwise I'm out of a job as well as you. S-sorry, but that's the way it is."

I stared at him for a long moment, waiting for him to say that he'd just been winding me up and it was all a joke. But, of course, he didn't. Instead, he just stood there, jingling the loose change in his pocket and not quite looking at me in his vague, abstracted way.

I snatched up my coat and stomped off, knowing that as soon as I told Mum, she'd have me back in Chez Cheryl's before you could say highlights, seeing as Sandra's feet were still giving her gyp, as she put it, in spite of her very expensive visit to that tip-top chiropodist.

Of course it was obviously creepy Gerald Crabshaw who'd made the complaint about me. He'd been livid when I'd asked him if he'd seen Marjorie the day she died, which was, on reflection, a pretty over-the-top reaction to such an innocuous question. Particularly as Donald had made it pretty clear I'd asked everyone in the bar the same thing.

Was Gerald, then, the person Marjorie had said she was going to have it out with, once and for all? The person, she said, who was not going to be allowed to get away with it – whatever 'it' was? The man who'd got her dander up? And was he, then, the person Marjorie had met after John Manning had ordered her off his land? It was well known that he and Marjorie weren't exactly best mates. Also well known was the fact that Gerald was as honest as a bent banker. Not to mention sleazy. And had eyes that were too close together.

As I walked home, along the village's deserted main street, I tried hard to remember what Marjorie had said that day in the salon. It beat thinking about what Mum and Dad were going to say when they found out I was out of a job. Again.

Marjorie had wittered away the entire time I was rinsing her hair, but I'd been so caught up with what I was going to put on my job applications, I hadn't really paid much attention, apart from murmuring the occasional, *'No? Really? And what did you do then?'*

Talk about making a drama out of a crisis. It was one thing after another with Marjorie, as though everything and everyone set out deliberately to annoy her. If it wasn't the shocking state of the footpaths, or corruption in the Planning Department, it was the latest power struggle in the Floral Art Society.

"He's not getting away with it," I could remember her saying as I unwound the rollers from her hyacinth blue curls. "He'll find I'm a force to be reckoned with once I've got my dander up. He's been allowed his own way for too long. Acting as if he owns the place. It's got to stop. And I'm going to make sure it does. It's about time someone in this village had the courage to stand up to him. And I'm the one to do it."

Who'd been acting as if he owned the place? Allowed to get his own way for too long? And what was it that had to stop? Did she mean Councillor Gerald Crabshaw, or Sir Gerald of Winchmoor, as he would no doubt like to be called one day?

The sound of my footsteps echoed along the quiet street until I came to the village pond, where the pavement gave way to grass. To one side of the pond was a rough patch of ground which had at one time, under an ambitious scheme piloted by our very own Councillor Crabshaw, looked set to be designated the Much Winchmoor Nature Reserve, on account of a couple of great crested newts that were thought to have been found in it. But when the newts turned out to be not quite so great, and definitely un-crested, Dintscombe District Council had had a change of heart and had withdrawn funding. Now it was nothing more than a bit of scrubby grass, a huge batch of brambles as high as your head and a couple of spindly bushes that had never recovered from being chewed by John Manning's cattle on the day of their freedom march.

I froze. Something, or rather someone, was there in the

shadows.

My fingers closed around my phone as a figure suddenly loomed out of the bramble forest and started towards me.

"Who's there?" I called, sounding a lot calmer – and braver – than I felt. I hit the torch button on my phone and waved it in front of me.

"Is that you, Katie? Are you all right, girl?" The unmistakable figure of Shane Freeman shambled out of the darkness, his elderly Labrador plodding on behind.

"I – jeez, Shane. You startled me." My heart was still pounding so loud I thought he could probably hear it. I directed the light towards the brambles, but could see no one else. "I – I thought I heard... who were you with?"

"Just Oscar here," he said. "I was telling the old fool to hurry up because I was freezing my – I was freezing to death, waiting for him to make up his flipping mind whether he wanted to do anything or not. Dogs, eh?"

"Your dog? But I thought—" For a moment, I'd been sure I'd seen two figures over there. But I couldn't see anyone else now, in the shadows.

"Nope. Just me," he said. "Now if you want to keep me company, while I wait for this damn fool of a dog to get on with it, you're very welcome."

"I – no thanks, Shane. I must get on," I said quickly and hurried off, with his soft laughter ringing in my ears.

"Katie?" he called me back, his face suddenly serious. "You're looking a bit nervous, sweetheart. Do you want some company? Straight up. No messing."

I shook my head. "Thanks, Shane. But I'm fine, honestly I am. It's just – well, this murder. It's got me jumping at shadows."

"Well, it shouldn't. They've got the guy who did it, so there's nothing to worry about, is there? Now, Oscar's finished at long last. How about I walk you home?"

"That's really kind, Shane. But, like I said, I'm fine. Thanks."

Of course I wasn't fine. And I was pretty sure the other figure I'd seen in the shadows hadn't been Oscar the Labrador but someone whose stocky outline put me in mind of the very man who'd been occupying my thoughts at the time. Councillor Creepy Crabshaw.

But what was he doing, skulking around the village pond at ten minutes to midnight? Not looking out for newts, great crested or otherwise. That was for sure.

My parents took the news of my dismissal from the pub with enthusiasm. Dad's reaction was understandable. Even though I'd taken on board the little lecture Donald had given me on a barmaid's need for discretion and hadn't breathed a word to anyone about who was drinking what, how much and with whom – apart from telling Will about his dad, of course, but that was different – Dad had never been keen on me working there.

He said it was because working behind a bar was a waste of my talents, education and training. But the real reason, I suspected, was that he'd been worrying about Mum finding out exactly how many pints of Ferret's Kneecaps Best Bitter made up what he called, 'just a couple'.

Mum's reaction was similar to Dad's, but for a different reason. "Thank goodness for that," she said.

"What's to be thankful for? Being fired three days into a job?" I muttered, still stinging at the injustice of it all.

"No, that's not good, I grant you. But I'm sure Donald must have had his reasons," Mum said, who was always ready to see the other person's side of things, particularly if it was to my disadvantage. "I've always found him a very reasonable man, if a bit on the drippy side. No, I meant from my point of view, it couldn't have happened at a better time. Sandra came back to work today, as you know, but had to admit defeat and go on home as her bunion is now infected. You should see it. It's the size of a cricket ball, and as for the colour…"

"Please, Mum. Spare me the details," I cut in quickly, as my mum could, and often did, go on for hours about the sorry state of Sandra's feet. "I get the picture."

"Well, then, tomorrow you can help me in the salon. To be honest, I was wondering how I was going to manage, especially as Friday's my busy day. I did think of asking young Millie Chapman, but she's not what you'd call reliable."

"And I am? That isn't what you said when Elsie Flintlock accused me of pouring cold water down her neck and giving her the 'new-monials' again," I pointed out.

"Yes, well, hopefully there won't be a repeat of that."

"But I was going to spend tomorrow doing job applications. It's more important than ever now."

"And one more day won't make any difference, will it? Not at this point in the week. They won't even look at your application until Monday at the earliest now, will they? Please, love, Fridays are always busy and I'm fully booked all day. I'll pay you the going rate."

It wasn't like I had much choice in the matter. And, without the pub job, I needed the money. Even though my mum's idea of the going rate was a million miles away from mine.

"Ok," I sighed, knowing when I was backed into a corner.

"That's settled then. Now, our first appointment is at half past eight so you'd better get off to bed, as you've an early start in the morning."

I sighed as I contemplated the train wreck that was my life. What had happened to it? Not only was I back living at home with my parents, with no job, no boyfriend, no money, no prospects. Now I was even being told by my mother what time to go to bed. Things couldn't get any worse, I thought.

But, of course, they could. And they did.

***

It was the first time in ages I'd put in a full day in Mum's salon and by the time I took what was laughingly called my lunch break at half past three, I was beyond exhausted. My feet ached, my back ached, my fingers ached, my brain ached, while the smell of perm lotion, shampoo and hair spray leached out of every pore.

In between listening to people moaning about their husbands, in-laws, children and how there's nothing worth watching on the telly any more, I managed to slip in the odd question about possible sightings of Marjorie Hampton on Tuesday.

But nobody I spoke to had the slightest idea who Marjorie could have been talking about that day. It could have been anyone. Almost everyone in Much Winchmoor had got Marjorie Hampton's dander up at one time or another, even our mild, inoffensive vicar who wanted nothing more than a quiet life, tending his begonias and watching Countryfile on the telly.

But the general consensus was that it was probably John Manning, as one of Marjorie's latest campaigns had been about the state of the local footpaths, in particular a blocked one somewhere on his land. Something that Will and John had sort of confirmed, although I wasn't telling anyone that.

As I left the salon and went into the kitchen to find something to eat, I decided to pass on what Mum described as the 'lovely quinoa and chickpea soup' she'd left for me. It looked marginally better than the gloopy frogspawn she was still trying to foist on me for breakfast but I preferred a hunk of cheese and a packet of salt and vinegar crisps. I was rounding it off with a couple of chocolate digestives when my phone went. It was Will.

"I thought you'd like to know, I've just been down to Yeovil and brought Dad back."

"Oh, that's brilliant," I mumbled through a mouthful of biscuit crumbs. "I knew they'd realise he's innocent eventually."

"He's not off the hook yet." There was a warning note in his voice. "It's more a matter of not having sufficient evidence to charge him, so they had to let him go. For now. They told him not to leave the area, though."

"So he obviously thought better of making that phoney confession?"

"Yeah. The solicitor I found for him finally made the old fool see sense."

"And how is he? Your dad, I mean. Not the solicitor."

"Yeah, I kind of figured that's who you meant. He's sober. And subdued. Keeps apologising."

"Oh. Right. Well, that's all to the good, isn't it?"

"Yeah, I suppose." He didn't sound terribly convinced. "Anyway, I wondered if you're going to be in the pub this evening? I thought I might drop in for a quick one. Just me. Not Dad," he added quickly. "He says he's on the wagon."

"Good for him. But, Will, you must be the only person in the village who hasn't heard. Donald fired me last night."

"The devil he did. Why?"

I decided not to tell Will it was because I'd been upsetting the customers by asking questions about Marjorie Hampton, because I'd then have to go on and admit that nobody had seen her after her encounter with his dad. Which I didn't think would do anything to lift Will's bleak mood. "He tried to make out I wasn't barmaid material at first, but the truth of the matter is, I was only a stand-in while his regular barmaid was off sick. A small thing that he somehow forgot to mention when he took me on. How do you like that?"

"Tough. You must be seriously cheesed off."

"Tell me about it. Especially as Mum's had me working in the salon all day. It was pretty dire working in the Winchmoor Arms, but this place is worse."

"Ok, so how about we go into Dintscombe this evening? There are new people in the Queen's Arms and they're really making a go of it. They have live music on a Friday night and it's that dreary folksy stuff you like."

"I'm sorry." I flexed my aching feet. A few more weeks of this and I'd be a martyr to them and able to compare symptoms with Sandra. "I've been slaving away since the crack of dawn and I've another couple of hours to go here in the torture chamber, by which time I'll be fit for nothing, except collapsing in the bath and then falling asleep in front of the TV. Or maybe even the other way round. Another time, eh?"

"Sure. Let me know if you change your mind."

"Ok, but don't hold your breath. Oh and Will?"

"What?"

"I'm glad we're mates again. I – I really missed you, you know."

There was a tiny pause. "Yeah. I missed you too," he said quietly, his voice suddenly croaky. "Enjoy your bath."

***

I ended the call and was about to put my phone away when it rang again. A number I didn't recognise came up.

"Is that Katie Latcham?" He had one of those soft Irish accents that could make a shopping list sound like a poem. "It's Liam O'Connor here, from *The Dintscombe Chronicle*."

My heart did a triple somersault. *The Dintscombe Chronicle* was the local paper and was among the first I'd sent my CV to when I came home. Dintscombe was a small market town five miles from Much Winchmoor and *The Chronicle* was a typical small town newspaper, more interested in advertising revenue than news. I'd gone there to do my work experience when I was at school and had enjoyed it.

Working on the local paper wasn't exactly top of my wish list. That, of course, was a job back in my first love, radio. But it sure beat working in the salon and I figured it could well be a useful stepping stone.

I held the phone closer to my ear and hoped he wouldn't hear the frantic beating of my heart.

Play it cool, Kat, I told myself. *He doesn't need to know how desperate you are.*

"Thanks for contacting me," I said in my best professional young woman about town accent. "I'm available for interview at any time and…"

"Grand. Well, we can do it right here and now, over the phone, if that's ok with you," he said. "And then if we are wanting a picture—"

"Sorry?" That wasn't quite the reaction I'd been expecting. "Why would you want a picture?"

"It's up to you. But it makes for a better story…"

"A story? You mean you're not ringing about my job application?"

"I'm afraid not. That's not my department. I'm on the news desk and I'm doing a follow-up on the murder in your village

97

this week. Thought I'd do a bit of a background piece. I understand it was you who found the body?"

"How did you get my number?" I asked frostily.

"Ah well, I did what I always do when I want to find out what's going on in a place. I went to the local pub. It was a bit quiet at lunchtime but I did have a drink with a very nice fellow called Terry, who says he's your—"

"Dad." I said with weary resignation. Was it possible, I wondered, to divorce your parents, particularly ones who gave your mobile phone number to strange guys who just happened to buy them a pint or two?

"He said you found the body, is that right?" Liam went on.

"Yes, I did. But I'd rather not talk about it." To be honest, I'd rather not think about it, either. Rather not wake up in the middle of the night, getting flashbacks. Seeing poor Marjorie's legs sticking out of the freezer over and over again. I'd rather not. But I did. And it still freaked me out. The last thing I wanted to do was talk about it to some sensation-seeking journo.

"Ah well, it's up to you," he said carelessly. "As a matter of interest, what job were you applying for? I mean, should I be worried for mine now, do you think?"

"Oh no. Nothing like that. It was no job in particular." I launched into the spiel I'd written and rehearsed so many times. This was my chance to put it into practice. "I was employed by a commercial radio station in Bristol until a couple of months ago and enjoyed the journalism side of it so much, I thought I'd go for a change of direction. In fact, I did a journalism module as part of my Media Studies course at college. I just sent in my CV to your paper on the off-chance."

"I see. Well, Katie…"

"I prefer to be called Kat, if you don't mind. Kat Latcham is the name I'm known by professionally."

"Is that a fact? Well, Kat Latcham, do you fancy meeting up some time and I can maybe give you the heads-up about possible openings for you at *The Chronicle*?'

"Wow, that's brilliant," I said, quite forgetting for a moment that I was trying to be all cool about it. "I – I mean, that's kind of you, Mr O'Connor."

"It's Liam. That's the name I'm known by," he paused and I could hear the laughter in his voice as he added, "Professionally."

"And would you be making fun of me now, Mr O'Connor?" I asked, with what I thought was a passable attempt at an Irish accent.

"Wouldn't dream of it, Kat Latcham. So, come on, now. How about tonight? There are new people in the Queen's Arms and they have live music on a Friday night. We could meet up for a quick drink and a chat. Shall we say 8 o'clock? I usually sit at the table near the window. You can't miss me. I'll be holding a copy of *The Chronicle*. Unless, of course, you'd like me to be wearing a red carnation?"

"A copy of *The Chronicle* will do," I said. Something told me I was going to enjoy meeting Liam O'Connor.

As I put my phone away, I realised I was no longer tired and my feet weren't aching any more. The thought that maybe, just maybe, I could get a job on *The Chronicle* put all thoughts of a quiet night in front of the television clean out of my head.

The rest of the afternoon zipped by as I went through in my mind which of my work pieces I would put in my portfolio to take along to show him. And then, of course, there was the vexed question of what to wear.

***

I decided to go for cool, casual but with a touch of sophistication. Skinny jeans, my favourite killer heel boots, my hair spiked and messy, just as I liked it. The regulars of the Winchmoor Arms might not get the way I dressed, but I was hoping Liam would. I was also hoping I hadn't overdone the Gucci Guilty. It was my favourite perfume, bought back in the days when I could afford such luxuries. I'd dabbed it everywhere in an effort to mask the smell of perm lotion which, in spite of a long and vigorous shower, I was convinced still clung to me.

I saw him the moment I entered the crowded pub. He was,

as promised, sitting at the table by the window, a copy of *The Dintscombe Chronicle* propped up in front of him. He was younger than I'd imagined, in his early thirties probably, with thick, dark hair that curled slightly over the collar of his white linen shirt.

He was eye-wateringly, drop dead gorgeous, with a smile that could power a lighthouse.

"Mr O'Connor, I presume?" I said.

"Indeed it it. It's good to meet you, Kat Latcham." His handshake was cool and firm. "First things first. What can I get you to drink?"

"A sparkling mineral water, please." I wasn't driving. Dad had not only given me a lift in to Dintscombe but had also given me the money for a taxi back. Conscience money, I called it, for giving out my mobile number to strangers in the pub. Although, now I'd met this particular stranger, I thought maybe I'd forgive Dad. This time.

Nevertheless, no alcohol. I wanted to keep a clear head. This was business, not pleasure, after all, I reminded myself. Although I couldn't help noticing the way his faded denim jeans clung to his slim hips as he stood up. Well, ok, maybe just a little bit of pleasure. And as for those long legs and those broad, powerful-looking shoulders…

After Ratface, I'd sworn I was off men for life. And I'd meant it. But, for someone like Liam O'Connor, whose clear blue eyes made you think of a summer evening's darkening sky, I could be persuaded to make an exception. Me and every other woman in the pub, I reckoned, as I noticed that mine wasn't the only gaze clocking his progress across the crowded room.

As I sat down, I became aware of someone watching not him, but me. It was Will, glaring at me from across the room.

"Will," I called. "What are you doing here? I thought you didn't like dreary folksy music?"

"And I thought you were planning a night in front of the TV," he snapped. "All you had to do was say no, Katie. You didn't have to make up phoney excuses."

"It wasn't like that—" I began. But it was too late. He'd

already stormed out of the pub, his face as dark as a thundercloud.

Chapter Twelve

"Sorry. Did I interrupt something?" Liam asked as he returned with the drinks.

"No. Just a mate of mine being a total idiot as usual." I reached into my bag and took out the folder containing some of my work and placed it on the table in front of him. "I've brought some of my stuff for you to have a look at. It's mostly pieces I did for the radio station, plus a few random bits I thought you might be interested in."

"I'd rather find out a little more about you, Kat Latcham," he said, looking not at the folder but at me. "You're working in your mother's hairdressing salon for the moment, I understand. I'll bet you hear all the local gossip there, don't you?"

"Tell me about it," I said. "My ears are still ringing."

"And what are the jungle drums saying about Marjorie Hampton?"

My hand stilled, the glass half way to my lips. "I told you I didn't want to talk about the murder. Is that why you asked me here, hoping I'd change my mind? This is all about you getting a scoop, isn't it? Nothing to do with a job at *The Chronicle*. Well, thanks a bunch."

I put down the glass, gathered up my folder and stuffed it back into my bag. I stood up, my cheeks flaming. Of all the naive birdbrains. What had I been thinking of? If I hurried, I could catch Will and snag a lift back with him. And maybe find out what was bugging him at the same time.

"Exclusive," Liam said quietly, looking up at me, a faint smile tugging at the corner of his mouth.

"Excuse me?"

"We say exclusive, not scoop. If you're going to become a journo, Kat Latcham, at least get the terminology right. Now, sit down and we'll start again. And yes, I would like to hear about how you found poor Marjorie Hampton. But no, I did not ask you here tonight for that sole purpose."

"So what exactly was your purpose?" I asked, still bristling.

"It's Friday night. The music's good and they do a decent pint in here, unlike that rubbish they serve in your local. I fancied a few drinks in the company of a gorgeous girl. Nothing more. Nothing less. Plus, of course, a little chat about job prospects with *The Chronicle*."

Gorgeous? Did he say gorgeous? And something about job prospects? My ruffled feathers slowly began to unruffle. I sat down. But I'd heard all about silver-tongued Irishmen who could charm the spots off a Dalmatian, and hardened my resolve.

"Yeah, right. We've never met before. For all you knew, I could have had a face like a horse and be covered in zits."

A face like a horse. Of all the stupid things to say. The one thing guaranteed to bring Marjorie Hampton's horsey features back to the forefront of my mind. I swallowed hard and took a long gulp of my drink. I spluttered as the bubbles went up my nose.

"Strong stuff, that mineral water," he commented. "Are you ok?"

"I'm fine. Sorry. You were saying?"

"How did I know you were gorgeous? Simple. I checked you out on Facebook. A good journalist always does his homework. Rule number one. Now, are you sure you wouldn't like something that won't make you choke this time? Something stronger?"

I smiled as the knot of tension that had been coiled inside me for days slowly began to unwind. "A good journalist should also know not to believe everything he reads on Facebook. And a Pinot Grigio would be lovely. Thanks." I added, as I came to the conclusion that keeping a clear head was seriously overrated.

Two glasses later and the knot had completely unravelled. Liam was great company and it was amazing how much we had in common, including our love of what Will called dreary

103

folksy music, as well as our desire to escape from small country villages and the small-minded people who lived in them.

"So what made you come back?" he asked.

I gave him a carefully edited version of why I'd had to return to Much Winchmoor. I didn't mind owning up to the redundancy thing, but I reckoned the being dumped for my flatmate bit was on a need-to-know basis only, otherwise I might as well walk around with 'loser' stamped on my forehead.

"That's tough," he said. "I know how I'd feel if I had to go back to the little village near Cork where I come from. You can't change your socks there without everyone talking about it and coming to the conclusion that you're part of an international sock smuggling ring."

"And are you?" I laughed.

"Ah well, now that would be telling, wouldn't it? And if I did tell you, I'd probably have to kill you."

"So how did you end up in Dintscombe, of all places? It's not exactly the hottest spot on the planet," I said. "Five pubs, a kebab shop and a nightclub that opens only when the owner's sober enough to remember to unlock the doors."

"Ah no, but, you see, I don't intend staying at *The Chronicle*. It's just a stepping stone. That's why I want to make a good fist of this murder story." He leaned towards me, his eyes shining with barely suppressed excitement. "It's the biggest thing to happen around here since—"

"Since last week's phantom knicker nicker? I saw the headlines in the paper."

He pulled a face. "Then you'll see what I mean. I need to make the most of this murder story. There's plenty of interest in it from the nationals. This could be the big break I've been waiting for."

"But I…"

He placed his forefinger on my mouth. Feather-light and cool against my lips. I only had to open my mouth, ever so slightly and – oh Lord, what was I doing? Here was I, off men for life, fantasising about how it would be if… And what was

104

he saying? Somehow I'd completely lost track of the conversation.

"…and I would hate to spoil a lovely evening by upsetting you again. So, there will be no more talk of murder, ok?" he was saying.

"Oh, but I don't mind talking about it." I was relieved I was able to catch up without making a total idiot of myself. "In fact, I'd like to. It's just the actual finding her that I don't want to dwell on. Sorry if I was touchy about it earlier but I think that will haunt me for the rest of my life." Despite the warmth of the crowded bar, I shuddered. Time to focus on something else. "John Manning didn't do it, you know. Although I seem to be the only person in the entire village who believes that. Apart from his son, Will, of course."

"And would that be the 'total idiot'– your words, not mine – who stormed out earlier? That was John Manning's boy?"

"That was Will, yes. You know John was released without charge this morning, don't you?"

He nodded. "That's because they'd held him for thirty-six hours. After that, they have no choice. They have to either charge him or release him. And obviously they've not got enough evidence to charge him."

"Or they've found evidence against someone else," I said. "Because he didn't do it, Liam. I know it as surely as I know my own name."

"And which name would that be, now?" he said with a grin.

"I'm serious. John Manning says Marjorie left him, very much alive and spitting mad, at half past three and I believe him. But I've asked almost everyone in the village now and nobody saw her after she went up to the farm. It's a complete mystery."

"Or nobody admits to seeing her." Liam said quietly, his face serious. "But, if John Manning is telling the truth, then somebody did. I think there's a very strong possibility that somebody's lied to you, Kat. The question is, who?"

"Gerald Crabshaw!"

Liam raised an eyebrow. "As in Councillor Gerald Crabshaw? The probable next leader of Dintscombe District

Council. The fellow who exchanges funny handshakes with my editor. What makes you think it was him, of all people?"

"Because he was the one who got me fired yesterday."

"Fired?" He looked confused. "I thought you worked for your mum?"

"I do now but—" I stopped as I remembered I was talking to a journalist. "This is off the record, right?"

The last thing I wanted was to see the pathetic details of my ill-fated career as a barmaid splashed across the local paper, not while I was actively job hunting.

"Of course," he assured me. "I told you before, as far as I'm concerned, I'm just enjoying a friendly chat with a gorgeous girl. Nothing more."

I knew it was just a bit of Irish blarney, but a frisson of pleasure chased down my spine and I had to force myself to focus. If I could persuade Liam to believe that John Manning was innocent, it would be great. He would, I reckoned, make a useful ally.

"Ok. Well, until last night I was working behind the bar of the Winchmoor Arms and I'd made a point of asking everyone I served if they'd seen Marjorie on Tuesday."

"And had they?"

I shook my head. "No one had. But when I asked Gerald, he went bonkers at me. Said I'd been accusing him of 'doing for her,' as he put it, which of course I hadn't. Why would I? It hadn't even occurred to me to suspect him."

I'd got his attention, that was for sure. His piercing blue eyes were fixed on me intently. "Go on," he said quietly.

"All I wanted was to find someone who'd seen Marjorie after she left John. Not track down her murderer. I'll leave that to the police, thanks very much. But an hour later, Donald fired me saying customers had been complaining. And the only customer who'd seemed remotely bothered by my questions was Councillor Creepy Crabshaw. Makes you wonder why, doesn't it?"

"It certainly does." He lowered his voice and leaned so close towards me I could smell the light citrus tang of his aftershave. "As a matter of fact, I've been hearing things about

106

Councillor Crabshaw."

"What sort of things?"

He shrugged. "Just local rumours. Unsubstantiated, of course. And certainly nothing I could go into print with. But even so, there have been whispers. And I've been cultivating a contact who I'm pretty sure is ready to dish the dirt on him."

"Then there is something," I breathed. "I knew it."

"Ah yes. But thinking it is one thing, proving it quite another. And I have to be careful because, like I told you, he's best buddies with my editor."

"Oh right. And that means he can get away with—" I stopped.

"With murder? Was that what you were going to say?" He was looking at me intently. "You don't seriously think he murdered Marjorie Hampton, do you?"

"Well, why not? It was no secret they absolutely hated each other and apparently, he blamed Marjorie for shopping him to the police, which resulted in him losing his licence for driving under the influence a while back."

"Yes, I heard about that. But hardly a reason for murder, I'd have thought. It was about eighteen months ago, wasn't it? Just before I started at *The Chronicle*."

"Probably. I wasn't here then either but Mum told me all about it. It was the talk of the village for weeks, apparently. Anyway, the other night in the pub Gerald had had a few and was ranting on about how Marjorie was going to come to a sticky end one day. And, believe me, he never said a truer word. Her end was as sticky as you could get. And no, before you ask, I don't want to talk about it."

The possibility of poor Marjorie's undignified death being splashed across the front pages of a newspaper for people to exclaim about over their corn flakes was too horrible to contemplate.

"Then don't talk about it," he said gently. "Would you like another drink?"

"No thanks. To be honest, I'm absolutely whacked. Mum's had me working in the salon since daybreak. All I want now is to go home and sleep for a week. Not that there's any chance of that as she'll have me back in there tomorrow morning. Apparently, there's a funeral in the village and all the old dears – I mean customers – will be in to have their hair done in honour of the occasion. I'd best be off."

"Some other time, then?"

My heart lifted. "I'd like that very much," I said demurely, trying not to sound too keen.

"I would offer to drive you home but..." he held up his drink.

"That's ok. I'll get a cab. Dad gave me the money. I think he's trying to make it up to me after I had a go at him about giving out my mobile number to strange men in the pub today."

I took out my phone and rang for a cab, and must have hit it just right. "There's one in the Market Place. He'll be here any minute."

"Look, if you'd like to leave that folder of work with me, I'll take a look at it," he said. "I'll be honest, there are no staff jobs going on the paper at the moment. The movement of staff tends to be the other way round, with falling circulation, loss of advertising revenue and threats of redundancy hanging over all our heads. But there may be some chances for freelance work, if you're up for it? It doesn't pay a fortune but..."

"I'm up for it," I said quickly, handing him my folder.

"Great. I'll get back to you on that. Oh, and Kat?"

"Yes?" His smile was doing funny things to my knees.

"I'm really glad your dad gave me your number, so I am."

So was I – but there was no way I was telling my dad that.

***

"That's it for a while, Katie," Mum said around half past eleven next morning, after what had already felt like a ten-hour shift. "The rush is over. I shan't need you now until one o'clock, if you'd like to take a break for a bit."

I didn't need asking twice. I slipped off my Chez Cheryl tabard and hurried away before she could change her mind. I decided to use the time to call Will but, as always, my call went straight to his voicemail. There was no point leaving a message because he never checked it. I glared at my phone in frustration. Why did he bother having a phone if the wretched thing was never switched on? I wanted to explain how I'd come to be in the pub with Liam last night – and also to ask why he'd stormed off the way he had.

I'd missed my run that morning, so I collected my bike from the shed. After standing around in the salon for hours, it would be good to stretch my legs by cycling up to the farm. But as I wheeled my bike out on to the pavement I heard someone call my name.

I turned to see Jules coming down the road. She looked so different from the last time I saw her I did a double-take. Her jeans looked as if they'd been sprayed on and were tucked into a pair of dead cool knee-high boots that made her legs look like they went on forever. With her hair pinned in a high ponytail and made up to the nines, she looked much more like the Jules I remembered.

"Hiya," I called. "You're looking good this morning. Going somewhere nice?"

"Hardly." She pulled a face. "I'm going to work. Donald phoned yesterday morning and asked if I wanted my job back. And with the baby and everything, I could hardly say no, could I? Eddie's on short time at the moment and things are pretty tight."

"Donald?" I stared at her. "You mean you're working in the pub?"

"Always did catch on quick, didn't you?" she grinned as she tossed her head, and sent her glossy pony tail swinging.

"But that was my job – I didn't realise..." The thought of Jules being the reason Donald had sacked me didn't sit very comfortably. "Donald, the rat, said I was just cover while his regular barmaid was off sick, a fact he somehow forgot to mention when he took me on."

"You've been working in the pub? I didn't know that." Jules had that look of studied innocence on her face that I remembered only too well. It had got her out of trouble – and, as often as not, me into it – many times in the past. "When?"

I was going to challenge her. Of course she knew. After all, nothing happened in this village without everyone else knowing and her grandmother was Olive Shrewton, a founder member of the Grumble and Gossip Group, so it was in her genes. But I shrugged and let it go. I hadn't liked working in the pub anyway and if there was half a chance of some work with *The Chronicle*, then it was all for the best.

"Actually, it was probably the quickest sacking on record," I told her. "I started work on Tuesday and he sacked me on Thursday night. Said I didn't have what it took to be a barmaid. Oh yes, and I upset the customers."

"The pig. He sacked me last Monday when I phoned in to say I was sick again. Which was nothing but the truth, even though I told him I had an appointment with the doctor next day and was hoping he'd give me something to help. Which he did, and I'm beginning to feel half human again now I can keep my food down. Mum reckons I'm carrying a boy this time. She could be right because I was certainly never like this with our Kylie."

"So how come you're working for him again, after he treated you like that?"

"I just told you. He said he'd been a bit hasty and offered me my job back."

"That was once he'd given me my marching orders, of course. Damn it, Jules, you should have told him what to do with his job. I would have."

"Yes, well, we don't all have your good fortune, do we?" she snapped, her cheeks scarlet, her eyes hot and angry. "No wonder you can't get people round here to think of you as Kat. Because underneath it all, you're still little Katie Latcham, running home to Mummy and Daddy when the going gets tough, aren't you? And yes, I dare say you would have told Dippy Donald where to stick his lousy job. You can afford to, seeing as your mum has fixed a job in her salon for you, even though young Millie Chapman really needed it."

"I – I didn't know." I looked at my old friend in astonishment, completely taken aback by her flash of anger which seemed to come out of nowhere. How stupid I'd been to think we could just pick up our easy-going friendship where we'd left off all those years ago. Was that why Will had been so angry with me last night? Did he, too, feel I'd taken our friendship for granted, assuming I could just move back home and expect everything and everyone would slip back to where they'd been before I left?

"And that's another thing," Jules went on. She'd obviously got up a good head of steam now and was really going for it. "I might as well get it all off my chest, once and for all. I've been wanting to say this for ages, even though Eddie tells me it's none of my business. It's about you and Will."

"Me and Will?" I echoed, gripping the handlebars of my bike like it was a life raft and I'd just jumped off the Titanic.

"You really hurt him, you know. That last time you were home with lover boy. I've never seen Will so cut up."

"You mean, the night after he and Nick had a set-to in the bar? I should damn well think I had a go at him. He – well, no, not just him. The pair of them behaved like a couple of complete idiots. I don't know what came over him."

"Don't you?" she snapped, eyes blazing. "Then you're blind as well as stupid. For pity's sake, couldn't you see? He might as well have had it stamped on his forehead. The guy was eaten up with jealousy."

"Will? Don't be ridiculous. Why would he be jealous?"

"He's fancied you for ever. You must have realised. Why else do you think he used to run around after you like a little puppy dog? Grow up. My Kylie shows more sense than you sometimes. Now, if you'll excuse me, I've got to go to work."

Will fancied me? As if. What was Jules on? I'd heard of pregnancy doing weird things to people, but this time she'd gone completely mad. And too far.

"Jules?" I called, as she walked away, her smart boots tapping an angry rhythm on the pavement.

"What?" Her face had that defiant look that I remembered so well. It was usually when she'd said or done something really stupid – or wrong. Or, in this case, both. "If you think I'm going to apologise…"

"No. I don't for a moment think that. I just wanted to say

111

that your Eddie was quite right for once in his life. It is none of your damn business."

Jules looked as if she was about to say something more but before she could do so, the sound of applause made us both whirl round. It was Gerald Crabshaw. He'd obviously been pinning something on the village noticeboard but must have turned at the sound of our raised voices. He looked like he'd just got the ringside seat at the fight of the century and was determined to enjoy every moment of it.

"That's the way, sweetheart," he called across to me. "That told her. Seconds out. Round two."

Jules glared at him. Then at me. "I'm late for work," she said and stomped away.

"No lunchtime shift for you, then, Katie?" he said, his fleshy lips pulled back in a horrible leery grin that made my flesh crawl.

I clenched my fists and stared defiantly at him. "You know full well Donald fired me on Thursday, seeing as you were the one who engineered it."

"Me?" He made a very poor fist of looking innocent. "Oh no, sweetheart, no. You've got that all wrong. That was nothing to do with me."

"Yeah, right. Of course it wasn't."

He sauntered across the road towards me, his little piggy eyes gleaming. "But, as it happens, Donald was quite right." He lowered his voice as he got closer. "You're not exactly barmaid material, are you? You don't have the build for it for one thing. Way too skinny. Whereas young Julie there," His fleshy hands drew elaborate curves in the air. "Well, she has assets in all the right places, don't you think?"

The creep. Without stopping to consider the wisdom of what I was saying, I snapped, "You know, Councillor Crabshaw, I don't recall you ever did say where you were the afternoon Marjorie was killed."

I had the satisfaction of seeing the smirk wiped off his face. "To quote what you said to your friend just now, it's none of your damn business," he said frostily.

"You know the police have let John Manning go, don't

you?" I pressed on recklessly. "Apparently, he didn't do it. Makes you wonder who did, doesn't it?"

I'd heard people say the blood drains from a person's face but, until that moment, I'd thought it was merely a cliché. But Gerald went from an angry mottled red to sickly grey in seconds. His eyes bulged and he looked as if he was about to keel over.

"And that's another thing," I went on with all the single-mindedness of a boxer who has his opponent on the ropes, and is impatient to deliver the knockout punch. "What were you and Shane Freeman doing, skulking about in the bushes beside the pond on Thursday night? Don't try to deny it because I saw you. And the way you were acting tells me you weren't hunting for newts or barn owls. So what was it? Fixing up another dodgy alibi, were you?"

"If – if you think…" he stammered. "It – it wasn't…"

Then, with the worst timing in the world, my pocket started vibrating and the theme music from Doctor Who rang out. As a ring tone, it's pretty pathetic, but it usually made me smile. Not that day. I took out my phone intending to turn it off. But before I could, Gerald Crabshaw turned tail and scurried off down the street as if a hundred hell hounds were snapping at his heels.

Chapter Thirteen

Talk about saved by the bell. Or, in Gerald Crabshaw's case, Dr Who. For a moment, it had looked as if he'd been going to say something incriminating, before the ringing phone gave him the chance to gather his scattered wits and scuttle away.

The caller was Liam.

"Hi there, Kat Latcham." His voice was as soft and beguiling as ever and went some way towards making up for Crabshaw getting off the hook. Particularly when he went on, "I was wondering if we could meet up? You see, I've been thinking about what we were talking about last night. A job with *The Chronicle*. Would you still be interested? It's only a one-off, you understand. But who knows?"

Play it cool, Kat, I reminded myself. Don't let him know you're dying to bite his hand off. "I could well be," I said, trying to make it sound like I had a hundred other fascinating job prospects lined up on the table. And was having trouble deciding which to go for. "About meeting up. When did you have in mind?"

"Tomorrow lunchtime, if you can make it. We could meet in Dintscombe. Do you have wheels?"

"Not any more." I cursed Ratface. I'd forgiven him for running off with my flatmate. I could even, given enough time, forgive him for taking my signed photo of David Tennant and my stash of £2 coins. But I would never, ever forgive him for pinching my car. When I lived near Bristol city centre, I could manage without it, but here in Much Winchmoor, where the local bus ran twice a day if it felt like it and the last one home left Dintscombe at twenty past six, a car was as necessary as breathing if you were going to have any life at all. Which I didn't. "And tomorrow's Sunday," I added. "Which is one of the days when the bus doesn't feel like it."

114

"I'm sorry? Feel like what?"

"Running. There are no buses between Dintscombe and Much Winchmoor on a Sunday. There's one this afternoon, though," I added hopefully. "I could maybe…?"

"Sorry. I've got a story I've got to follow up. Tell you what, I'll come and collect you tomorrow morning. Will 11.30am be ok for you?"

OK for me? I'd have agreed to meet him at dawn, if that was what he wanted. "That will be fine," I said, in a brilliant imitation of a woman in total control of herself, when the reality was that only an iron determination stopped me punching the air like I'd just scored the winning goal in the last second of the Cup Final. "So, what sort of job is it?" I asked, casual-like.

"Nothing official, I'm afraid, although, as I said, who knows where it may lead? The thing is, Kat, I need someone in the field to do some – well, let's call it background research."

"If it's background research you want, I'm your woman," I said quickly. "When I worked for the radio station, I did most of the research for their flagship morning programme."

I crossed my fingers tightly behind my back as I spoke. After all, it was only the tiniest of tiny white lies. He didn't need to know that most of the 'research' I actually did consisted of trying to sweet talk the station's vanishing advertisers into coming back. But I did once do a whole piece on threats to axe the local bus routes that Brad said was 'sparky and showed promise.'

"I'll fill you in tomorrow," Liam said.

Despite the fact that I was holed up in Mum's salon, the rest of the day passed in a happy haze. Happy, that is, apart from the realisation that everybody I talked to denied having seen Marjorie Hampton on the afternoon of her murder. And that I still appeared to be the only person in Much Winchmoor to believe John Manning was innocent – apart from Will, of course.

I even stayed cool when conversation in the salon reverted yet again to my love life and job prospects. Let them talk, I told myself. This time tomorrow, I could be taking my first steps towards a decent career and getting my life back.

Not to mention I'd be spending time with a guy who made me forget I was sworn off men forever.

I didn't even mind that Will, as usual, wasn't answering my calls and was ignoring my texts. Or that I had to spend Saturday night with my parents watching an episode of *Midsomer Murders* that was so old, John Nettles was skipping around like a two-year-old.

Next morning, I was getting ready to meet Liam – a process that involved trying on everything in my wardrobe, at least twice, and deciding that none of it was right – when my phone rang. I groaned when I saw Liam's name come up. He was phoning to cancel. I knew it.

"I'm terribly sorry, but something's come up," he said. There was an edge of excitement in his voice. "A breaking story which I'm going to have to cover. I'm waiting for the photographer now and won't have time to drive all the way out to pick you up."

"But I could drive in?" I said, unwilling to pass up on my big break.

"I thought you said you didn't have a car?"

"I don't. But I could borrow my mum's." Hopefully, I could have added. But didn't. He seemed to take forever to make up his mind.

"Ok then," he said eventually. "You see, there's something I need you to do for me. And if it all works out, I'll makes sure the editor knows about your contribution. Maybe we'll even get to share the by-line, who knows? So, will you do it?"

"Providing it's legal." I refrained from adding that, depending on his definition of illegal, I could perhaps even then be persuaded. Instead, I said: "You haven't told me what it is yet, Liam."

"No time now. I'll explain when I see you. And of course it's legal. Trust me, I'm a journalist." He gave a low chuckle that made my toes curl and got me thinking of chocolate. Rich, dark, and melting slowly on my tongue. I was almost lost in the fantasy when his next words jerked me back. "Do you know Dintscombe Memorial Park?" he asked.

"I should do," I laughed. "I had my first cigarette in the bandstand there when I was at school. I was sick for a week."

"Well now, if I promise not to ply you with tobacco, would you meet me in the lay-by next to the entrance and I'll explain? Only it will have to be soonest. Like now. I really do need your help, Kat. So if you could get here as quickly as you can, that'll be great. And bring a camera if possible. No big deal if you can't. So, are you up for it?"

Was I ever! I didn't waste time trying to find Dad's precious digital camera, which he'd probably locked away in the bank's safe deposit box until their next jaunt to the Italian lakes, and hoped my phone would do.

Five minutes later, after promising to treat Mum's sugar pink car like it was made of spun glass, I was bowling along the narrow lane that led out of Much Winchmoor on my way to meet Liam, praying that the Much Winchmoor community speed watch team hadn't decided Sunday was a good day to take to the lanes with their speed guns. Or that Will hadn't decided to take his tractor out for a nice leisurely chug around.

***

The only time Dintscombe High Street showed any signs of life was on Wednesday mornings. Then the streets would be packed as everyone poured into town for the weekly market. The rest of the time it was as dead as the proverbial dodo and not nearly as interesting. Forget the economic downturn. The blame for turning Dintscombe High Street into a wasteland lay squarely at the door of Dintscombe District Council, when it decided to grant planning permission for an out-of-town retail park a few years earlier.

The problem was, it wasn't really out of town, but a mere hop, skip and a jump from the High Street. And it was no surprise to anyone, except the Council, when the retail park lured the few shoppers there had been away from the High Street and into its characterless, cloned units.

Which was the reason why, even on the brightest, sunniest

days, the centre of Dintscombe could best be described as dreary. But on a chilly grey Sunday in early March, it went off the scale of drabness. I drove along the deserted High Street, which was totally devoid of life, except for a few scruffy pigeons scavenging among the overturned rubbish bins, a legacy from last night's night revelries which, as far as I could see, consisted mainly of the challenging game of who can kick the rubbish bins the furthest.

You can't say the drinkers of Dintscombe don't know how to enjoy themselves on a Saturday night, I mused, as I turned off the High Street and into Park Road. As I pulled in to the lay-by near the imposing wrought iron gates at the entrance to the park, a legacy of the town's more prosperous past, my heart gave a little skip. Liam was waiting for me, the collar of his leather jacket turned up against the stiff breeze that sent a discarded crisp packet skipping along the pavement.

He had to all but fold himself in two as he shoehorned his long legs into Mum's tiny car, which became even tinier the moment he got in. At the same time, I became acutely conscious that he was wearing the same tangy aftershave he'd worn on Friday night and I wished I'd taken more time getting ready. Wished, too, I'd worn that skimpy blue top I'd decided against at the last minute.

"This is your car?" he asked with a frown.

"No. It's Mum's," I said. "She's the Cheryl—"

"Of Chez Cheryl. Yeah, I kind of got that, seeing as it's written all over the car in gold, glittery letters."

"Mum has this idea that if she drives around in an eye-catching car, people will see it and think, 'Oh yes, I must go and get my hair done. Chez Cheryl sounds a fun place.'"

He raised an eyebrow. "And do they?"

I shrugged. "Not so you'd notice. Although, as Dad says, at least it stops the boy racers pinching it."

"He's not wrong there." He gave a flicker of a smile. "The only thing is, Kat, I'm not sure it's quite suitable for the job I had in mind for you."

Not suitable? My bubble of excitement burst. What had the car got to do with anything? "Don't tell me," I forced a laugh and was pleased at how casual my voice sounded. "You're a boy racer at heart and wouldn't be seen dead in a sugar pink car?"

That flicker of a smile again. "Something like that. But what's more to the point is that it's a very conspicuous car, which might make it a very effective marketing tool for a hair salon but is probably not too well suited for a surveillance job."

"Surveillance?" That bubble of excitement popped to the surface again. "As in private detectives? Stake-outs and that sort of thing? Is that the research job you were talking about?" It certainly sounded a lot more interesting than colour-coding the towels in Mum's airing cupboard, which is what I'd be doing if I'd stayed at home.

All I had to do was convince him that the car and I were both up to the job. "But I'll be very careful, I promise. Stay deep in the shadows. I'm sure it won't be a problem. And look, this car is so small, it's virtually invisible."

"Hardly that." He glanced at his watch and frowned. "Well, it looks like I have no choice. I'm running out of time. Mike will be here any minute."

He tapped his long, slender fingers on the dashboard in front of him and appeared to be deep in thought. Finally, he nodded like he'd just made up his mind about something. I crossed my fingers.

"Ok. Here's the deal. Do you see that house over there?" He leaned across and pointed to a small, grey stone cottage with diamond-paned windows and a neat pocket handkerchief front garden on the other side of the road. "It belongs to a woman called Doreen Spetchley. Do you know her?"

I tried not to think about how close his face was to mine and forced myself to concentrate. "I, um, no. No, I don't think so. The name doesn't ring a bell. Should I?"

"Probably not. She's got a senior post in the council planning office and I received a tip-off about her yesterday. A disgruntled colleague whom she'd passed over for promotion said it might be worth my while checking out who she's arranged to meet up with this afternoon. But my contact wouldn't, or couldn't, say where that meeting would be. Or with whom. Although I've got my suspicions."

"Do you think it's Creepy Crabshaw?" I asked.

"I don't know and that's the truth. My contact just said they thought I'd be interested in seeing who the deputy head of the planning department is having cosy little meetings with out of office hours."

"So what do you want me to do? Wait and see who comes calling?"

"Exactly. Hence my concern about the car."

"I'm sorry. Dad was using his so it was the Pink Peril or nothing. But I'll be really careful and stay out of sight, I promise. What are you going to do?"

"That's why I called you. I've been here for an hour already, but there's a massive fire on the industrial estate and the photographer's going to pick me up from here any minute. Could be a big story – there's hints about it being arson – so I can't afford not to be there. So, how about it? Not your usual research job, I admit. But a pretty important one. Are you up for it?"

"Try and stop me."

"Did you bring a camera?"

"I'm afraid not. You said to hurry and I didn't want to waste time hunting for Dad's. So I've only got this." I showed him my phone.

"That'll probably be good enough. I was going to use my phone. Any pictures we do get won't be for publication. Just as leverage to persuade one or the other, or preferably both, to give me an interview. My contact was pretty sure the meeting was at Doreen Spetchley's house, so all I want you to do is take pictures of whoever turns up."

"What about if the meeting is somewhere else? Do you want me to follow her?" I asked eagerly.

"No way," he said firmly. "Let's face it, that would be almost impossible driving around in a car like a big pink marshmallow. She'd spot you a mile off."

"But if she's on foot? I could follow her then, couldn't I?"

He gave me a long, straight look. The kind of look people

give you when they're trying to work out how to say something they know you're not going to like. He was right. I didn't like.

"Your jacket. It's about as inconspicuous as your car," he said. "And as for your hair, well, let's face it, you don't merge into the background, do you? Certainly not in Dintscombe on a grey Sunday afternoon."

He had a point. My jacket was the pink sparkly one. I'd been in such a hurry to leave the house, it was the first one I'd come to. As for my hair, well, the evening before, I did what I often do when I'm feeling a bit low. I coloured my hair and had opted for two contrasting tones – purple and a pale, silvery blue. I fiddled in the glove compartment, hoping to find a bobble hat or something that I could cram on. But my mother's a hairdresser. She didn't do hats. Least of all bobble hats.

"I'm sorry." I mumbled, feeling pretty silly. "I didn't know. If you'd said—"

He smiled and touched my arm lightly. "Hey, don't be. You look amazing. It's probably a dead-end story anyway. If Doreen goes out, chances are, it'll be to a car boot sale or something, so don't worry about it. But if the meeting is here, and you can manage to get a shot, preferably of them both, that would be fantastic. If not, well, at least we tried."

I felt a warm glow at the way he said 'we tried'. Like we were a team. "How will I know it's her?"

"She lives alone," His voice had an edge of impatience to it. "Who else would it be opening her front door?"

"Yeah, of course. Sorry. I just thought…"

"She's in her mid-fifties, slim, about five foot six, with grey hair pulled back in one of those bun things."

"Ok. I'll do what I can," I said. "I'll call you and—"

"Sorry. Got to go. This looks like Mike. I really appreciate this." He touched the back of my hand briefly and sent tingles zinging up my arm. "I owe you one, Kat Latcham, so I do."

As he and the photographer drove away, I settled down to watch out for Doreen Spetchley. It wasn't quite what I'd expected when Liam had talked about a research job. But a job was a job, and who knew where this one would lead? I took my phone out and set it to camera.

The only problem was, sitting there with nothing to do but watch that little cottage for signs of life gave me plenty of time to sit and think. And, as they had done several times since yesterday afternoon, my thoughts came back to Jules. And what she'd said. She'd got it all wrong, of course. All that stuff about running home to Mummy and walking into a job that was meant for someone else. I didn't run home. I'd crawled there, with my tail firmly between my legs, and I'd had to put up with no end of grief from Dad about it. As for the job, didn't she realise my mum was virtually blackmailing me into working for her? Millie Chapman was welcome to the job – and I'd told Mum that. Several times.

But most of all, Jules had been wrong about Will. He and I were like brother and sister. We used to talk to each other about everything, even each others' romances – or, as was more often the case, lack of romances. Even when I left home and went to college, we'd take up where we'd left off when I came back in the holidays. Arguing, bickering, but underneath it all the best of mates.

Until I met Ratface Nick. And everything changed. For a start, I didn't come home anything like so often and, when I did, Will was cold and distant, if not downright rude. And it had hurt. Ok, so he didn't like Ratface. Well, I didn't like Amy Snelling, and Will had gone out with her for ages. But I didn't go round talking about 'punching her lights out', like Will had threatened to do to Nick.

As for this thing Jules had said about him fancying me, that was the most ridiculous thing I'd heard since the vicar's wife suggested a mass abseil down the church tower to raise money for the bell fund. In fact, not only was the thought of me and Will ridiculous, it was downright uncomfortable. For pity's sake, it would be like fancying your own brother. Besides, how can you fancy a man you could beat at conkers? Or who sat behind you in primary school and tied your plait to the back of a chair? Or laughed himself silly when a cow head-butted you into a ditch?

I wished he was here beside me, so we could have a good laugh about how Jules's raging hormones had turned her brain to porridge. She'd be seeing little green men on the village pond next.

As if on cue, my phone pinged with a text message. It was from Jules. An apology. Of sorts. *"Sorry. Was a total cow yesterday. Bad day. Weird things in pub. CU later? xx"*

There was still no sign of activity from Doreen's cottage and I was getting bored, to say nothing of having a numb bottom from sitting in the same place for too long. I replied to Jules, saying I'd call her tomorrow. I still hadn't heard from Will so I texted him. Yet again. I tapped out another apology. Another explanation. In case he hadn't got the first one. *"Why don't u answer my txt? Did u get it? Srry abt Fri night. Not what u thought. Liam offered me work 4 Chronicle. Cldnt say no, cld I?!! Am working now!!!! Tell u ltr. How's yr dad? Kat. xxx"*

He probably wouldn't answer that one either. One of these days, Will would maybe catch on that texting is meant to be a two-way process. But at least I'd tried. I'd just hit send when I saw the front door of the cottage open. It was Doreen Spetchley. It had to be. Liam's description was spot on. I watched with dismay as she hurried out and got into the small blue hatchback that was parked on the drive.

Obviously the meeting was not at Doreen's house after all. What to do now? Liam had told me not to attempt to follow her on foot or in the car, but I couldn't just sit here and do nothing. I tried to phone him but just got his voice mail. There was nothing for it. Surely, as long as I kept a couple of cars between me and Doreen, it would be easy enough to follow her without being seen? Goodness knows, I'd watched enough detective programmes to know how it was done.

I waited for Doreen to drive past. Mindful of what I'd seen them do on the television, I allowed another car to pass before pulling out, earning myself a blast on the horn from the irate driver of the massive 4x4 I'd just cut in front of. Not the best of starts at being inconspicuous, particularly as the racket he made was loud enough to wake up everyone in Dintscombe cemetery.

I focused so hard on keeping my eyes firmly fixed on Doreen's little blue hatchback that its image was probably permanently etched on my retinas. It helped me ignore the fact that I had a 4x4 the size of a small tank welded to the rear bumper of Mum's little pink car as I drove along.

Chapter Fourteen

Since the latest round of cutbacks, policemen in and around Dintscombe were rarer than hens' teeth – which was lucky for me. If one had been about that Sunday afternoon, he'd have pulled me over for erratic driving quicker than you could say, 'could you blow into the bag, please, madam?'

The 4x4 driver's patience ran out at the first set of traffic lights, when he rocketed past me with another ear-splitting blast and a mouthful of abuse which thankfully I couldn't hear, owing to the ear-splitting blast.

Not that I blamed him. One moment, I was crawling at a snail's pace in an effort to keep at least one car between me and Doreen, the next I was racing along, the engine of Mum's little pink car screaming as I hurried to catch up. Tailing someone looked so easy on TV but the reality was a nightmare.

At one point, I got stuck behind a bus – needless to say, it was not heading for Much Winchmoor – and, for one horrible moment, thought I'd lost Doreen completely. But the patron saint of surveillance operatives must have been looking out for me at that moment, because I was able to nip past the bus in time to see Doreen indicating left.

As we left the town and got out on to the bypass, I was able to relax a little and allow a few more cars between us. But then I began to worry about what I'd do if Doreen was heading for Much Winchmoor. It would be impossible to follow her along the narrow lanes that led into the village without being noticed. I gave a sigh of relief when I saw the blue hatchback indicating it was getting ready to leave the dual carriageway at the turning before the one for Much Winchmoor.

I was pretty sure I knew exactly where she must be heading. The narrow road led up to Compton Wood, a rambling, mostly neglected stretch of woodland used only by a few local dog walkers and bird watchers. It had to be there. It was the perfect spot for a secret assignation. Excitement fizzed through my veins as I turned off the main road.

I pulled in at the bottom of the hill that wound up through a tunnel of trees to a small car park near the top. The last thing I wanted to do was catch up with Doreen part way up the hill. Suddenly I got a mirror-full of flashing headlights, and pulled over as close to the hedge as I dared, to let a silver Porsche streak past.

I turned my head away quickly as I recognised the impatient driver. It was Gerald Crabshaw. I didn't have him down as a bird watcher and he was well known for his dislike of dogs. So I reckoned my guess about Doreen Spetchley's mystery man was the right one. Liam was going to love this.

I waited until Gerald's Porsche disappeared, then drove after him. I knew every inch of this area well, as Will and I used to come up here collecting hazelnuts and blackberries when we were kids. I remembered that, just before the turning into the car park, there was a field gate with a bit of a pull-in. I drove as quietly as I could, parked in the gateway and got out, being careful not to slam the car door as I did so.

Then I crept up the remaining few yards towards the car park. It was set back from the road, in a dip that, according to Will, was once a small quarry. The overgrown hazel bushes, sycamores and brambles that surrounded it would make a perfect screen. Even though the trees were not in leaf, there was still enough cover for me to be able to peer down on the car park without being seen.

Just as I'd hoped, there were only two cars there. Doreen's little blue hatchback, and Gerald's sleek silver Porsche. The two of them were standing by Gerald's car. Doreen's long thin arms were draped around his neck, laughing up at him, as she pulled him towards her. She looked like she'd been stranded on a desert island and he'd just rocked up to rescue her.

It looked very much like Doreen Spetchley and Gerald Crabshaw were having an affair. More to the point – and this was the bit that was going to interest Liam – a senior member of the Planning Department and a member of the Council's Planning Committee were tangled together like tights in a washing machine. What a story. And what a picture. They were so engrossed in each other, I could have used a flash and they wouldn't have noticed.

I edged my way through the tangled undergrowth, the smell of wet leaves filling my nostrils with each cautious step. But they were obviously not cautious enough because, with the next one, my foot slipped from under me and I had to drop quickly to my knees to stop myself from tumbling all the way down the slope.

They broke away from each other at the sound and looked in my direction. I flattened myself on the ground so that now it wasn't just the smell of wet leaves filling my nostrils, but the wet leaves themselves. Then, the biggest stroke of luck. A couple of wood pigeons, obviously as startled by the sound of my near-fall as Doreen and Gerald had been, clattered out of the bushes just above me. With my heart still thudding, I peered down at the car park and saw that Gerald and Doreen had obviously decided the noise came from the wood pigeons, and were once again engrossed in each other.

I felt in my pocket for my phone and only just stopped myself from groaning out loud. It wasn't there. I'd only left the wretched thing in the car. How could I have been so stupid?

I was about to go back and fetch it when there was a sudden dramatic change in the body language between the two lovebirds. Doreen pulled away from him, her hands to her mouth, her head going from side to side, like she couldn't believe what she'd just heard. Even without hearing her actual words, I could see she was obviously in some considerable distress. Whatever Gerald had said to her, she didn't like it one little bit.

He looked as twitchy as a canary in a cattery but made no move to comfort her. Then Doreen moved towards him, both hands outstretched as if she was imploring him. This time, he was the one shaking his head as he backed away. Then he turned and scuttled back to his car.

The throaty roar of Gerald's look-at-me Porsche set the wood pigeons off on another panicked flight as he exited the car park, sending up a shower of loose stones as he did so, before roaring off down the hill. I could only hope that in his hurry, he wouldn't notice Mum's car in the gateway.

Doreen was still standing in the middle of the car park, shaking her head as she stared after him. Then she stiffened and strode towards her car. Even from a distance, I could see she'd gone from being desperately upset to hissing, spitting rage. Talk about hell hath no fury. There was no doubt I was looking at a woman scorned – and one who'd just decided she was not going to take it lying down.

She jumped in her car, then she, too, roared out of the car park and rocketed off back down the hill, heading, I assumed, back to Dintscombe.

I disentangled myself from the undergrowth, brushed as much of the wet leaves and mud off as I could, then made my way back to Mum's car, where my phone looked reproachfully up at me from the passenger seat. I was so busy blaming myself for being such an idiot that, at that moment, my brain wasn't totally in gear. If it had it been, I might have remembered I'd failed my driving test the first time round because of what the hatchet-faced examiner described as an 'inadequate' three-point turn, and I'd have driven up to the car park to turn round. Instead, I attempted to do it in the narrow gateway.

It was soon apparent there'd been no significant improvement in my three-point turning skills. In fact, I lost count of how many shuffles it took, and began to think panicky thoughts of Mum's little car being wedged across the narrow lane forever. Then, just when I was starting to breathe again at what was surely the final shuffle, my muddy shoe slipped on the accelerator and I went back too way too fast. There was an ominous crunch as the back of the car connected with the heavy metal gate.

That little pink marshmallow car was top of Mum's best loved list, ahead of the cat, George Clooney and my dad. But I was sure to drop off the list completely, and was going to be sweeping the salon floor and unwinding perm rollers for the rest of my life, when Mum saw what I'd done to her precious car.

Still feeling shaky, I drove down the hill and made my way back along the lane. As I reached the bypass, I turned right to go back to Dintscombe. I told myself I was concerned about Doreen and wanted to check she'd got back safely. Or maybe, even, bump into Liam if his fire had burnt itself out. But the truth was, I was not in any great hurry to face my mother and needed a bit more time to think up a convincing story.

When I drove past Doreen's cottage the little blue hatchback was parked safely on the drive. I pulled in to the lay-by at the park entrance again and called Liam. I pushed the worry about the car firmly to the back of my mind and focussed on the job in hand.

"Any news?" he asked.

"You'd better believe it," I said, tingling with excitement. "She was only meeting our esteemed Councillor Crabshaw."

"I knew it," he breathed. "I knew there was something dodgy about that fellow. I'll bet you she's been passing on confidential stuff to him. It has to be something like that. Remember that new retail development?"

"You mean the so-called 'out of town' one, that turned out to be so close to the centre, the High Street now looks like a ghost town with more boarded-up shops than open ones?"

"That's the one. The Planning Committee was seriously misled about the original application and I'm pretty sure your Councillor Crabshaw had something to do with that. If he was in cahoots with someone senior in the Planning Department, that makes it seem even more likely."

"They looked like they were into more than just cahoots," I said and couldn't help adding, "or, put it this way, they looked as if things between them were pretty hot, judging by the way the two of them were tangled up together."

"On her front doorstep?" Liam sounded surprised. "I wouldn't have thought Gerald Crabshaw would have been that indiscreet."

"Ah no. Well, actually he wasn't." I'd been hoping I

wouldn't have to tell him, but it was too late now. I'd started so I had to finish. "I, I know you said not to but I – well, the thing is, I followed her."

"You followed her?" Liam's voice crackled with annoyance. "Damn right I told you not to. That was a pretty stupid thing to do."

"They didn't see me, honest," I said quickly. "They met in the car park up in Compton Woods. I know the area well from when I used to play up there as a kid, so I parked in a gateway and made my way up through the bushes. I used to be very good at tracking when I was a Girl Guide, you know."

"Did you now?" He sighed then, to my relief, laughed softly. "Well, you showed initiative, that's for sure. Even so, you might have been putting yourself in danger. I would hate to lose my bright new research assistant when I've only just found her. Promise me, next time, you'll do what I say. "

Next time? There was going to be a next time? Bright new research assistant? I glowed in the warmth of his praise. Suddenly, the worry of having to tell Mum about the car faded into insignificance. "I promise. But if I hadn't followed her, I wouldn't have seen them cuddled up together. And that's not all. They were cosy for a while, but then he must have said something to upset her, because they suddenly broke apart and he beetled back to his car and drove off. She stood there for a while, looking shocked. Then she seemed to pull herself together. She looked spitting mad as she drove off. I was actually a bit worried about her, which is why I came back here to her cottage, just to check she got home in one piece. Which she did, thank goodness."

"You've done a brilliant job." I glowed some more until he went on, "Did you manage to get any pictures?"

"Ah well, the thing is…" Now for the tricky bit. Should I confess I'd left my phone in the car or try and brazen it out? I decided to go for a half truth. "It was really difficult. I couldn't get too close in case they saw me."

"Not to worry. You've given me something to work on now. I'm grateful to you."

I glowed yet again. "How's your fire going?" I asked.

"Pretty good. Everyone's being a bit tight-lipped at the moment, but that says to me it's pointing towards arson. We've been told we'll have a statement any moment now. So, once again, I'm just hanging around waiting. The story of my life."

"I'd happily swap with you," I said wistfully. "I've got to go home and face my mother."

"Ah now, you're not telling me you've gone and dinged the pink marshmallow, are you?"

"I'm afraid so. I was doing a three point turn and, well, let's just say, there was an incident between the car and a metal gate and the car came off worse."

"That's tough. And I'm sorry I can't put that down on my expenses for you, otherwise I would. However, I do have a mate who's very good at knocking out dents. He'll do you a good job and not rip you off."

"I'll bear it in mind, thanks. I've got a feeling being ripped off is the least of my worries and that I'm going to be paying for my error of judgement in unpaid labour in the salon for the rest of my life."

Chapter Fifteen

I took my time driving back to the village and, once there, turned up the hill towards the farm instead of going home. Putting off facing my mum? You bet your life I was. But I was also concerned that Will hadn't been in touch, so I thought I'd call in and see if he was about. He wasn't. But his father was.

It was difficult to decide whether John Manning looked better or worse than the last time I'd seen him. Then, he'd been white-faced, unshaven and shocked as he was driven away in the back of the police car. Now, he was still white-faced, but clean-shaven, his hair smoothed tidily back and his clothes, though crumpled, looked clean.

But his eyes were as empty and haunted as ever.

"It's good to see you home again, Mr Manning," I said. "How are you?"

"How am I?" He frowned as if he was having to dig deep to find the answer to that particular question. "I'm sober. That's what I am. But where are my manners? Come along in, Katie, please do. Will's off on the farm somewhere but he'll be back shortly, I'm sure. He hasn't had his lunch yet."

I followed him down the long gloomy passage and into the kitchen, which was tidier than the last time I'd seen it. It had lost that cold, unlived-in feeling, thanks to the range that was giving out a gentle, comforting warmth. A cat was curled up in the chair next to it and fixed me with a warning glare, daring me to try to move him.

John stood on one side of the large deal table, I stood on the other. We stared at each other for a long, awkward moment. I swallowed hard. Jeez, this was awkward. What did I say now? A mumbled, "I – I hope you're feeling better," was the best I could come up with.

He shook his head. "Anything but, lass," he sighed.

"Anything but. At least the drinking stopped me thinking and feeling. But now, I don't know. I just don't know."

My heart contracted with pity for him. He looked so lost and broken that I forgot the awkwardness and just wanted to make him feel better. "Have you seen a doctor?" I asked gently.

"Of course not. What would he do? Tell me to give up drinking, that's what." The knuckles on his hands showed white where he gripped the back of the chair. "The police still think I killed her, you know."

"Then they're wrong. Because you didn't," I said fiercely.

"No. No. You're quite right, I didn't. And Will tells me how you've gone around defending me to everyone, for which I'm grateful. Even though you were wasting your time. Because, you know, when they put me in that police cell and shut the door, I thought… for a moment then, I thought maybe I had. Maybe I had killed her but couldn't remember." I had to strain to hear him as his voice dropped to a hoarse whisper. "And that was what scared me most. It also made me see what a monster I'd become. That I could have killed someone and not even remembered it. I thought, too, how ashamed and disgusted Sally would be. That was what Marjorie said to me that day, you know, and she was absolutely right. Which was why I was so furious with her. Because I knew she spoke nothing but the truth."

"But you didn't kill her."

"I swear to God I didn't. But I came damn close to killing myself with my stupid drinking. And where would that have left Will? To lose both parents within a year? Goodness knows what would have happened to me if the farm shop hadn't been locked that afternoon. I'd have probably ended up with alcohol poisoning."

"How do you mean?" I asked uneasily.

He gestured to me to sit down, then pulled the chair out and sat down opposite me, his head bowed. He never once looked up as he spoke. "After I'd had the run-in with Marjorie, I stormed into the house, grabbed the whisky bottle and went up to my room. But there was only a bit left in that bottle, so I went out across the yard to the farm shop, where I used to keep a stash. But I figured Will must have found it – he'd found all the ones in the house –and locked the door to keep me out. Goodness knows what state I'd have been in if I'd found those bottles. As it was, I drank enough to blot out the whole of the rest of that day."

"You don't remember going into the pub that night? I was working there behind the bar. I served you. Several times."

He shook his head. "I don't remember a thing until I came round next morning with you and Will standing over me and Will asking me what the hell I'd done."

"Wait a minute," I said. "Go back a bit. You said Will must have found your stash. Where did you say you kept it?"

"In the farm shop. Down behind one of the freezers. I assumed he'd been in there, found it and locked the door to keep me out."

"But Will hasn't been able to set foot in the place since his mother died." John looked up and winced as I said that. But I kept going. "He told me he tried a few times but just couldn't face it. The day we found poor Marjorie, that was the first time Will had been in there since – since Sally…"

"He couldn't face going in the shop?" He rubbed his hands down his face, his eyes deeply troubled. "Poor lad. I – I didn't know. He always seemed so together, I thought he was ok. That he was handling things. If I'd known…" His voice trailed away.

I sighed. "Don't you two ever talk to each other? About things other than the farm, I mean? No, I don't suppose you do. It's not your way, is it?"

John shook his head. "I didn't know," he repeated the words like they were some kind of mantra. "I didn't know."

"But, hang about, if it wasn't Will who locked the door, then who was it?" I asked. My stomach lurched as I realised the implication of what I was saying.

John caught on at the same time. His face went even whiter, his eyes widened with shock. "You mean; the murderer was in there? At that very moment when I tried the door? That he—?"

The chair made an ugly screeching noise on the floor as he

stood up. He paced about the room. "Oh, dear God," he muttered, more to himself than to me. "What have I done? What the hell have I done?"

"Come and sit down again," I put my hand on his arm and steered him gently back towards the chair. "And John, you haven't done anything."

It was the first time in my life I'd ever called him anything other than Mr Manning, but the use of his Christian name came naturally, my only thought was concern for him. He looked so terrible, I was afraid he was going to keel over.

"Can I get you anything?" I asked. "Tea? Brandy?"

He shook his head violently. "I swear, Katie, on Sally's grave, I will never touch alcohol again for as long as I live. As for you saying I didn't do anything – you don't get it, do you?"

I did get it. But I'd rather been hoping he hadn't. He was beating himself up enough as it was.

"Well, yes, but—" I began but he cut in, his voice harsh.

"I didn't do anything, and that's just the point. If I hadn't been so stinking drunk, I would have gone back to the house and found my key. Had I done so I might just have saved Marjorie's life. Because whoever it was that locked that door…" He swallowed hard. "It wasn't me and it wasn't Will. So it could only have been the murderer, couldn't it? While I was trying the door, he was – he must have been – well, you know. If I'd had my wits about me, I could have, I should have prevented it. Although what the poor woman was doing in there in the first place, heaven alone knows. If only I'd..."

Helpless, I could only stare at him as his voice trailed away. I searched desperately for something to say that wouldn't make it worse for him.

"See?" He looked at me intently. "You think so too."

"No. No, of course I don't. You can't torture yourself like that," I said, as I struggled to get through to him, to say something, anything, that would take the haunted look from his eyes. "We can all blame ourselves for one thing or another. If I'd listened to her more carefully that morning, maybe I'd have been able to tell the police who she was going to have it out with. Who had got her dander up, as she put it."

"Oh, that one's easy. She was talking about me."

"No, she wasn't. I'm absolutely certain about that, because she'd already had a go about you," I felt my cheeks redden. "I'm sorry. I – I didn't mean—"

"It's ok." He gave a wry smile. "I think I can guess exactly what she was saying about me. I'll say this for Marjorie, she'd never say anything behind your back that she wasn't prepared to say to your face. And say it to my face she did."

"That's true. But she hadn't arranged to meet you that afternoon, had she? That just happened by chance when she was passing the farm and saw you crossing the yard. So what exactly did she say?"

"Well, she said Sally would be ashamed of me," he said.

"No. I don't mean that. I mean, at the beginning. What made her come into the yard and have a go at you in the first place?"

He screwed up his face in concentration. "Something – it was something to do with the state of the bridle path. The one we call Pendle Drove. Said – yes, that's it. I remember now. She said something about what a disgrace it was, that it was ankle deep in mud and impassable. And how Will and I should know better than to go driving our vehicles up and down it – and didn't we know what legs were for?"

"And had you been driving up and down it?"

"Well, I hadn't. Can't speak for Will, although I can't think why he would. That drove goes all the way around our boundary and comes out on the land at the back of old Jack Shrewton's barn. It was the way the local farmers used to take their cattle, back in the old days, to get to the other side of the village. But nobody ever goes along there now. We certainly don't, unless we're checking the boundary fences. But as we've had no stock grazing there for a while, there's no reason we should. So I don't know who's been churning up the lane, but I'm pretty sure it wasn't us. One of those damn hooray Henries in their four-wheel drives, off-roading, I expect."

Then I remembered. Something about Marjorie that had struck me as odd when I'd first seen her body. Apart from the fact that she was half in, half out of the freezer, of course.

"Her shoes," I said. "They were covered in mud. When she was in the salon earlier that day, they were so highly polished you could see your face in them. But when we found her, they were caked in mud. So that mud could only have got there that afternoon. That was what she was doing up here, then. She must have started to go along Pendle Drove but couldn't get through because of the mud. But why? What was she doing there? Had she gone there to meet someone, do you think?"

He shrugged. "She didn't say. And, if she had, how come she ended up in my freezer?"

I gave up. The whole thing made no sense. "I don't know," I said wearily. "It must have been after she left you, mustn't it? Did she say anything? Anything at all, to give us a clue as to where she was going? Or with whom?"

He shook his head. "Not that I can recall, I'm afraid. But to be honest, she could have said she was off to have tea with Elvis and it wouldn't have registered, I was that hopping mad with her."

"Hmm. Not likely. I don't think she approved of Elvis either," I said, trying to lessen the tension, if only for a moment.

His brief smile didn't reach his eyes. "I've made a terrible, terrible mess of things, haven't I?" he sighed. "It wasn't until I saw Will, when he came to collect me from the police station, that I realised how selfish I've been and how much I've let fall on his shoulders. I vowed there and then that if I get out of this mess without going to prison, I'll work my socks off to make things right again between us. I can hardly look the lad in the face, and that's the truth."

"And have you told him that?" I asked gently.

"No. But I will."

"Promise?"

"I promise." He reached out and took my hand in his large, work-worn one. "Thank you for believing in me, Katie."

I blinked back a tear. "That's what friends are for," I said gruffly.

"Yes. Yes." His eyes, I was glad to see, looked a little less bleak, as if talking had lightened some of the heavy black cloud that was weighing him down. "You're a good girl. Sally always said you were one of the best, and she was a good judge of people, was my Sally. I'm so glad you and Will have made it up."

I shrugged. "Yeah, well, you know what we're like. Fighting like cat and dog one minute, best mates the next. Always have been."

"Do you know, Sally always hoped that you and Will might make a go of it one day?"

"A go of it? What? You mean..." I swallowed hard and felt my cheeks burn as I suddenly realised what he was getting at. Jeez. I hadn't seen that one coming. He'd got it all wrong about Will and me. "There's nothing like that between us, you know," I said quickly. "Nothing at all. We're just mates, that's all."

"There's not? Then I'm sorry to hear it," he murmured. "Sorry, too, if I embarrassed you. You see, girl? It's not always good to talk, is it? There are some things that are better left unsaid."

"Maybe you're right."

I flashed him a quick, awkward smile as I stood up to go. He came out into the yard with me and pointed at the back of the car. "Looks like your mum's been in the wars."

"Worse," I said. "It was me. Had a disagreement with a gate."

He bent down, looked closely at the dented boot lid and shook his head. "That's a bad one, that is. What did your mum say?"

"She doesn't know yet," I said grimly. "I'm on my way to tell her now. She's going to go mad."

He shook his head. "Can't help you this time, Katie," he said as he straightened up. "Looks a bit more serious than when you buckled your front fork riding your bike into the pond."

I flashed him a smile and started the engine. "No? That's a pity. Guess I'll just have to go home and face the music."

I was impatient to be gone. Will could well be back any minute and I wanted to be well out of the way before he did.

After John's comments about me and Will 'making a go of it' as he'd put it, facing Mum with her crumpled car suddenly seemed the less awkward option.

As I passed the pub on my way home, I was surprised to see Gerald's car tucked away in the far corner of the pub car park. And, parked next to it, a battered old pickup. I slowed down to get a good look and recognised the burly figure of Shane Freeman in the driver's seat. He had the window wound down and was smoking a cigarette, at the same time drumming the fingers of his other hand on the steering wheel, like he was getting fed up with waiting.

But who was he waiting for? Gerald, maybe? I remembered seeing the pair of them hanging around by the village pond the other evening on my way home from work, although Gerald had disappeared as I approached. But where was Gerald now? And what were the pair of them up to?

There were two ways in to the Winchmoor Arms. The door that led in off the High Street opened into the Lounge Bar, while the one in the car park, to the side of the building, opened into the public bar. I checked my watch. It was almost 4 o'clock. Way past Donald's normal closing time. And the public bar door, like the one in the front, was firmly shut. If I hadn't known otherwise, I'd have assumed Gerald had had a heavy lunchtime session and had decided to leave his car and walk home.

So, was Donald having a lock in? It wouldn't be the first time. But on a Sunday afternoon? Hardly likely. The pub didn't open on Sunday evenings and Donald was well known for favouring those few quiet hours to take the opportunity to catch up on the complete week's *Countdown*.

I stopped the car to get a closer look and, as I did so, the public bar door opened and Gerald came out. As he started across the car park towards his car, Shane Freeman climbed out of the pickup, ground out his cigarette with the heel of his boot and began to amble across towards him. As he did so, Gerald saw me and stopped as abruptly as if he'd just walked into a door. He motioned Shane to stay where he was, hurried across to where I was parked and wrenched open the car door.

I gave a startled yelp as he thrust his angry face into the car. It was so close to mine I could see the tracery of thread veins across his nose. Smell the sourness of whisky on his breath. I shrank back but my head connected with the headrest and I could go no further.

"What the hell do you think you're doing?" he roared. His angry voice reverberated around the tiny interior and made my ears ring. "Are you following me?"

"Of course not. Why would you think that? I'm on my way home. I'd just stopped to take a phone call and—"

"It was you, wasn't it?" he snarled. "You were up in Compton Wood earlier. Don't try to deny it, you stupid girl. I saw you. Let's face it, this ridiculous car is hard to miss. I wondered what your mother was doing up there on a Sunday afternoon. But of course it wasn't her. It was you, wasn't it?"

"I – I was trying to find my dog." As excuses went, it was a pretty lame one. But the best I could come up with in the circumstances.

"You don't have a dog." His voice went up several decibels and I began to fear for my ear drums. And, from the redness of his face, for his blood pressure.

"I – no. Did I say my dog? I meant Elsie Flintlock's little dog. Prescott. You know how he's always running off. I – I've just taken him home. Elsie was ever so grateful. Well, I must be off. Mum will be wondering where I am."

"Good idea. Oh, and Katie," I felt the headrest creak as I shrank back against it as he leaned in still further. Another inch and he'd have been on my lap. "Keep your sticky little beak out of things that don't concern you. Ok?"

As he did so, something within me snapped. I stopped cowering back, sat up straight and faced him. I've never had much time for bullies. I'd learnt, the hard way, when I was eleven and Will was off school with tonsillitis, and so unable to defend me like he usually did, that the best way to deal with bullies was to stand up to them.

Ok, so I got a bruise on the top of my arm the size and colour of a Victoria plum for my pains, but the bully had an even bigger one on his cheekbone and his eye swelled up so much, it closed completely. And I got detention for fighting on the school bus. But it had been worth it, even if I did have sore knuckles for a week, and Will said I was all sorts of a fool for mouthing off to the hardest kid in the school. But the bullies never bothered me again.

And they weren't going to start now. I held up my phone and took Gerald's picture. He jerked back as if stung and I clicked again. It wasn't his best look, that was for sure, and I could understand he wasn't happy about it. But I felt his language, and some of the names he called me, were wholly inappropriate considering we were within shouting distance of the church. And it was Sunday afternoon.

"And there are more pictures where that one comes from, Councillor Crabshaw," I cut in crisply, when it looked as if he was never going to run out of swear words. "Of you and a certain lady. With a lovely shot of Compton Wood in the background. Now what was her name? It'll come to me in a moment. By the way, does Mrs Crabshaw know where you were earlier this afternoon? What did you tell her? That you were out for an afternoon of bird watching?"

The way he clenched his fists, I could see another punch to the forearm heading my way. So I quickly closed the door, started the engine and drove off. I was glad he couldn't see how much I was shaking, although maybe he could have worked it out from the way Mum's little car jerked its way down the High Street in a series of bunny hops a kangaroo would have been proud of, never mind a rabbit.

As I turned into our road, I looked back and in my rear view mirror I could see Gerald's face, scarlet with rage. While Shane Freeman stared after me, his mouth hanging open.

Chapter Sixteen

What was it about this bloody place that people felt they had the right to stick their noses in everyone else's business all the time? Was there something in the water, he wondered?

This time, they'd gone too far. Well, one of them had, at least.

Did that stupid, stupid girl think he was going to let her spoil everything he'd worked for, schemed for and risked everything for – just so she could run around playing cops and robbers?

It was about time she found out that murder wasn't a game. And he was just the person to teach her. It would be his pleasure.

"So, she likes to be called Kat, not Katie, does she?" he murmured to himself. "Well, little Miss Call-Me-Kat Latcham. Have I got plans for you. You're about to find out exactly what curiosity did to your namesake.'

He leaned back in his chair and smiled. Murder was like learning to drive, he reflected. The more you did it, the easier it got.

Chapter Seventeen

The confrontation with Mum, painful though it was, wasn't the cause of my sleepless night. I crawled out of bed next morning, feeling, and looking, I realised as I peered at my morning face in the bathroom mirror, as if I hadn't slept a wink. Because every time I drifted off, images of Marjorie, half in, half out of the freezer, complete with woolly grey tights and mud-encrusted shoes, became superimposed on Gerald Crabshaw's angry face. Sometimes I saw him in the bar, ranting on about Marjorie. Other times it would be when he'd stuck his head in the car yesterday, and accused me of following him. But each time, his snarling message had been the same. The same words. The same fury.

'Keep your sticky little beak out of my business. Remember what happened to Marjorie. Stupid, stupid girl.'

I would then be jerked back to wakefulness, bathed in sweat, my heart banging against my rib cage like a startled canary. Gerald was Marjorie's killer. I was sure of it. The thing was, what to do about it? Should I tell Ben, or PC Newton, as I had to remind myself to call him?

"You should eat something," Mum said. She was still ploughing her way through her frogspawn porridge, which that morning looked more like wallpaper paste and she was, as always, eager to share its benefits with me. I shook my head. Even chocolate biscuits had no appeal.

And yet, sitting there in Mum's familiar kitchen, my fears, which had seemed so real and frightening in the small hours, started to seem a bit over the top. Or even just plain daft. The truth, I realised, was probably something much more mundane. Yes, Gerald was a nasty piece of work, a total sleaze-bag, in fact. And, as Liam suspected, it was highly likely he was abusing his position as a member of the planning committee to get up to something iffy. It would probably also explain his fling with Doreen Spetchley. The rather plain, grey woman was not his usual type at all, I wouldn't have thought. But what do I know?

Like all bullies, he was nothing but bluster. Look how he'd pulled back yesterday when I'd stood up to him. I was willing to bet that what had set him off was mentioning I'd seen him with Doreen. Even if I hadn't named her. He was trying to cover up his affair. Nothing more sinister than that.

Marjorie's killer had to be a stranger. Some maniac who'd come across her, alone and vulnerable, around Pendle Drove. The poor soul had simply been in the wrong place at the wrong time.

Even so, although I decided against telling Ben Newton, I thought it would be a good thing to tell Liam about the threat Gerald had made. I tried his phone several times that morning, but each time got his voice mail and decided against leaving a message, apart from asking him to call me.

Ten minutes later, my phone rang. I snatched it up but was disappointed to see the caller was Jules, not Liam.

"Fancy coming round for coffee?" she asked. "Well, coffee for you. I still can't face it."

The truth was, I couldn't face another lecture from Jules. I glanced around the empty salon. "I'm not sure I can get away," I said quietly. "Mum would have me scrubbing the floor with a nail brush if she could find one."

"That bad, eh?"

"Worse. The thing is, you see, I had a little prang in the car yesterday and she's making me work it off. Another time, eh?"

"For goodness sake, go," Mum said, coming in behind me. "Get out from under my feet for a bit, or I really will have you scrubbing the floor with a nail brush. You're looking peaky this morning. It's a lovely day out there. Go and get some fresh air. Just don't take my car."

She was obviously still working on a suitably grim penance for that. Floor scrubbing would probably be the least of it.

"OK, Jules," I said. "It looks like I've just been given some time out for good behaviour. I'll come round, shall I? Unless you want to come here?"

"You come to me. I've got some chocolate digestives I need to share, otherwise I'll end up as wide as I'm high by the time this baby is born."

I laughed. "Chocolate digestives? You remember my weakness, then?"

"I remember all your weaknesses, girl," she said. "But I won't go on about them, I promise. And I'm really, really sorry about Saturday. I was way out of order. Forgiven?"

The sun might have been shining but a keen wind was blowing as I stepped outside. I shoved my hands in my pockets and made my way towards the small housing development at the far end of the village where Jules and Ed lived. Ten minutes later, I was moving a pair of fairy wings and a glittery plastic tiara from a chair in Jules's cramped, chaotic kitchen. The fresh air had restored my appetite and I was on my second biscuit when Jules said, "I meant what I said. I'm sorry for letting rip on Saturday. You had every right to tell me to mind my own business. Eddie says living with me at the moment is like living on the edge of an active volcano, just waiting for the next eruption."

"He said that?" I was impressed. Ed must have paid more attention in geography lessons than I'd given him credit for. "Have you told him about the baby yet?"

Jules nodded. "I had to, didn't I? Now that Gran and Elsie knew about it. Actually, he was pretty cool about it. More cool than I am to be honest, but then, he's not the one being sick every single day."

"Still bad, eh?"

"The tablets the doctor gave me last week are helping a bit but it's still not great. But hey, I didn't ask you round here so I could whinge on about morning sickness. I wanted to say I was sorry. To your face."

"Which you've done, so let's forget it, eh?" I said quickly, eager to change the subject. I didn't want her harping back to me and Will again. "Hey, what did you mean in your text when you said something weird happened in the pub at lunch time on Saturday?"

"What did I mean?" Jules frowned as she thought back. "Oh yes. That's right. It was Creepy Crabshaw. I wanted to ask you what on earth you did to him to freak him out like that. He came in to the pub not long after I did, in a right old state. Ordered a neat double whisky and his hands were shaking that much I thought he was going to spill it. Then he knocked it back like he was dying of thirst. And yet, less than five minutes earlier, when he spoke to us—"

"Overheard us having a spat, more like it."

"Whatever." Jules flicked some chocolaty crumbs from her blouse. "But he was his usual pervy self, wasn't he? So what did you say to him to set him off like that?"

"Me? Nothing much." I cast my mind back. What was it? It wouldn't have been about Doreen. That was yesterday. "Well, I had a go at him about getting me the sack, which he denied. Not that I believed him. Then I asked him where he was the afternoon Marjorie was killed. That didn't go down too well, as you can imagine."

Jules's eyes widened. "Hey, if they hadn't arrested John Manning, it would almost make you think he'd done it, wouldn't it?"

"John was released without charge yesterday. And Gerald didn't look too pleased when I told him that, I can tell you." Suddenly, all my doubts from my sleepless night came flooding back. "He could have done it, you know," I said slowly.

"No way." Jules gave a shriek of laughter. "I was just joking when I said that. He's all mouth and trousers, that one. Say boo to him and he'll run a mile. Come on, Katie…"

"Kat."

"Sorry. Keep forgetting. Come on, Kat. This is Gerald Crabshaw we're talking about. We've known him all our lives. And whilst he's a right pain in the proverbial, particularly since getting himself elected councillor (and that was only because no one else wanted to do it) he's no murderer. Think about it."

"No. Of course he isn't. You're quite right. He hasn't got the bottle, for a start." I decided against telling her how I'd seen him up in Compton Woods with Doreen. I didn't want to tell anyone. At least, not until I'd talked it through with Liam. Instead, I said, "It's just that I saw him yesterday afternoon, about 4 o'clock. He came out of the pub and threatened me. Said if I didn't stop poking my nose into his business, I'd come to a very sticky end, or words to that effect. And the thing that spooked me was not only the look on his face as he said it – I've never seen him so angry – but the fact that he'd said the same thing to me before, almost word for word. Only then he'd been talking about Marjorie. And it was the day before Will and I found her body."

Jules chewed her fingernail as she thought about what I'd just said. "Ok, yeah. That's a bit weird," she acknowledged. "But even so, he was only mouthing off, surely? You know what he's like. He was always going on about Marjorie, particularly since he got done for drunk driving and reckoned it was her who'd tipped the police off. Which, knowing Marjorie, it probably was."

"But if it wasn't Gerald, then who was it?" I said, completely forgetting that an hour or so ago, I'd decided the killer was a total stranger. "Hey, what about Shane Freeman? He was hanging around the pub, looking as shifty as you like. And the other night in the pub, when I asked him if he had an alibi for the time Marjorie was murdered, he looked even shiftier than usual. In fact, he told me later that he was doing local drops that day so would have been in the area."

Jules's snort of laughter sent digestive crumbs arcing across the kitchen. "For goodness sake, what are you on, girl? Shane-the-Pain? Much Winchmoor's answer to Reggie Kray? He was born looking shifty. That doesn't mean a thing. Although I have to say, he was flashing the cash in the pub on Saturday. And he's bought himself a new motor, so they were saying."

"Has he now?" I frowned. "Well, what if…?"

"What if nothing," she cut in. "You've been watching too many *Midsomer Murders*, that's your trouble. You need to get out more. If it wasn't John Manning who killed Marjorie, then my money's on some passing tramp. Maybe he was dossing down in the farm shop, she disturbed him, he lashed out, not meaning to kill her, but when he realised what he'd done, he dumped her in the freezer and legged it."

Jules' common sense approach had just lifted a huge weight from my shoulders, particularly as I'd come to a similar conclusion earlier that morning. "Yeah. You're probably right." I admitted.

"Aren't I always?" she smirked.

Not always. She'd got it totally wrong about Will and me. But not, I reckoned, about Gerald. I decided against saying anything to Ben, because I might then have to explain to him what I'd been doing up in Compton Woods yesterday afternoon, which could lead to some awkwardness. "I expect I just caught Gerald on a bad day," I said.

"You're not kidding, he was having a bad day. According to Elsie Flintlock, he'd had a right go at poor old Donald, as well," Jules said. "Gave it to him 'hot and holy' was how she put it."

"What about?"

"I don't know. I wasn't there. Donald had sent me out to the store room and when I came back Gerald had gone and Elsie said that he'd yelled at Donald and stormed out."

"Did she say what he'd yelled?"

"She may have done. I wasn't really paying attention. You know how she goes on. I find the best thing is just to tune it out. Here, for goodness sake have another of these," she pushed the packet of biscuits across the table. "Otherwise I'll eat the lot."

"I thought you said you couldn't eat a thing?" I said.

"Anything except chocolate digestives."

I reached across for another biscuit but, before I could take one, my phone rang. It was Liam.

"Sorry," I said to Jules. "I've got to take this. Hi, Liam. Thanks for ringing back."

"No problem. Sorry it took so long but things have been pretty hectic here this morning. What's up?"

I glanced across at Jules, who was straining to hear every word, while at the same time pretending she wasn't. "Can we meet sometime today? So that I can give you... the, um, results of that research I did for you yesterday. I've had some further thoughts on it I'd like to discuss with you."

"Today could be tricky," he said. "Tomorrow's better."

"Tomorrow will be fine."

"Then how about we – look, sorry. Kat, I've got to go. Mike's making frantic signals at me. Looks like something big may have come in. I'll call you."

"Great. See you then. Bye."

Jules was grinning at me as I ended the call. "Research, eh? Is that what they call it now?"

"That was a guy from *The Chronicle*," I said primly. "It's purely business."

"Now, would this be the dishy Irishman who was asking after you in the pub the other day?"

"You think he's dishy? I can't say I'd noticed," I said in what I hoped was a casual voice.

"Hah, not much you hadn't. I can tell from the way your cheeks have turned the colour of beetroot. You never could keep a secret from me, Kat Latcham. It was him, wasn't it?"

"Yes, and Dad gave him my mobile number, can you believe it? He could have been an axe murderer for all Dad knew."

"What did he want you for?"

"My body. What else?" I laughed.

"Yeah, well. That goes without saying. But you know he's got a bit of a reputation, don't you?"

"For what?" I knew I shouldn't ask, but couldn't help myself.

"For loving and leaving them. You remember Ginny Mason in the year below us at school? Curly hair and freckles. Had a thing about Johnny Depp. She went out with him for a while, things were really serious between them, or so she thought. Then he dropped her like a stone for no apparent reason. Then there was the girl who works in Dintscombe Library, and after that…"

"Ok. Ok. I get the picture," I said, more rattled than I wanted to let on. "There's nothing between me and Liam. Nor likely to be. Yes, I did meet him on Friday night, but it was

149

strictly business. As a matter of fact, he offered me a job."

"On *The Chronicle*?" Jules looked impressed. "Doing what?"

"Well, it's just helping out with the odd bit of background research at the moment, which is what I wanted to talk to him about. But who knows where it might lead?"

"With Liam O'Connor, I think I can probably guess," Jules said, her face suddenly serious. "You will be careful, Kat, won't you?"

"What, like you're my mother all of a sudden?" I said, trying, but failing, to hide my annoyance.

"No. But I am your friend. And I wouldn't want you to get hurt. You know he's going around asking all sorts of questions about the murder, don't you?"

"Well, of course he is," I said. "He's a journalist. Asking questions is what he does."

"That, and making up the answers if he doesn't get the right ones," Jules said.

"Well, don't you worry about me. I can take care of myself," I said as I gathered up my things and stood up.

"Oh no. Now I've upset you again. Me and my big mouth. Oh, for pity's sake, Kat, don't go off in a strop again."

"I'm not in a strop, honest," I said. "But I really do have to go. Mum will have steam coming out of her ears if I'm not back soon."

"So how did you come to prang her car? I'll bet she gave you grief. That car's her pride and joy."

I rolled my eyes. "Tell me about it. If you must know, I reversed into a gate." Again, I decided not to tell her where the gate was or what I was doing when I reversed into it. "But you know how Mum is about that wretched car. I'll never be able to borrow it again and will have to spend the rest of my life apologising to her. Thanks for the coffee and biscuits. I'll see you soon, ok?'

"Yeah, let's do that," Jules said as she opened the front door to see me out. As she did so, we saw Will coming down the road towards us. I had to stop myself turning round and bolting back into Jules's kitchen.

"Kat, listen. What I said yesterday, about Will having a thing for you?" Jules said quickly, putting a hand on my arm. "I wouldn't want you to get the wrong impression. That Will's some sad loser, pining away for you."

"No, of course I didn't think that." I forced a laugh. "I didn't think that for a nanosecond. You forget, Jules, I know Will a lot better than you do."

Jules took her hand away and waved at Will. She lowered her voice and went on, "In fact, according to Eddie, he's seeing this vet who works in the practice in Dintscombe. Name of Anneka, or something like that. She's Swedish, Eddie says."

"That's great. I'm pleased for him."

Of course I was pleased for him. But why, then, did I have this weird feeling, the sort you get when you put your foot on a step that isn't there?

It was my disturbed night catching up on me. That was all.

Chapter Eighteen

"Hi Will," Jules called out. "What are you doing hanging around here on a Monday morning? Have you been given time off for good behaviour as well?"

"Something like that," he grinned.

"Got time for a coffee?"

"Sorry, I can't stop. I came to find Katie. Her mum said she was down here."

I shot him a worried glance. "You were looking for me?" It would have to be something pretty heavy to drag him away from the farm on a Monday morning. "What for?" My heart missed a beat. "It's not your dad, is it? They haven't…?"

"No. He's fine." He looked across at Jules then back to me. I'd always been able to read the expressions on his face. This one was saying that whatever he had to say to me, he'd prefer not to do so in front of Jules. I gave a small nod to show I'd got the message.

"Are you on your way back?" he went on. "Only if you are, I'll walk with you."

"And I've got a million things to do," Jules said as she turned to go back indoors. "See you both."

As we walked off, I looked back in time to see a curtain twitch inside the house. Jules might well have a million things to do, but watching Will and me was obviously right up there at the top of that list.

"So come on, out with it." I asked once we were safely out of earshot. "What was so important that you had to come and seek me out, rather than phone? You haven't lost it again, have you? Honestly, Will, you're the limit."

"No, I haven't."

"Then where is it? No, don't tell me. Let me guess. On the dresser in your kitchen?"

"Something like that. If you must know I was coming down to see your mum anyway. I had a nice leg of lamb I thought she might like. I know how your dad enjoys his roast lamb and, after what happened the last time I went to find a piece of meat for your mum…"

"Oh no, please, Will. Don't remind me. As you say," I went on quickly before the flashback to that moment could take hold. "Dad's certainly very partial to roast lamb. And if it gets Mum off her current diet and back on to real food, you'll have done us all a favour. So, does that mean the police have let you back in the farm shop, then?"

"No. It's still taped off. This one comes from the freezer in the barn. The police were rooting around again this morning. From the little bit they let slip, it doesn't look like they've found the murder weapon yet. They've now been able to rule out Dad's shotgun, which is a huge relief."

"I can imagine. And your dad is ok, isn't he? I mean, you weren't just saying that because Jules was there?"

"No, honest. He's a lot better. He's still very shaken by it all, of course. Well, we both are."

"Yes, I know how you feel."

I never used to have a problem over what to say to Will. In fact, he used to complain that I never stopped talking. But for the moment, I couldn't think of a thing to talk about. Well, not strictly true. I had plenty to say. My problem was, where to start? We walked on in awkward silence for a while. Then we both spoke at once.

"Look, I'm sorry about—" I said.

"You see, the thing is—" he said. We both stopped, and he gestured to me to carry on.

"I just wanted to explain about Friday night," I said. "In the pub. With Liam."

"Liam?" His eyes darkened.

"Liam O'Connor. He's…"

"A reporter on *The Chronicle*." His eyes darkened even further, his face creased into a scowl. "I know who he is. He's been plaguing the life out of me and Dad, asking us for an interview. Wanting all the gory details and…"

"Ok. Ok. Chill," I cut in as I could see him building up a good head of steam. "But I just wanted to tell you that the meeting I had with him that night was business, not pleasure, ok?"

"Oh, really?" One eyebrow shot up. "From where I was standing, it looked like you were enjoying a whole heap of pleasure."

"And if you'd looked a little more carefully, birdbrain, you'd have seen that I was drinking mineral water and had a file full of my work with me. Hardly the stuff of a hot date, is it?" I glared at him. "Besides, what were you doing in there? You always said you hated that hippy, drippy folksy music. Your words, not mine."

He grinned at me as we crossed the road and in to the village's main street. "I do. But they serve a good pint in there."

"Yes, that's what Liam said." And, of course, the niggly little voice inside my head went on, Anneka or whatever her name was, probably liked hippy, drippy folksy music. They went for that kind of stuff in Sweden, didn't they? So where had she been on Friday night? Had she stood him up? Was that why he'd been in such a foul mood?

We walked on in awkward silence for a few more minutes. "Well, I'm glad your dad's ok," I said eventually. "I was worried about him."

Will stopped and turned to face me. His face was serious and he looked like he'd just made up his mind about something. "As a matter of fact, that's what I wanted to talk to you about. Well, not about him, as such. But what you and Dad were talking about yesterday." He looked down at his hands. "He – he told me, you know."

I felt a rush of heat travel up my face. So John had told Will that Sally had always hoped he and I would 'make a go of it', as he'd put it, had he? Great. Absolutely great. How was I going to get out of this one? Talk about embarrassing.

"Oh, well, that's parents for you, isn't it?" I mumbled, scuffing the edge of the pavement with the toe of my boot. "Always making plans whether you want them to or not."

"Plans about what?" He stared at me blankly. "Sorry. You've lost me."

"It doesn't matter," I said quickly. "I was just wittering. You know what I'm like. Forget it. What – what were you saying?"

"Dad said you'd told him how I hadn't been able to face going in the shop since – since Mum died." He plucked at the fastening of his coat with restless fingers. "He, he also said you'd told him that he and I should talk. About how we felt about losing Mum. And all that."

"And did you?" I asked gently.

He nodded. "Sort of. He said he thought I blamed him for being so wrapped up in the farm that he hadn't noticed Mum's illness. Can you believe that? As if I would."

"Maybe he blames himself?"

"That's just as daft. And I told him so. He then said he'd no idea about the strain I'd been under and that he felt really bad about it. Promised to make it up to me. He's sober, you know. Hasn't touched a drop since he was arrested."

"I know. He told me."

He placed his hands on my shoulders, his expression serious. "You're a star, Katie Latcham, that's what you are."

"I didn't do anything…"

"You believed in him when no one else did. And you cared enough to talk some sense into him. Into both of us, for that matter. And for that we're both really grateful. Thanks to you, we've cleared the air a bit. Dad and I are both as bad as each other when it comes to talking about how we feel about things. And people."

I opened my mouth to make some light-hearted remark, in an effort to break the tension that had sprung up between us, but nothing came out. Instead, I stood as if frozen, staring up at him, and wondering why I'd never noticed before how, in this bright spring sunlight, his eyes were the colour of cornflowers and how he had a little fan of white lines in the corner of each eye, made, no doubt, by screwing up his eyes against the sun when he was working.

"Th-that's blokes for you," I finally managed to say, in a voice that didn't sound remotely like my own.

"Yes, well." He cleared his throat and raked his fingers through his hair. "So this morning, good as his word, Dad said he'd handle things on the farm today and that I was to take you somewhere for lunch. As a thank you. From us both."

"Oh, there's no need," I said quickly, relieved that the moment of weirdness between us, whatever it was, had passed. "I only did what any mate would have done. Besides, I'm just on my way to see Elsie Flintlock."

"I'm sorry, but my lunch invitation doesn't include her," he said.

I laughed, relieved to be back on a more familiar footing with him. "Thank goodness for that. It's just that she – she's got something for me. Something I need for this research work I'm doing for *The Chronicle*. The one I was talking to Liam about on Saturday night. You know, old folks' memories and all that sort of thing."

It wasn't exactly a lie, but I was uncomfortably aware that it wasn't exactly the whole truth either, and was relieved when he didn't follow it up.

"It's always wise to put a time limit on a visit to Elsie, otherwise you'll be there all day." He looked at his watch. "How about I pick you up about twelve, and we'll take a run down to the coast? I thought we could go and see if that cafe on the beach still does those amazing crab sandwiches. I haven't been there for ages."

I scrabbled around frantically for a convincing-sounding excuse. For a reason I couldn't even explain to myself, I didn't want to go to lunch with him. Even if it was to my most favourite beach cafe in the whole world. Was it because of John telling me how he and Sally had hoped Will and I might make a go of it, as he'd put it? Or Jules telling me about Will and the sexy Swedish vet? Or – and I had to admit, I was feeling pretty snarky about this one – was it because Will was asking me out, not because he wanted to, but because his dad had told him to?

"Will, I'd love to," I lied. "But the problem is Mum. I'm working for her all this week. Well, the rest of my life probably. I suppose you know what I did to her car? I should

156

imagine she's told the whole world by now. It'll be on the front page of *The Chronicle* next week, I shouldn't wonder."

"I saw the damage. You must have given something a hefty clunk. What was it?"

"A metal gate. I was trying to do a three point turn and got it a bit wrong." I decided not to tell him the metal gate had been up near Compton Wood, nor what I was doing there. That information was on a strictly need-to-know basis and I decided that Will, like Jules, didn't need to know. "So, I don't think Mum would be too happy if I skived off."

"Your mum said she's fed up with you grumbling at everything, from her choice of music to the colour of the curtains…"

"I didn't grumble about the curtains. I simply suggested, very tactfully, that the salon needed a bit of a makeover, that's all. Which is nothing but the truth. As for the music, how would you like to spend all morning listening to Des O'Connor? She says the customers like him. But honestly…"

"Anyway, she said she's tired of you mooching about the place and would be much obliged to me for taking you out from under her feet," he said. "So, are you up for it? Or have you got something more exciting planned? More business meetings with smooth-talking Irish journos, maybe? You haven't told me anything about this job he's talking about. What exactly is it?"

Time, I decided, for a quick change of subject. I had also run out of excuses. "Twelve o'clock will be fine," I said, as I waited for a small minibus to drive past before I crossed the road. "Can you pick me up from Mum's?"

"Better had. I'd hate to start Elsie Flintlock's tongue wagging again."

"Hah! I don't think that would be possible. That would be to assume it ever stopped wagging in the first place."

***

Elsie opened her front door and screamed. "Come back here NOW!"

I flattened myself against the porch wall as something small, fast and hairy hurtled towards me, shot through my legs and disappeared out of the front gate.

"Would you like me to go and get him back?" I asked.

"No point. The little monster will be half way to Dintscombe by now. He'll come back when he's hungry."

Elsie's little dog, Prescott, whose brown and white fur always reminded me of a worn-down toothbrush, was of dubious parentage and even more dubious temperament. He was notorious for biting first and asking questions later.

"Did you want something?" Elsie asked. "Or are you one of those detractor burglars? You know, one of you keeps the poor old soul talking on the doorstep, while the other goes round the back and helps himself to all her valuables. We were warned about it by that young policeman who looked as if he shouldn't be allowed out without his mum. He came to talk about crime pretension at our last Young Wives' Group meeting."

"If you mean a *distraction* burglary, then of course I'm not here for that," I said indignantly. "I, I just popped round for a chat, that's all."

"A chat?" Elsie couldn't have looked more surprised if I'd said I'd dropped in for a quick game of carpet bowls. She folded her arms and gave me a challenging look. "Now what would you and I have to chat about?"

I gave a little shiver, hoping she'd take the hint and invite me in. No chance. "Well, I've just seen Jules," I said. "And she was saying how Gerald and Donald had a bit of a set-to in the pub yesterday lunchtime and that you were there. Is that right?"

Elsie looked at me, her small pointy head cocked to one side like a little bird, her eyes bright and inquisitive. "Why would you want to know that?" she asked. "Last week, you were quizzing me about Marjorie Hampton and now you're on about Mr High and Mighty, Call-Me-Councillor Crabshaw. What is it with you?"

I shrugged and avoided those all-seeing eyes. "I was just curious, that's all."

"Curious?" Elsie gave a cackle that would have done credit to the Wicked Witch of the West. "Well now, young lady. You know what curiosity did, don't you?"

"Killed the cat?"

"And what were you insisting on people calling you the other day? Kat, was it?" Her face became suddenly serious, her eyes shrewd. "You be careful, Katie Latcham. People can get very funny when folk go around asking questions about them. And people aren't always what they seem, you know."

"Who do you mean?"

"I'm naming no names. But let's just say, there are some people who don't like others prying into their business. They don't like it at all."

That was rich, coming from Elsie, of all people. But I bit back the comment and merely nodded.

"Well, if you must know," she leaned forward, her eyes gleaming as they always did when she was about to pass on a particularly juicy bit of gossip. "Donald said something to Gerald Crabshaw about paying his dues. At which, Gerald all but stamped his feet and left. Donald gave me one of those silly, embarrassed grins he does and said something about people who don't pay their bar bills, and what makes them think he is made of money, that he can extend them unlimited credit? Anyone would think there was Bank of Much Winchmoor over the front door, he said, the way some people took advantage of his good nature."

Donald said Gerald owed him money? So, not only was Gerald having an affair, he was running up debts too. A shiver of excitement chased down my back. What if I was right all along? The evidence was indeed beginning to stack up against Gerald Call-Me-Councillor Crabshaw.

The question was: should I tell Liam before or after meeting Will for lunch? In the end, I decided to leave it until later. Liam had said something about a big story breaking, hadn't he? And I didn't think he'd meant lost cats or stolen underwear.

"Hurry along now," Elsie smirked. "You don't want to keep young Will Manning waiting, do you? If you ask me, you've been doing that for quite long enough."

I stared at her. Centuries ago – I'd bet next month's salary on it if I had one – Elsie Flintlock would have been burned at the stake as a witch. "How did you know I'm meeting Will?"

Elsie cackled. "If you will hang about chatting on street corners, you must expect people to take notice."

"You were in the minibus, weren't you?" I said, remembering one had swept past as I'd waited to cross the road. "But I still don't see…"

"My friend Olive is a very good lip reader," Elsie said, as I felt my cheeks begin to burn. "And I don't think you're in a position to go around accusing folks of having a wagging tongue, do you? Now, you go off and meet your young man and forget all about asking questions. Like I said, people aren't always what they seem. He's not the empty headed, harmless fool he appears to be."

Before I could point out to Elsie that Will was not my 'young man,' she'd closed the door. I stood on the doorstep for a few moments, thinking hard. So Elsie had seen this other side to Gerald Crabshaw, just as I had.

Which brought me back to the question that had been bugging me since the small hours of the morning. What to do about it?

Chapter Nineteen

"You ok?" Will asked as he took my hand to help me across the tumble of rocks at the entrance to the beach.

"More than ok." I took a deep lungful of the crisp, salty air that was blowing straight off the sea into my face. "I'd forgotten just how much I love it down here."

Dried seaweed crackled beneath our feet as we crossed the morning's tideline, and my nostrils filled with that unique, evocative smell you only ever find on the sea shore. As we scrunched across the shingle I felt the tension I'd lived with for so long begin to ebb away while the salt-laden wind caught at my hair and blew away the last fragments of my disturbed night.

Even the problem of what to do with my suspicions about Gerald Crabshaw faded, as I decided to call Liam about it later and see what he advised. But until then, I pushed it to the back of my mind and simply enjoyed the way the early spring sunshine painted the cliffs the colours of deep golden honey and sent a thousand diamond-bright glints dancing off the sea. All around there was nothing to be heard but the mewling cries of the seagulls and the rhythmic swish and pull of the receding tide. Bliss.

Much Winchmoor with its murder, gossip and intrigue seemed a zillion miles away as Will and I walked along the shingly beach. It seemed the most natural thing in the world to remain hand in hand as we walked. Two good friends, enjoying each other's company, on a near-deserted beach in early spring. Nothing more.

"Let's see if you are still as rubbish at this as ever," Will said, as he sent a pebble skimming across the sea, skipping over the surface of the water like a swallow in flight.

"That's not fair. You've probably been practising," I said, as my pebble sank like the proverbial stone after three pathetic bounces.

"Oh yes, of course. I get the chance to come down here most evenings—" His sarcastic comment was cut off abruptly as a larger than expected wave caught him unawares, dousing his jeans from the knees down and leaving me helpless with laughter.

"Right. You've done it now. Prepare to be soaked." Before I could run away, he grabbed me, pinned my arms to my sides and dragged me down to the water's edge.

"No, please, Will, don't," I screamed, kicking out in a futile attempt to free myself. "These are my best jeans. They'll be ruined. Please. I'm begging you. Put me down. Please."

He stopped, inches away from the water's edge and set me on my feet, although his arms were still around me. I looked up at him. I'd forgotten how tall he was, how lean and muscular, how safe I felt with his arms around me. Safe, that is, now he'd decided against throwing me in the sea.

He was holding me so close, I could feel the thudding of his heart beneath his sweater. My breath caught in my throat.

"Will?" I must be seriously unfit if larking about on the water's edge for a couple of minutes left me feeling like I'd just run a marathon. "We – we are all right now, you and me, aren't we?"

"How do you mean?" He sounded like he'd just run the marathon with me.

"I mean, we're still mates, aren't we?"

I staggered slightly on the damp shingle as he took his arms away. "Yeah, we're still mates," he said quietly, then with a complete change of tone called, "come on, race you to the cafe. Last one there buys lunch."

Over lunch, our conversation was light and undemanding with none of the awkward pauses there'd been earlier that morning. We agreed the sandwiches were even better than we remembered, the crab meat filling more succulent, the bread crustier and the chips must have been cooked by angels – my words, not his. It was like the days out we used to have. Before things got complicated.

"Do you want a coffee?" Will asked as the leggy young waitress cleared our plates.

"Maybe later." I stretched like a cat. "Ah, that was so good. You're not in any rush to get back, are you?"

"No rush at all," he smiled. "In fact, there's something I want to say to you, Katie – no, sorry, don't bite my head off. I mean Kat, of course. But do you have any idea how difficult it is to remember to call you that when I've known you all my life as Katie?"

"It doesn't matter," I said, as I scanned the sweet menu, then realised I couldn't eat another thing. "I've almost given up trying to get people around here to do it. Are you having a sweet? The Dorset apple cake's always good."

He shook his head. "I'm done."

"Me, too, more's the pity. The thing is," I said. "Going back to this name thing. The longer I stay in Much Winchmoor, the less Kat and the more Katie I become."

"And is that such a bad thing?" he asked, his face suddenly serious.

"Yes. It is." I was desperate to make him understand. "You see, Will, Katie is all about my past. But Kat is, or rather was, my future. It was my chance to put dumpy, frumpy Katie Latcham behind me and do what Gran used to encourage me to do, and spread my wings. Be someone new."

Will laughed, like I knew he would. "Dumpy, frumpy Katie? You wouldn't be fishing for compliments by any chance, would you?"

"From you? I'd be fishing forever, waiting for those, wouldn't I? No, I was just trying to make you understand." I gave up. There was no point. He didn't get it and I didn't want to waste the rest of this lovely day by arguing with him. Instead, I shrugged and said, "I expect you think that sounds barmy?"

"Totally nuts. But then, I always knew you were." He picked up one of the small packets of sugar that were jammed into a glass in front of us and began to twist it between his fingers. When he looked up, I was surprised by the uncertainty in his eyes. He looked like he was weighing up whether or not

163

to say something and couldn't quite decide.

For once, I didn't say anything and waited for him to carry on. Which he did, eventually. "You know how you said Dad and I aren't very good about talking about our feelings—"

He broke off as my phone began to ring. I glanced at it. The caller was Liam. Bad timing or what? Whatever Will was working up to say, it looked pretty serious. I hit the button to send the call to voice mail.

"Anyone important?" Will asked.

"It was Liam," I said, aware that Will's scowl seemed to be a knee-jerk reaction to the very mention of Liam's name. Not surprising, really, if he'd been badgering Will and his dad about the murder. "I'll call him later. Now, what were you saying? Something about your dad?"

"Well, not about him, really." He concentrated on folding and refolding the sugar packet with clinical precision. "I was —"

This time it was the ping of a text message that interrupted him. Once again, it was from Liam. It read: *"Pls call me. NOW. V URGENT."*

"I'm sorry, Will," I said. "Whatever it is, it sounds really, really important. I'll have to call him."

Will pushed his chair back and stood up. "It's ok," he said stiffly. "I'll go and get the coffee. You still take it black with no sugar, I suppose?"

***

Liam answered at the first ring. "What's so urgent that it can't wait until I've finished lunch?" I asked, trying but not quite succeeding in keeping a flash of irritation out of my voice.

"Did you tell anyone about following Doreen yesterday?" he asked, his voice low as if he was anxious not to be overheard. "Anyone at all?"

"No. Of course not. Why would I?"

"Then don't. Don't tell anyone."

"Well, it's not something that's likely to come up in

164

conversation, is it? But why the urgency? I don't understand."

"I can't explain now. There's a big story breaking and I need to be there. In fact, I needed to be there ten minutes ago but I wanted to touch base with you before I did. Can you still meet me tomorrow?"

"I'm not sure. I think Mum's got me enslaved for the rest of the week. But I'll see what I can do because there's something I need to talk to you about."

Beyond the cafe window, I watched a group of seagulls swooping down low across the sea, filling the air with their ear-splitting shrieks. For one fanciful moment, it seemed like their cries were mocking me. I shivered as all my worries about Gerald Crabshaw came crowding back.

Liam gave an impatient sigh. "Look, do you want this job or not?"

That got my attention. A jolt of excitement shot through me. "You mean a real job? With *The Chronicle*?"

"It's possible. But I've got to go. I'll call you tomorrow about where and when to meet."

"I'll be there, whatever suits you," I said hurriedly "I'll sort something with Mum. And Liam?"

"What?"

"Thanks. For thinking of me. For giving me a chance. That means a lot."

"It's only a maybe. You do realise that, don't you?"

"Yes, but…"

"I'll call you tomorrow."

***

"Good news?" Will asked, as he placed a steaming mug of coffee in front of me. "You've got that smirk on your face you always get when you've done something you're pretty pleased with."

"I do not smirk."

"Always have done. Ever since I've known you. In fact, we used to call you Smirker Latcham at school. Did you know that?"

"No you didn't. I refuse to believe that. Anyway, that's so unfair. I have nothing to smirk about. The job's anything but a done deal. Just a chance. A 'maybe' is what Liam called it. That's all."

"What job?"

"Working for *The Chronicle*." I reached across and touched his hand, unable to stop myself smiling. "Keep your fingers crossed for me. This is so what I want."

"What, covering dog shows and parish council meetings? That's all there ever is in that blasted rag. Do you remember how we laughed that week when the lead story was about some celebrity chef buying a pound of carrots off a stall in Dintscombe Market?"

"Don't you just wish that was this week's lead?" I said sombrely, as my feel good mood plunged like my poorly executed skimming stone had earlier. "It's not hard to guess what it's going to be."

Will covered my hand with his. "I thought we agreed we weren't going to talk about it?' he said softly.

"You're right, we did, didn't we?" I said. "But it's sort of become the elephant in the room, hasn't it?"

"And we weren't going to talk about elephants either," he said firmly. "So, tell me, does this mean you're going to be *The Chronicle*'s crime reporter now?"

"Of course I'm not, birdbrain. I know jolly well it's going to be dog shows and parish council meetings. But I don't mind. I enjoyed the journalism part of my course and, though I say it myself, I was pretty good at it. This is it, Will, I can feel it. My ticket out of Much Winchmoor."

He sat back in his chair, his expression unreadable. "And is that so very important to you? To get away from Much Winchmoor?"

I sighed. "It's ok for you. Your family's as much a part of this village as the duck pond. In fact, I dare say there were Mannings in Much Winchmoor when the Romans were rampaging around the country. You belong here. But I don't."

"Now you're just being a drama queen," he said. "You belong here as much as I do."

"But that's the thing. I don't anymore." I inhaled the fragrant steam of the coffee and took a sip. I scrabbled around to find the right words that would make him understand how I felt. "It's like, oh, I don't know. It's hard to put into words but, although I'll always love Much Winchmoor, it doesn't feel like my home anymore. I feel sort of out of sync with everything and everyone. Like I'm on the outside, looking in. And when I look into my future, I don't see myself living here, married with two-point-four children, doing the school run, running the play group or whatever it's called now."

"Would that be so bad? Jules seems happy enough."

"But I'm not Jules. I want something different. I worked really hard at college. I know you think I just racketed around the whole time, but I didn't. And I want to be able to use the skills I worked so hard for. That's why this job on *The Chronicle* is so important. It's a stepping stone. Once I've got something like that on my CV, I'll be able to move on."

"You've got it all worked out, haven't you?" There was an edge to his voice that hadn't been there before. It was like he'd suddenly got fed up with the entire conversation and gone all moody on me again. I wanted so much to get him to see where I was coming from.

"I wish I did have it all worked out," I said. "But, you see, that was where I went wrong with my job at the radio station. I didn't plan ahead enough. The warning signs were there but I ignored them. And, looking back with the benefit of hindsight, there were plenty of them. I should have started job hunting right then. If I'd done that, I'd have gone from one job straight into another, rather than wallowing about in the black hole of unemployment I'm in now. And the longer that gap is on my CV, the harder it will become. You do see that, Will, don't you?"

"I suppose. Well, I'll keep my fingers crossed for you, then," he said, although I'd have preferred it if he'd said it with a little more conviction.

"Thanks." I finished my coffee and pushed the empty cup to one side. "Now, that's enough of me. What was it you wanted to tell me?"

He shook his head and lifted his jacket from the back of his chair. "It was nothing important. Are you ready?"

"For a rematch on pebble skimming? You bet I am. Because I have to warn you, boy, I was letting you win earlier."

"No, I meant ready to go." He shrugged on his jacket, his face as dark as the bank of storm clouds that was building up out of the sea. "Back to that place where you feel you don't belong. I have livestock to sort out."

I stared at him, dismayed by his abrupt change of mood. "But I thought the plan was we were going to stay here for the afternoon? That your dad was taking care of things on the farm?" I was almost running in an effort to keep up with him as he strode ahead of me, out of the cafe and across the car park. "Maybe we could take a walk along the cliff path. What do you think?"

"Sorry. No can do. I've got to get back. I've got a million and one things to do. Besides, that rain is heading our way."

He drove back to Much Winchmoor mostly in silence, only giving monosyllabic answers when pressed to do so, until I finally got the message and stopped trying to make conversation. And they said women were the moody ones, I thought. They'd obviously not met Will Manning on one of his off days. He could make Mr Grumpy look like Little Miss Sunshine.

And, to make matters worse, the rain he'd predicted arrived within minutes of us driving out of the car park. I hated it when he was right.

He pulled up outside our house, turned towards me as if to say something. But before he could do so, my phone rang. He pulled back with an exclamation of annoyance.

"You'd better answer that," he said as he reached across and opened the passenger door for me.

I got out, figuring that in his present mood, he was likely to push me out if I didn't move. "Ok, then. Thanks for…" I began, but he didn't wait to hear the rest, leaning over to slam the passenger door and roaring off up the road. I watched him for a moment, then realised my phone was still ringing.

"Hello? Kat?" I didn't recognise the breathy voice. "It's

Amy. From school, remember? You were asking if anyone had seen Marjorie Hampton?"

My heart quickened. I forgot about Will and his mood. "Yes. Yes, I was. Did you remember seeing her, after all?"

"No. But, as I said, my mum lives just opposite her. She used to live the other side of Dintscombe but moved here six months ago to be nearer me and the kids. I saw her this morning and remembered I'd told you I'd ask her if she saw anything that afternoon..."

"And did she?" I prompted, wishing she'd get on with it.

"She saw someone go up to Marjorie's cottage. Said he seemed an unlikely sort of visitor for Marjorie to have, which was why she remembered it. A big fellow, loads of tattoos, and a scruffy leather jacket."

"Shane Freeman!" Excitement surged through me. "Do you think it was him?"

"Do you mean the guy with the old Labrador? Drives a lorry?"

"That's him. Always wears this battered old leather jacket, whatever the weather."

"It could have been, I suppose. Mum doesn't know many people in the village. Like I said, she hasn't lived here that long."

"So what time was this?"

"It would have been a little after four, because she'd just come in from work. She works in that big new supermarket on the edge of town."

"So Marjorie must have been at home at 4 o'clock, way after the time she saw John Manning," I said. "I knew it. That puts him in the clear. That's brilliant."

But my relief was short-lived. "Well, I'm not so sure," Amy's voice held a note of caution. "Mum says she didn't actually see Marjorie. Which is why she was keeping an eye on this man. But, here's the thing, Kat. Mum says she saw the two of them the day before. And Marjorie was having a right go at him. She said something about how it had to stop and that she was going to tell the police. Mum is now in quite a state, wondering if, when she saw him the next day, he was going back to kill Marjorie. She said he'd looked pretty angry the day before."

I shook my head. "He couldn't have. Marjorie wasn't killed at her cottage, remember? I think when Shane called on her, the poor soul was already dead. All it means is that Shane Freeman is up to something. But it wouldn't have been murder. And it doesn't put John Manning in the clear, either. Just emphasises the fact that Marjorie did not return to her cottage that day."

"No, I suppose not."

"Has your mum told the police this, yet?" I asked.

"She's been away visiting my aunt in Wales since then. Only got back this morning and didn't know anything about the murder. She's pretty shocked, as you can imagine. You don't expect that sort of thing in a quiet little village, do you? I thought—" she broke off, as from somewhere behind her came the sound of all hell breaking loose. "I've got to go. Marlon. Give that back to Skye this minute!" She gave an embarrassed laugh as she ended the call. "Kids, eh? Who'd have them?"

Not me, I thought as I let myself into the house, my ear drums still ringing from Skye's scream of outrage. Not in a million years.

***

Mum and Dad were in the kitchen when I got in. Dad was reading the paper and Mum was cooking.

"You've got a bit more colour in your cheeks, love," Mum said. "All that fresh air must have done you some good. But you're much earlier than I expected. I thought you were staying down the coast for most of the afternoon and wouldn't be in for dinner."

"So did I," I grumbled, as I shrugged off my coat and rooted around in the cupboard for the biscuit tin. All that sea air had given me an appetite and those crab sandwiches now seemed a long time ago. "But Will had to get back. Apparently, the farm can't survive without him. What it is to be indispensable."

"Never mind. And put that biscuit back, because you're just

in time for dinner. I've been trying out a new recipe."

My heart sank. Dad looked up from the sports pages, his face anxious. Even the cat looked uneasy.

"I thought Will said he brought you a leg of lamb this morning?" I said, sniffing the air but smelling nothing remotely like roast lamb. In fact, the air smelt like nothing I've ever smelt before, which was always a bad sign when Mum was on one of her health crusades.

"I'm keeping that for next Sunday. I think I'll invite Granny and Grandad over. You know how they love a nice Sunday roast. And they were only saying the other day that it's ages since they saw you."

"Great," I said sounding more enthusiastic than I felt. I've never had the same easy relationship with Mum's parents that I used to have with Gran Latcham, and knew that the lamb wouldn't be the only thing getting a roasting on Sunday. My appearance, my job prospects, my failure to catch and hold on to a man and give them lots of lovely great-children, would all be under scrutiny. I'd be found wanting in every way.

"And I thought maybe Will and John would like to come as well," Mum went on. "What do you think?"

"Who knows?" I said gloomily. "I've given up trying to work out what Will Manning does or doesn't want to do." I lifted the lid of the saucepan that was bubbling away on the stove and stared suspiciously at the pink sludgy mass inside, while Dad muttered something about getting a pie in the pub later. "What is it?" I asked.

"It's a low carb beetroot risotto, which you make with cauliflower instead of rice," Mum said brightly. "It tastes better than it looks, honest."

I reckoned it would have a job to taste worse than it looked. Although if the smell was anything to go by, it probably did.

"Thanks, Mum, but I'll pass too, if you don't mind," I said quickly, promising myself that I'd sneak in and help myself to some bread and cheese when she was safely out of the way. "Will and I had a huge lunch. I'm still stuffed."

As I spoke, I glanced over her shoulder at the television in the far corner of the kitchen. I gave a little gasp, like you do when someone punches you in the stomach. Hard. The tin of biscuits clattered to the floor.

"Katie?" she looked anxiously at me. "Are you all right? You've gone as white as a sheet. What is it, love?"

I couldn't answer. Couldn't move. Just stood there, staring at the screen. The early evening local news had just started and there was a reporter standing in front of the blackened shell of a building.

"Oh yes, the fire. Nasty, wasn't it?" Mum said as she turned round to see what I was looking at. "It was somewhere in Dintscombe, although they didn't say exactly where. There was quite a bit about it on the lunchtime news. Apparently, the alarm was raised by a passing motorist in the early hours of this morning. But by the time the fire engine arrived, it was too late."

"God, that's awful." I managed to croak as I knelt down to pick up the biscuit tin, glad of the chance to drag my horrified gaze away from the screen.

"But that wasn't the worst of it," Mum went on. "They found a body inside, although they haven't identified it yet. I was trying to work out where the cottage was. What do you think? Looks as if it might be down by the park, if you wait for them to show a longer shot."

But I didn't need to wait for the longer shot. I knew exactly where the burnt-out cottage was. I should do. I'd spent enough time, the previous day, sitting in Mum's little pink car, staring at it. I also had a pretty good idea of the name of the casualty.

It was Doreen Spetchley's cottage. It was, therefore, a safe bet that the body they'd found inside would be identified as that of Doreen Spetchley.

Chapter Twenty

"Katie? What is it?" Mum asked. "Aren't you feeling well, love?"

Mum's anxious voice barely penetrated the fog in my mind as I struggled to make sense of what I'd just seen.

"What is it?" she repeated. She took the biscuit tin from me and placed it on the table. "Come along, Katie. Speak to me. You're beginning to worry me, standing there like you've seen a ghost."

"Is it something on the telly, love?" Dad asked. "Something about the fire?"

"Oh, no, it's not someone you know, is it?" asked Mum. "Is that why you're looking so upset?"

I shook my head as I took a step back from their volley of questions. "No. No. I didn't know her."

"Her?" Mum frowned and looked anxiously at Dad.

"How do you know it's a she?" he asked. "They said they hadn't identified the body yet. Do you know something we don't?"

"No, of course not," I said quickly. The last thing I wanted to do, at that moment, was tell them about Doreen. At least, not until I'd spoken to Liam. I forced myself to calm down and tried to think things through clearly and calmly. "But, face it, there's a fifty-fifty chance I'm right, isn't there? Look, I'm sorry, but I've got to make a phone call."

"But we're just about to eat," Mum protested although Dad was already shrugging his coat on and heading for the front door.

"But I told you, Mum, Will and I had a huge lunch. I really couldn't eat a thing."

And that was nothing but the truth. Even if Mum had been serving Will's lamb, cooked pink the way I liked it, with those lovely crunchy roast potatoes she did so well, I wouldn't have been able to force it down. In fact, there was a good chance I'd never be able to eat again.

I hurried out into the back garden and, when I was sure I was well out of earshot, keyed in Liam's number.

"Hi Kat. Sorry I had to cut you short earlier—"

"That doesn't matter," I cut in quickly. "I've just seen the news on the television. About Doreen Spetchley. At least, I'm assuming it was her body they found in the fire. And that this was the big story that was breaking the last time we spoke?"

There was a slight pause. "It was. And I'm afraid it's looking highly likely it was her body. She lived alone. There's no formal identification yet, though. It's going to have to be done on dental records, unfortunately."

I shuddered at the thought of that tall, grey woman being identifiable only by her teeth. Horrible to think that the last time I'd seen her, she had been furiously angry – but very much alive.

"What happened?" I asked. "Does anyone know?"

"My money's on an electrical fault. The fire broke out in the small hours of this morning, so that's the most likely explanation. But the police are being tight-lipped, as usual. The only information they'll give is that their investigation is ongoing."

"They said on the television that they're asking for anyone who saw anything to contact them. Do you think I should tell them about Doreen meeting Gerald Crabshaw?"

"But that was ages before the fire, so it can't possibly have any relevance, can it?" he said. "Besides, are you going to explain what you were doing, spying on her? Or following her up to Compton Wood? Because, I have to warn you, Kat, it's not going to look good on your CV. Not good at all."

"I realise that. But even so…"

"Trust me, Kat," his voice was low and measured. "You will achieve nothing by going to the police. Except leaving yourself wide open to a whole heap of awkward questions. Now, correct me if I'm wrong, but I would say that since finding Marjorie Hampton's body, you've had enough of answering awkward questions, wouldn't you? It's up to you, of course. But my advice would be to say nothing. Because at the end of the day, there is nothing to say, is there?"

"No. I suppose not," I said slowly, although I was not entirely convinced. "But I wanted to tell you something about Gerald Crabshaw. He threatened me, you know."

"He did what?" Liam asked sharply. "When?"

"It was yesterday afternoon. I saw him in the village after I got back from Compton Wood. We had a few words and he told me to stop poking my 'sticky little beak', as he called it, into his business. And he said it in exactly the same way he'd talked about Marjorie Hampton, the day before she was killed."

"Just bluster, that's all. He's a load of hot air, that one."

"Yes, but there's something else. I've found out that he has financial problems. According to my source, he and Donald – that's the landlord of the village pub – had quite a set-to about his bar bill. And then, of course, there was the row that he had with Doreen Spetchley. It's all beginning to stack up against him, wouldn't you say?"

"What I would say, Kat, is that you should back off," Liam said sharply. "This isn't a game, you know. This is the real thing. Two women have died."

My stomach lurched. "Are you saying Doreen was murdered as well?"

"No, I'm not. At the moment, the police are treating her death as an accident, but what I am trying to say is that somewhere out there is a very desperate person, someone who will stop at nothing to cover his – or her – tracks. Someone, too, who may not appreciate somebody like you going around asking awkward questions. So, my advice to you is to forget all about Gerald Crabshaw."

"But if he's guilty…"

"Then the police will deal with it. That's their job. And I might as well tell you, I'm putting my investigation into him on hold for the moment. At least until the police have finished looking into the fire. The last thing I want is to tread on their toes. And that's the last thing you should want as well. Believe me, I know what I'm talking about."

"Yes, ok. I take your point. To be honest, I'm more than a little relieved. The whole thing was giving me nightmares. So, I suppose this means there's no point in us meeting up tomorrow now?"

"There's every point in us meeting up. Is 11 o'clock in the coffee shop in Dintscombe High Street convenient for you?"

"I'll be there," I assured him. "What sort of job are we talking about? It's not another surveillance job, is it?"

"Hardly. But I'll explain tomorrow. However, I should warn you, it has nothing to do with murder, corruption or anything like that. Something much more mundane, I'm afraid."

With the image of the blackened wreckage of Doreen Spetchley's cottage still fresh in my mind, I reckoned I'd settle for mundane any day.

***

"I'm so sorry I'm late," I said, as I hurried into the coffee shop a little after ten past eleven. "The bus was late, then there are temporary traffic lights on the main road that took ages and…"

"It doesn't matter a bit," Liam closed his laptop and stood up. "I'll get you a coffee. You look as if you could do with one. How do you like it?"

"Black, no sugar, please." I watched him as he threaded through the crowded tables and made his way up to the counter. Tall, slim and elegant in a casual, unstudied way, with his faded denim jeans and soft leather biker jacket, he drew admiring glances from most of the women there.

So Liam thought I looked as if I could do with a coffee, did he? What was that supposed to mean? I took an anxious peek in the mirror on the wall opposite. I looked – and felt – a mess. The succession of sleepless nights I'd had were written in the dark circles under my eyes, the pallor of my skin and the lankness of my hair.

Liam, on the other hand, looked like he was fairly crackling with life. There was an air of suppressed excitement about him and the sparkle in those clear grey eyes was like sunlit frost on a crisp winter day. No wonder every woman in the coffee shop was lusting after him. I'd probably be doing so myself if I had the energy.

"So, how are you?" he asked as he placed the coffee in front of me and took the seat opposite.

I shrugged. "I've been better. I'm not sleeping too well at the moment. I keep thinking of Doreen. First Marjorie, now her, and it's really freaking me out, the thought that I'm involved in some way with both. I'm beginning to think I must be jinxed."

"Of course you're not jinxed. You just had the terrible bad luck of being in the wrong place at the wrong time, that's all."

"Correction. Wrong places at the wrong times. Plural." I pointed out.

He shrugged. "Like I said, bad luck. I think the best thing to do is to forget all about that and concentrate on something different. That is, providing you were serious about working for *The Chronicle*?"

"Of course I am," I said, my tiredness miraculously slipping away. "So, what is it? Another research assignment?"

He grinned. "Nothing so exciting, I'm afraid. Just plain, boring, run-of-the-mill stuff, as I warned you."

"That's ok. After the week I've had, I'm more than happy to settle for boring and mundane."

"OK. But don't say I didn't warn you. There's a meeting of Much Winchmoor Parish Council tonight and when I told Mike – that's the editor – about you, he was willing to let you have a go at covering it for us. You'll be paid lineage – that is, so much per line, at standard NUJ rates. It won't earn you a fortune, but it'll be a start. Something to put on your CV. How about it? Are you interested?"

"I certainly am." I thought how Will had teased yesterday about how *The Chronicle* was nothing but parish council meetings and dog shows, and couldn't wait to tell him. "And the dog show? Would you like me to cover that too?"

"Is there one? Well, you can, if you like. It's up to you. What Mike's trying to do is set up a network of local correspondents in the area, who report on things of interest in their own villages. You would be the first. If it works out, he's hoping to extend it to more villages."

"Local correspondent, eh?" I laughed. "You mean, I'd be a sort of Kate Adie?"

"Yeah, I suppose so. Although I have to say, you're a whole lot better looking than her."

Suddenly, I forgot the rings under my eyes, the pallor of my skin, the lankness of my hair. If Liam thought I looked ok, that was good enough for me. "I can't thank you enough, Liam," I said. "I'll do a good job, I promise."

"Sure, I know you will. And I'll be on the end of the phone if you need any help. As for thanking me, you can do that by holding your nerve and not saying anything about Sunday. If it gets out that I asked you to put Doreen Spetchley under surveillance, that'll be my job on the line and yours will be over before it even started. Ever since the phone hacking scandal, Mike's been as jumpy as a kitten about anything that smacks of press intrusion."

***

It took me longer to get ready for the Parish Council meeting than if I was going on a hot date. Out went the ripped jeans and skimpy tee shirt. In came a skirt I'd found lurking in the back of my wardrobe, and the only remotely sensible sweater I possessed that didn't have a rude slogan scrawled across the front of it. As for my hair, three shampoos later and I'd finally got rid of most of the purple and green stripe that I'd only sprayed on because I knew it would wind up Mum's customers. I'd got that right at least – which is more than can be said for the makers of the spray-in colour, who'd promised that it would easily wash out. But, at least after three washes, it had faded to a more subtle shade of lilac with just a hint of sludgy green.

The care I took over my appearance was a measure of how important this assignment was to me. It was only a parish council meeting, in the village school. But it felt like the first positive step on my road back to a decent job – and out of Much Winchmoor.

I was way too early, of course. I left my bike propped against the school wall and checked my bag for the third time that evening. Notebook, pen, spare pen. That, according to Liam, was all I needed.

I took my time, dawdling across the school playground where Jules and I had first met when we started school at the age of five. I lingered under the climbing bars, still there, although the surface beneath them was now a strange rubbery one rather than the bone-crunching tarmac that had been there when I'd swung above it as a harum-scarum kid who, egged on by Will, didn't know the meaning of the words, 'be careful'. Just in front of the main door that led into the school were the lines marking out a game of hopscotch and, for one second, I was tempted to see if I could still do it.

I was so pleased I resisted the temptation as, seconds later, I heard the click of the gate as someone came in to the playground from the car park.

"You!" Gerald Crabshaw halted in mid-step, one hand still holding the gate, while his face contorted with rage at the sight of me. "What the devil are you doing here? You're following me again."

"How can I be following you?" I said, sounding a lot more courageous than I felt. "I was here before you. So I could accuse you of following me."

"And what are you doing here?" he scowled.

"If you must know, I'm here for the Parish Council meeting. I'm covering it for *The Chronicle*."

"What?" His short humourless laugh was more of a sneer. "You? Working for *The Chronicle*? Barmaid to journalist in one day, eh? Well, let me assure you, your new job won't last any longer than the previous one. I'll see to that. I'm a personal friend of Mike Chalmers and I'll be having a word with him. This is harassment, that's what it is."

"What's going on here, Gerald? Is something wrong?" A tall, white haired man, whom I recognised as a retired solicitor who lived in the High Street, came up behind us. I'd done my

179

homework and knew his name was Stuart Davies and that he was the Chairman of the Parish Council.

Gerald whirled round. "Good to see you, Stuart. I was just sending this – this person on her way."

"Are you here for the meeting?" Stuart smiled kindly at me. Then he turned to Gerald. "Members of the public are welcome to attend council meetings, as Councillor Crabshaw here well knows," he said.

"Oh, I'm not a member of the public. I'm from *The Chronicle*," I said quickly, and couldn't resist adding: "I'm the newly appointed local correspondent for Much Winchmoor."

"Are you, indeed? How splendid. Come along in then. It's really rather chilly out here, isn't it?"

"If she goes in, I won't." Gerald Crabshaw's voice bristled with scarcely contained anger.

Stuart turned to face him, his expression bland. "That's your choice entirely, Councillor Crabshaw. As you know, as our District Councillor, you are always welcome to attend our meetings. So, too, are members of the Press who represent the public. Now, shall we go in?"

Gerald Crabshaw swore, turned round and stalked off in the direction of the car park, slamming the gate behind him so hard it shook on its hinges.

"I'm sorry," I said. "I don't want to cause trouble."

"Don't worry. You haven't. To be perfectly frank, my dear, the fellow's a complete pain in the you-know-where. But that's strictly off the record, ok? I'm delighted that we're finally going to get our meetings covered in *The Chronicle*, if only to let people in the village know what we as a council do, and, hopefully, to get more of them involved. So, come along in and I'll introduce you to the Clerk. She's the one who does the real work around here." He opened the door for me, ushered me in and added in a low voice, "be prepared to be bored rigid."

But as it turned out, I was nothing of the sort. In fact, I was so busy taking notes, trying to keep track of who said what, that an hour and a half flew by in no time as the pages of my notebook filled up nicely. I kept reminding myself that the more I remembered, the more it would earn me in lineage.

Compared with dispensing pints or rinsing off perm lotion, this was going to be a far easier way of earning money.

Or so I thought.

***

An easy way to make money? I found out next morning that the previous night's confidence was sadly misplaced.

I was sitting at my laptop, the notes from the previous night's meeting scattered all across the table in front of me, and panic churning my insides. Pages and pages of hieroglyphics and weird, meaningless initials that meant absolutely nothing to me. Who was FS? And what did I mean by 'fdsly'?

My head was aching with the effort of trying to make sense of it all. Then there was the small matter of trying to recall all the things I'd learnt in college, things you had to check when writing a report. Then there were those questions I had to ask – and answer – each time I drafted a piece. What were they, now? Something like who, what, where, when and why?

After a few abortive attempts, I began to produce what I hoped would be acceptable copy. I was struggling to decipher the notes for my third story, an account of a number of complaints that had been received about overgrown footpaths in the area, when it suddenly occurred to me. Last night I'd been too busy just trying to keep up with my note-taking to realise the significance of the item, but now, this morning, I realised that the people who'd taken the trouble to complain to the Parish Council – and Marjorie Hampton's name was not among them – could also have spoken to her about it, knowing her interest in the village footpaths.

Excitement fizzed through my veins. This, surely, was something worth following up. I didn't have the names of the people who'd complained, but I was sure the Clerk would have. I was about to call Liam to see what he thought about it when Mum yelled up the stairs.

"Katie? Will you come down here, please? Now?"

Her voice had that she-who-must-be-obeyed quality about it that made me sigh, so I hit the save button and closed my lap top. I looked at my watch. How unfair was that? Just when I was getting stuck in to my 'proper' job, and the 11 o'clock shampoo and set must have decided to arrive early.

"Katie?" Mum's voice had a strange edge to it that I couldn't identify. She sounded pretty stressed, that was for sure. "Are you coming? Hurry up and come down. There's someone here to see you."

"Ok. I'm coming, I'm coming. What's the rush?" I muttered as I hurried down the stairs. Then I stopped dead, a sick feeling in the pit of my stomach. A policeman was standing in the kitchen, filling it up with his big, dark blue presence. He turned as I came into the room. Then I saw it was Ben and started breathing again.

"Oh, hi Ben," I said brightly. "Mum, you remember Ben Newton from school, don't you?"

"This is not a social call, Katie," he said, and something in his voice made my heart skip a beat, before continuing at a fast, erratic pace that couldn't possibly be good for it.

He took his notebook out and flipped it open. "Were you driving a pink Fiat Panda in Dintscombe on Sunday afternoon? Vehicle registration number…"

As he reeled off the number, Mum's face paled. She looked anxiously across at me. "That's my car," she said. "And Katie was driving it with my consent. Is there a problem?"

"If you don't mind, Mrs Latcham, I'd prefer it if your daughter answered the questions. Were you driving that particular car in Dintscombe on Sunday afternoon?"

I nodded, hoping against hope I'd been captured on CCTV going through a red light or something. "Yes." My voice came out as a high pitched squeak.

Ben moved forward. Gone was the mate I went to school with. In his place was PC Newton, grim-faced and serious. Something told me he wasn't interested in me jumping red lights. I took an instinctive step backwards.

"Then would you care to explain what you were doing, parked outside a house in Park Road, Dintscombe, for over an hour on Sunday afternoon?" he said. "A house which has subsequently burnt to the ground?"

Chapter Twenty-One

I stared at Ben as my brain turned to porridge and my legs to jelly. I put out a hand to grab the back of the nearest chair. What to do? What to say? The only thing I could think of was Liam, warning me that his job, as well as mine, would be on the line if the editor found out that he'd asked me to watch Doreen Spetchley that afternoon.

"I'm sorry. I didn't quite get that," I said, playing for time in the hope that my brain would start functioning again. "What was I doing where?"

"In Park Road, Dintscombe." He didn't quite succeed in hiding his impatience. "The lay-by, just outside the entrance to the park, to be precise. Your car was seen there."

"My mother's car," I hurriedly corrected him before Mum could. "But, yes, I remember now. Of course I do. I'd stopped to take a phone call. After all, that's what we are told to do, aren't we? Not to answer our phones while we are driving. Which of course I don't. Ever. So – so when this call came in, I pulled in to take it."

"Really?" He lifted one dark, heavy brow and I couldn't help wondering if he spent hours in front of the mirror practising that particular *yeah-yeah-I've-heard-that-one-before* look. "It must have been a pretty long phone call. According to our information, you were parked there for well over an hour."

"I was?"

He nodded. "According to a very security-conscious neighbour. He became so suspicious about the length of time you were there that he took the trouble to take a note of your registration number, as well as a very accurate description of the vehicle. And he wondered, as indeed do we, exactly what you were doing all that time?"

"Yes, well, I admit I stopped there for a few minutes, but I wouldn't have thought it was that long. Maybe there was another car that came along when he wasn't looking. I can't believe he sat at his window watching me for a whole hour. That would have been bonkers."

"Indeed. But how many other bright pink cars are there in the area with 'Chez Cheryl' painted down the side?"

I shook my head. What did I do now? Hold out my wrists and say something like 'it's a fair cop'? Think, Kat, think, I urged myself.

"Exactly,' he said. "Now, shall we start again? What were you doing, parked in the lay-by for over an hour, on Sunday afternoon?"

I sighed and rubbed the back of my neck. "Well, if you must know," I said with what I hoped was a sheepish grin. "It's all a bit embarrassing."

Behind me, I heard Mum's sharp intake of breath. I looked at her, then looked back at Ben and shrugged.

"Don't worry about that," he said. "It won't be anything I haven't heard before."

"But it might be something—" I took a deep breath and went for it. I was hoping Mum would have taken the hint and left us to it. But she sat there, looking from one to the other of us, like she had a front row seat at a Wimbledon final.

"OK, here's the thing," I said. "I – I signed up to an internet dating agency and had arranged to meet this guy in Dintscombe. On Sunday. I remembered all the safety advice I've been given and agreed to meet him at the entrance to Dintscombe Park. I waited for over an hour. But he didn't turn up. Pathetic, isn't it? I was stood up."

I might have been making up the story, but I wasn't making up the embarrassment I felt. It was not helped by the fact that I could feel my mother's eyes on me all the time I was speaking, although I didn't dare look at her.

"You signed up to an internet dating agency?" For a moment there, he wasn't PC Watkins but plain Ben again. The same Ben who, a couple of days earlier had asked me out. Or, at least, I thought that perhaps he had. I gave a silent groan. Could things get any more embarrassing?

"Yes. Do you need to know which one?" I asked, hoping desperately that he wouldn't. To my relief, he shook his head.

"That won't be necessary, thank you, Miss Latcham," he said stonily, all po-faced and formal again. There was a deep silence in the kitchen, broken only by the hum of the fridge as he seemed to take forever to write in his notebook. I could imagine what he was writing. "Sad loser who has to use the internet to get a date." Well, better that than knowing what I was really doing there. For my sake – and Liam's.

"While you were there, waiting for your no-show date, did you happen to notice anyone visiting the cottage opposite?" he asked.

"You mean, the one that burned down?" My eyes widened. "Wasn't that a terrible thing to happen?"

"Did you see anyone?" he repeated, his expression as stony as ever. He made no attempt to answer my question.

"No. Apart, that is, from the lady who lived there. At least, I suppose it was her. A tall, thin woman with her hair in a bun. She came out while I was waiting there, got into her car – a small, blue hatchback of some sort, I think – and drove off. Oh Lord, was it her body they found in the fire?"

He didn't quite say, 'I'm the policeman and I get to ask the questions. Not you,' but he certainly looked as if he'd have liked to. Instead, he asked, "You say you saw her? What time was this?"

"I'm not sure exactly. But I guess it would have been round about half past three. She drove off in the direction of the High Street." I stopped myself from adding that I didn't know where she went after that. I'd already told one outright lie and a couple of half truths. I didn't fancy racking up any more.

He took out a card and held it towards me. "Well, if you think of anything else, perhaps you'd contact me on that number?"

"You've already given me one of those, remember?"

"Oh yes, of course," he said. "At the Manning farm. You do seem to make a habit of being in the wrong place at the wrong time this week, don't you?"

Somehow I didn't think now would be a good time to tell

186

him about my suspicions about Gerald Crabshaw. So I just gave him a weak smile.

As Mum went to let him out, I sat down in the nearest chair with a thump as my legs finally gave way.

"Well now, what on earth was that all about?" Mum demanded as she came back into the kitchen, a look of steely determination in her eyes. "Internet dating? I don't believe that for a single second, even if he did. What's going on, Katie? What were you really doing in Dintscombe on Sunday afternoon? That same day you crunched my car. You never did explain exactly how it happened. Was it something to do with that poor woman who got killed in that fire? Come on. Out with it. I think it's time for some answers, young lady, don't you?"

"Later, Mum. I'll tell you later, I promise. But first I must make a phone call. It's really important."

At that moment, the door to the salon pinged. "You're going nowhere, except to shampoo Mrs. Tinley," Mum said firmly. "That's her now. Go on. We'll finish this little chat later. I don't know what you're up to, Katie, but whatever it is, it's giving me a very bad feeling."

She was getting a bad feeling? I thought as I followed her into the salon. That was nothing to the feeling I was getting.

***

It was over an hour before I got the chance to slip away from Mum's ever-watchful eye on the pretext of getting a fresh batch of towels from the airing cupboard. As soon as I was out of earshot I called Liam.

"I had a visit from the police," I said quietly the second he answered. "Apparently, I was seen on Sunday."

"The devil you were!" His voice shocked me with its harshness. "Didn't I tell you not to follow her?"

"Yes, you did," I said, stung by his tone into speaking louder than I'd meant to. I lowered my voice again, not wanting Mum to hear. "But I was seen when I was parked in the lay-by, not when I was following her. And you needn't worry. I kept your name out of it. Just came up with some daft story "

"I am so sorry, Kat, I surely am," he said, his voice back to its normal lilting Irish cadences. "I didn't mean to bark at you. I was worried about you, that was all."

I suppressed the retort that it had sounded more like he'd been worried about himself, not me, as he went on, "and if you will insist on driving a car that looks like a marshmallow on wheels, I'm not surprised you were seen. You can't say I didn't warn you."

But this time there was no censure in his voice, just a little gentle teasing. I shrugged and let the prickle of annoyance go.

"You did indeed," I said. "Well, apparently, a 'security conscious neighbour' was how the police described him, saw me parked in the lay-by and got suspicious because I was there so long. So he took down my registration number which he then passed on to the police."

"So what did you tell them?"

I groaned at the memory. "I had to think quickly. I said I belonged to an internet dating agency and that the guy I'd arranged to meet had stood me up. Made me sound a right loser, but better that, I thought, than telling the truth. At least that way, we both get to keep our jobs."

"Ah yes, now," Liam said slowly. "About that. The thing is, I've been meaning to call you all morning but there hasn't been a chance. I'm sorry, Kat, but I'm afraid there's been a bit of a problem."

"What sort of problem?" Even as I asked the question, I had this niggly feeling I wasn't going to like the answer.

"Mike called me into his office this morning. It appears he's having second thoughts about the whole idea of using village correspondents. Or community correspondents, as he was going to call them, as he thought it sounded more inclusive. He was really taken with the idea. But that was yesterday. Now today, he's had a change of heart, and thinks it could create problems."

My stab of disappointment was like a physical pain. "What sort of problems?" I asked, trying to remember to keep my voice down.

"He didn't say. And why are you whispering?"

"Because I don't want my mother to hear. I'm in enough trouble with her as it is. I'm supposed to be fetching some towels and she'll yelling up the stairs for me any moment."

"Then you'd better go."

"No. I need to know about my job. Or lack of it. This is down to Gerald Crabshaw again, isn't it? You said the other day that he and your editor exchange funny handshakes, which I take it means they both belong to the same mutual backscratching club. In fact, only last night Gerald boasted about getting me fired from not one but two jobs."

"Last night? How do you mean?"

"At the Parish Council meeting. I turned up, as agreed, and he was the first person I saw. He told me to go home."

"So you didn't cover the meeting? Well, at least that was one good thing. I would hate to think you'd done all that work for nothing."

"But of course I covered the meeting. As a matter of fact, the chairman came along and insisted that I did so. Gerald threw a hissy fit and did this 'either she goes or I do' thing. And when the chairman called his bluff, he went off in high dudgeon. I tell you, Liam, I am so not his favourite person at the moment."

Liam sighed. "Did I, or did I not, tell you to keep away from him?" The prickly note was back in his voice again.

"And I did," I said indignantly. "It wasn't my fault he turned up for the meeting last night, was it?"

"No. I suppose not. But trouble does seem to follow you around, Kat. Maybe it's best you forget about going after a job on *The Chronicle*, at least until things settle down."

"But that's so unfair," I protested. "None of this is my fault. Besides, I've already written up two pieces from last night's meeting and am about to start on a third, about the footpath obstructions. Stuart Davies – he's the Chairman – is going to think it pretty odd if, having made a point of insisting that I stay and cover the meeting, my stories don't appear in next week's paper, isn't he?"

189

"Katie?" Mum's voice came up the stairs. "What are you doing up there, for goodness sake? Mrs Marshall is waiting for her coffee. Black, two sugars. Not too strong."

"Sorry, Mum. Just coming," I called, then went back to Liam: "Sorry. I've got to go."

"Ok. And Kat, I think you're absolutely right. None of this is your fault. And Stuart Davies might think it strange if the stories didn't appear. You go ahead, write them up and email them in. I'll square it with Mike. Would you like to email them to me first and I'll give them the once over, then forward them for you?"

"Would you? That would be brilliant. Thanks, Liam, you're a star," I breathed, suddenly seeing a glimmer of light in a day that had started badly and got progressively worse. "As I said, this is the second time Gerald Crabshaw has tried to get me sacked. I must have got him really rattled again, just like that time in the pub when I asked him where he was the day Marjorie was killed. If you could have seen his face when he saw me last night. Talk about if looks could kill. He – oh, my God."

The pile of warm towels in my hand felt like ice, as a chill ran through my body.

"What's wrong?" Liam asked anxiously.

"I – I've just remembered something. Something that will prove he was lying about his alibi. Gerald Crabshaw killed Marjorie Hampton, Liam, and I think – no, I'm sure – I can prove it."

"What on earth—?"

"No, I've got to go. Mum will be sending out a search party if I don't. And besides, I need to think this through and check out a few things out before I say any more. Check my sources, like a good journalist should. Isn't that what you told me?"

"Indeed I did. But I also told you to be very careful. Gerald Crabshaw's a nasty piece of work. Not that I'm saying he's a murderer, mind you. But he's definitely hiding something, the very least of which is his affair with Doreen Spetchley. Something that, after this latest news, he'll be even more anxious to cover up."

"How do you mean? What latest news?"

"I've just come from a police press conference. They don't think Doreen's death was an accident. The post mortem showed she was dead before the fire started and they're treating her death as suspicious. Now, if you're right about Crabshaw, there's no saying what he'd do if you challenged him. Promise me you won't."

"Don't worry. It's not Gerald I'm going to see. But someone who can prove he was lying about his alibi. And when I've done that, I'll go to the police and straighten everything out."

"Damn it, girl," he growled. "You will not."

I bristled at his tone. "I don't think—" I began but he cut in.

"Now, listen," he said, his voice low, urgent. "We need to get together and talk this through before you do anything, or say anything to anyone. Understand? I'm tying up a few things here, then I'll be on my way over to Much Winchmoor anyway. I've been trying all morning to get hold of Gerald Crabshaw to interview him, but have drawn a blank every time. I'm just hoping he hasn't done a runner because, if he has, it will be down to you interfering in things you know nothing about. So promise me that if you do see him, you won't approach him, follow him or antagonise him in any way but will contact me. Got that? I'd hate to think you'd blundered in and scared him off."

Blundered in? I drew in a sharp breath. What sort of an idiot did he think I was? "Of course I wouldn't *blunder in* as you put it," I said indignantly. "I'm not a fool, you know."

"That's your opinion," he snapped, then went on quickly before I could protest. "And I don't need to remind you, do I, that Gerald Crabshaw is my story? And it's very unprofessional of one journalist to pinch another's story."

"But I wasn't—" I tried to interrupt, but he wouldn't let me.

"In fact, to put it bluntly," he said sharply, no trace of that lovely Irish warmth in his voice any more, "this is my big chance, Kat, my ticket out of this hell hole, and I'll not have it wrecked by a little girl like you playing at being a journo. So keep out of it, ok? Back off. Go back to your little old ladies and their perms, and leave the real work to the professionals.

191

Do you understand?"

Before I had chance to come back with some withering put-down, he ended the call.

Chapter Twenty-Two

I was seething as I put my phone back in my pocket. *Go back to your little old ladies and their perms. Leave the real work to the professional*s. Of all the patronising things to say. How dare he? He'd been all silver-tongued charm when he'd wanted something, but he'd just shown his true colours. It seemed that Will had been right about Liam all along – and that annoyed me as much as anything.

Liam had used me from day one. He'd first made contact with me because he thought I'd give him all the gory details about finding Marjorie's body. Then, when he'd realised that wasn't going to happen, he encouraged me to think there was a job going on the paper when there obviously wasn't, just because he needed someone to watch Doreen Spetchley's house. What an idiot I'd been, willing to risk anything for a 'maybe' job on his precious paper. Believing him when he'd said it was a chance for us to work together on the story, maybe even sharing a by-line.

He would no more think of sharing a by-line with me than a kidney. What a naive, gullible idiot I'd been. And to think I'd covered up for him by not telling Ben Newton what I was really doing outside Doreen's house on Sunday.

Well, I was going to put that particular bit of misinformation right, for a start, I decided. I fished in my pocket for Ben's card, but stopped as I realised that I, of course, was the one who'd been lying to the police. Not Liam. All he had to do was deny any knowledge of me – and, to be fair, he'd never asked me to follow Doreen. In fact, he'd been furious with me when I told him I had. So I was the one who'd be in trouble. Not him.

On the other hand, there was something that had occurred to me that the police might be very interested in. But I needed to check it out with Jules first.

"Katie?" Mum's voice, as she called up the stairs again, was several decibels higher this time. "Are you coming? Mrs Marshall would like her coffee this morning, not tomorrow, if it's all the same to you."

It was almost half past one by the time I managed to get away. Jules would, of course, still be working, so I planned to catch up with her in the pub. Thankfully, Mum bought my story about how I'd promised to let Jules have a couple of books I'd been talking to her about. She didn't need to know that the last time Jules and I had been talking about books was when she'd blackmailed me into doing her English Lit homework for her.

After the cloying perm lotion and hair spray-laden atmosphere of the salon, it was great to be outside. It was one of those glorious sunny days you sometimes get in early spring where everything is sharp-focussed and bright, when the sky is so blue it makes your eyes ache. In the bank at the bottom of our back garden, clusters of primroses were opening up, encouraged into flower by the warmth of the sun. Just the sight of them put me in a better mood. Yesterday's storm, when Will and I had been on the coast, seemed a million miles away.

Perhaps whatever had been bugging Will then had passed over too, like the storm. I decided to go up to the farm after I'd seen Jules, to see if I could find out what had been getting him down. Now we'd got back to our old, easy ways (yesterday afternoon excepted) I didn't want to let things fester on, like they had before.

I fetched my bike and was about to pedal off in the direction of the High Street when I heard the throaty roar of a powerful car coming down the road behind me, and I pulled over to let it pass.

It was Gerald Crabshaw. After last night's run-in at the parish council meeting, I was in no hurry for another showdown with him. I hoped he'd just keep on going, but no such luck. He stopped the car a few yards in front of me and clambered out. And something about the purposeful way he strode towards me told me that my day was about to get a whole heap worse.

"Katie. Just the person I was hoping to see," he called out.

And you're just the person I was hoping not to see, I could have said but didn't. Instead I gave him my falsest, brightest smile and got ready to pedal off as fast as I could.

"I'm so sorry," I said. "I can't stop. I'm late as it is."

With a turn of speed I'd never have believed him capable of, he lurched towards me. Before I'd realised his intentions, he'd grabbed my handlebars with both hands and hung on grimly, like a red-faced matador wrestling a bull by the horns.

It was a ridiculous and – I don't mind admitting – rather scary situation. I was stuck, straddled across the bike, one foot on the floor, the other on the pedal. I could do nothing. Go nowhere. Not without letting go of my bike.

I looked around desperately. Who would see me? Or hear me, if I yelled? The days when people stood around gossiping on the streets of Much Winchmoor were long gone, along with the shop, the village bakery and the post office.

"Look, Katie, I just need a little chat, that's all," he said, in a creepy, whiney tone I'd never heard before. "I didn't mean to startle you."

"You didn't," I lied. "So if you could just let go…" I yanked on my handlebars but his grip was firm. If it hadn't been so scary, it would have been quite funny, the sight of two adults tussling over a bike, like a couple of kids in the playground, arguing whose turn it was to ride it.

"Please. Hear me out," Gerald went on, his face getting redder and redder with the effort of holding on. "I want to apologise for last night at the Parish Council meeting. I don't know what came over me, I really don't. I'd had some bad news, you see." Suddenly he loosened his hold on my handlebars. His shoulders slumped and he looked so unhappy that I almost felt sorry for him. "A dear friend of mine was tragically killed, but even so, there was no excuse for taking it out on you. I'm deeply, deeply sorry, my dear."

Gerald Crabshaw apologising? Had I wandered into some parallel universe by mistake? There'd be a squadron of pigs flying overhead next.

"That's ok… There's nothing… to apologise… for." My voice came out in jerky little puffs as I tried pull my bike away, without losing too much dignity in the process. "If you'd just… move… I really… am late."

"No, wait. Please. This won't take long; I've come up with a way to make things up to you a bit. Forget last night's Parish Council meeting with its mind-numbing ramblings about pot holes and missing cats' eyes. I've got a story for you that could well turn out to be the scoop of the century. Isn't that what you journalists say?"

I bristled. "Actually, the editor's having second thoughts about employing me, thanks to you."

He had the grace to look uncomfortable. "Well, yes, I'm sorry about that. But don't worry, I'll talk to Mike, I promise. Trust me, Katie, this story will be a big one," his piggy little eyes gleamed. "I mean, as in front page of the nationals. Mike will be desperate to take you on, but this will get your CV out there. You'll be able to take your pick."

I didn't believe a word of it. I'd already been made a fool of once today, thanks to my so-called journalistic ambitions. It wasn't going to happen again. "Sorry. It sounds great, but, if you could just let go…"

"Look, I know we got off on the wrong foot, but how about we meet up later and I give you all the gen, and you can make up your own mind what you do about it? The story's a cracker, Katie. I can promise you that."

A cracker? I was about to tell him no, but then thought with an inward smirk how Liam had been trying all day, without success, to get an interview with Gerald. And here was the man himself, practically begging to talk to me. What if he was on the level?

He must have seen the indecision in my face, because he went on. "Listen, I've got to pop into Dintscombe quickly, then I'll be dropping in to the pub for a quick one. Why don't we meet there in, say, an hour?"

"But the pub will be closing soon," I said.

He shook his head. "Donald's expecting me. There's no way he'll close, if he thinks there's a chance of selling another pint or two."

I remembered the way Gerald had threatened me the day before, and was about to say no way, when I stopped and thought about what he'd said. I looked at him closely. Certainly there was none of the usual swaggering bluster about him today. In fact, he looked as if he'd shrunk since last night. His eyes had a vacant, dazed look, his skin pale and sallow. Maybe he really was grieving for Doreen.

What harm could it possibly do? The memory of Liam's stinging words still rankled. If I could get one over on him, then so much the better. And it would do no harm to my standing with Mike, the editor, would it? If, of course, what Gerald was saying was true. Which I very much doubted. Even so, it might be worth going along with him for now. I'd be safe enough, meeting him in the pub, after all. What did I have to lose?

But before I could say anything, his patience must have run out because he scowled and jerked on the handlebars so hard I almost overbalanced. "For heavens' sake, girl, what's to think about?" he snapped. "I suppose the story's not enough for you, is that it? You want money as well?"

"What do you mean? I don't…"

"You saw us, didn't you? Up in Compton Wood. I thought at first it was your mother parked in the gateway and wondered what she was doing there. But it wasn't her, was it? It was you."

I backed away as far as I could without falling over, flustered by his sudden change of tone. Gone was the penitent, apologetic man. In his place, the arrogant pushy one I knew so well. Once again, I looked around at the deserted village street.

"I – I don't know what you mean, honest," I said quickly, my heart thudding so loudly I thought he must be able to hear it. "And why would I want money? If I'd seen something up in Compton Wood – which I didn't, I swear – I wouldn't say anything, I promise, least of all try to blackmail you." My words tumbled over each other in my rush to convince him. "Look, I've got to go. My friend will be wondering where I am and start sending out search parties."

"You'd better not say anything," he snarled, now reverting completely to type, "Else it will be the worse for you."

I was scared, of course I was. Why else would I be standing there, gabbling like an idiot? But there was something about the way he spoke that lit a fuse in me so that, for a moment at least, I forgot my fear and felt only blind, reckless fury, as I remembered Marjorie and Doreen.

"Oh right," I flashed. "Is that how you deal with everyone who gets in your way? First Marjorie, and now Doreen. Lost a dear friend, was that how you put it? How could you do that to someone you pretended to be fond of?"

"Don't be ridiculous. You can't think I had anything to do with either death. Besides, Doreen's was just a tragic accident."

"That's not what the police are saying," I said.

"Oh and of course, I'm forgetting, you have a direct line to the police, don't you?" he sneered.

"I have my sources. In fact, one of them's a particularly good friend of mine. And he was saying that Doreen Spetchley did not die in the fire. That she was dead before it started."

Of course Ben Newton hadn't said anything of the sort to me. The information had come from Liam via the police press conference. But it wouldn't hurt Gerald to think I had a good friend in the force.

"Suspicious circumstances, they're saying," I went on while he stood, open-mouthed, looking like I'd just punched him in the stomach.

His face went from white to grey, and all fifty shades in between. He stepped back from the bike as if the handlebars had suddenly become searing hot, all the while staring at me, with the half-desperate, half-spoiling-for-a-fight look of a cornered rat.

I took my chance, yanked the bike towards me, then pedalled off as fast as I could, the anger that had given me that little spurt of courage now evaporated.

"Katie, come back," Gerald shouted after me as I put on a turn of speed that would have impressed Bradley Wiggins. "There's something you need to know—"

I wasn't planning on hanging around long enough to find out what it was he thought I needed to know. I reckoned I could probably guess. As I got near the Winchmoor Arms, the door opened and Elsie and Olive came out.

I jumped off my bike and on to the pavement as Gerald's look-at-me Porsche roared past, making enough noise to wake up all the residents of St Bartholomew's church yard.

"What's got up his nose?" Elsie asked, staring after him.

I shrugged, hoping they couldn't see how my hands were shaking as I leaned my bike against the pub wall. "Who knows?" I said, as I waited for my heartbeat to return to normal.

"He looked like the devil himself was at his heels," Olive said. "You know what they say, drive like the devil…" she shrugged. "Or something."

"Boy racer!" Elsie yelled after him.

"And what about you, dear?" Olive asked, turning to me with a smile. "Did you and your young man have a nice day at the beach yesterday?"

I was about to ask how she knew where Will and I had gone but decided to save my breath.

"He's not my young man," I said shortly. "But yes, thank you, we had a good time. Excuse me." I inched past them.

"No point going in there. Donald all but threw us out," Elsie said with a sniff. "Asked if we were going to sit there, nursing our drinks and toasting our toes in front of his fire, all afternoon. And did we think he had money to burn?"

"Yes," Olive chimed. "And then he said if we didn't have anything better to do, then he did. He was quite grumpy, which is unusual for him. He's usually very friendly, in his own quiet way. Missing his wife, I dare say."

Elsie snorted. "Missing his wife? That's not very likely. I expect he just wants to go and put his feet up. So there's no point in you going in there, hoping to be served, young lady. Number one, I don't hold with young people drinking themselves silly in the middle of the day when they should be doing a decent day's work like the rest of us. And, number two, he'll probably refuse to serve you anyway, seeing as how he sacked you. So I'm saving you the embarrassment of being refused."

"He didn't sack me. And I'm not going in for a drink," I said. "I just want to see Jules."

"Then he'll definitely chuck you out for distracting his staff when they should be working," Elsie chortled as she pulled a bright pink woollen hat that looked more like a tea cosy over her newly-permed head. "Come along, Olive. Let's get home before I catch them new-monials again. How these youngsters get away with standing around with practically nothing on, I don't know. Don't know they're born, some of them."

"I hear your mother's got a dent in her car, dear," Olive said. "Was she very upset? Thinks the world of that little car, does Cheryl, doesn't she?"

"Olive! Are you coming, or are you going to stand there all day gossiping?" Elsie demanded.

Olive gave me one of her sweet, apologetic smiles and hurried after her friend, whose tea cosy hat bobbed up and down as she bustled off down the deserted High Street.

I glanced at my watch. Jules should be out any moment but I didn't want to hang around outside in case Gerald came back. I reckoned I'd risk Donald's bad mood.

***

It took a while for my eyes to get accustomed to the gloom of the bar after the brightness of the street. At first I thought it was empty. Then I heard the sound of chinking glasses and saw that Jules was behind the bar, unloading glasses from the glass washer, while from the back kitchen came the reassuring sound of Donald, banging around.

"Blimey, Kat, you look like you did that day we got chased by John Manning's bull." Jules looked at me anxiously. "What's wrong? Do you want a drink?"

I shook my head. "No thanks. I'm just a bit freaked out. I don't know what would have happened if Elsie and Olive hadn't chosen that moment to come out of here. An unlikely pair of rescuers but, boy, was I pleased to see them."

Jules's eyes widened. "What happened?"

"He threatened me. Again."

"Who?"

"Gerald Crabshaw. He's quite mad, you know. Completely bonkers. Did you know he was having an affair?"

"Now why doesn't that surprise me? He'd chase after anything in a skirt, the old lech," Jules said as she began placing glasses on the shelf above the bar.

"Yes. Nothing unusual there, as you say. But it was who he was having the fling with that's the big deal. It was only that woman who died in the fire in Dintscombe yesterday. Not only that, but I'm pretty sure he broke up with her with just hours before the fire."

She put the glass down. Suddenly I had her full attention. "You're kidding."

"Course I'm not. But that's not the half of it. Because of something you said, I'm pretty damn sure I've got proof that he killed Marjorie. I knew there was something that didn't quite fit but I couldn't put my finger on it. Then this morning I did. And that's why I wanted to come here and check it out with you before going to the police."

"Check what out?" Her eyes danced with excitement as she leaned across the counter towards me. "And what sort of proof? Stop talking in riddles, girl. You always were one for spinning out a story."

I chose to ignore that. "Remember when you were late picking Kylie up from school? The day Marjorie Hampton was killed?"

She pulled a face. "Tell me about it. Her teacher still hasn't forgiven me. Neither has Kylie."

"And why did you say you were late?"

"Because the main road was closed by an accident for most of the afternoon and the bus had to go around all the villages. It took forever."

"Exactly. That's what was niggling around in the back of my mind for ages, only I was too dumb to make the connection. Don't you see? Donald and Gerald were each other's alibis for the afternoon of Marjorie's murder. One of them, I can't remember which, said they were at a meeting about the site of a possible new playing field out on the bypass that day. But you see, they couldn't have been, because the road was closed. There was no way they could have got there. They were lying."

"Donald?" Jules looked anxiously in the direction of the kitchen and lowered her voice. "Surely not. He'd never have the nerve…"

"He would if he was desperate enough. It's my bet Gerald's got something on Donald to force him into backing up his story. And that's why Gerald got me sacked from the pub. It all makes perfect sense now. I think the site meeting line was the first story they came up with and it was only later they realised the road was closed and then had to change it to something else. Which they probably did. Only, of course, I'd been told the first version. It's just a pity it took me so long to remember it."

"So they told porkies about where they were," Jules said as she took more glasses from the glass washer "Perhaps they had some dodgy deal of their own going on. I've seen Gerald in a huddle with Shane Freeman on several occasions, and it didn't look like they were discussing Bristol City's chances this season. The word around the bar is that, since Shane's been on the continental run, he's the go-to man for cheap cigarettes and booze. But that doesn't mean any of them had anything to do with Marjorie's murder."

"Maybe not," I agreed reluctantly. "But it's a bit iffy to start giving false alibis during a murder investigation, wouldn't you say? If whatever they were doing was innocent, why lie about it?"

Jules looked worried. "You've got a point. So, what are you going to do about it?"

"Tell the police, of course. It's up to them what they do about it, but I think they'd be very interested in the fact that our Councillor Crabshaw lied about his whereabouts the day Marjorie Hampton was killed, don't you?"

Before Jules could say anything, Donald rushed into the bar, his expression grim.

"Juliet, I'm so sorry," he said. "That was the school on the phone just now. I'm afraid your Kylie's had an accident. Only a bit of a bump on the head, they say. Nothing to worry about, but they think you should come up right away and take her home. That she'll be—"

But before he could deliver the rest of the message, Jules was gone, leaving the door wide open behind her.

Chapter Twenty-Three

Donald walked across the dimly-lit bar and quietly closed the door that Jules had left open in her rush to get to Kylie.

"Oh dear, children can be such a worry, can't they?" he murmured as he made his way back across the room, straightening up a couple of stools as he did so. "Always into something. I must say, I'm often quite relieved that Joyce and I were never blessed."

"Poor Jules." I fastened my coat and stood up, ready to leave. "She looked quite frantic."

"I'm sure little Kylie will be fine." Donald went behind the bar and carried on unloading the glass washer where Jules had left off. "I couldn't help but overhear your conversation just now, what with the pub being so quiet."

And you straining your ears to hear, I could have added. But didn't.

"Publicans do a lot of that, you know," he went on, straightening the glasses on the shelf above him. "Overhearing things they aren't meant to." He closed the glass washer then pulled out a stool and sat down, one elbow leaning on the bar. He looked like he was settling down for a good long chat. "Sometimes people act as if I'm not there, you know. The invisible man. I've heard them going on about me being the 'grey man', taking the mick about how Joyce shouts at me, things like that. Sometimes, I can be standing right there by the bar. But they just don't notice me."

"I'm sorry." I had no idea what I was apologising for, but it felt like he was expecting it. And I did, indeed, feel sorry for him. Whatever Gerald had bullied him into doing was none of his choosing, I was willing to bet. But maybe he hadn't overheard the bit where I was speculating about his involvement. I hoped not, anyway.

"I heard what you said about Gerald Crabshaw – and – and me," he went, his head bent as he straightened up the already straight beer mats along the counter.

I swallowed hard. He had heard us after all. Jeez, this was awkward. "I'm sorry," I said again, with an embarrassed laugh. "You know what us girls are like when we get together. Just talking a load of nonsense, that's all. Dad always says…"

"I've had my suspicions about Gerald Crabshaw for some time now, same as you have." Donald cut across, his words coming out in a rush, like he'd suddenly made up his mind to say something.

"You have?" My heartbeat quickened and I took a step towards him. "Suspicions about what?"

But before he could answer, my phone rang. Talk about bad timing. Just when Donald was about to open up. I looked down at it quickly, about to switch it off, when I saw with a jolt that it was Will. He never phoned me during the day. In fact, he never phoned me at all if he could help it.

"Will? What's wrong?" I said anxiously. "Is it your dad?"

"No. Nothing like that. Where are you?"

I hesitated. If I told him the truth, he'd want to know what I was doing there. And if I told him that, then he'd come across all bossy older brother again and tell me not to. Just when I was beginning to get somewhere.

"Where am I? You phoned me to ask me where I am?" I said, my voice tinged with impatience. "Well, if you must know, I'm on my way to see Elsie Flintlock again. You know, that research job I went to see her about yesterday? Well, she said she'd look out some old photos, and for me to come back this afternoon, which is what I'm doing."

"Oh right. It's just – well, I thought we might catch up later this evening?"

"I'm not sure—" I began but he cut in.

"I need to see you, Katie," he said. "I have something to tell you. It's important. I should have told you yesterday but…"

"But you went off in a strop. I remember," I said. "Ok, I'll see you this evening. But, Will…"

"Sorry. Got to go. There's someone at the door. I'll see you later, then. About seven? I'll call for you."

He ended the call and I looked across at Donald, who was watching anxiously.

"Trouble?" he said.

I shook my head. "Just Will."

"That's ok then." He reached down behind the counter and took out a bottle and two glasses and placed them on the counter between us. "Sit yourself down, Katie, why don't you? Unless, of course, you're in a hurry to go off and see Elsie Flintlock? Who, by the way, I'm pretty sure I heard making plans to go into Dintscombe with Olive this afternoon."

"No, that's ok. I'll catch up with Elsie later," I said. "I'm in no rush. I just don't like Will checking up on me like he's my dad, or something."

He gave a flicker of a smile. "I don't blame you. You've been having quite a time of it lately, haven't you? I can see you're not your usual chirpy self at the moment. Would you like a drink? Something to put the colour back in your cheeks? I'm having one. I don't do this often but it's been one of those days. And I prefer not to drink alone."

"No, thanks. I don't…" I began, but changed my mind. Donald was being unusually kind and it seemed churlish to refuse. Besides, he looked as if he wanted to talk. About Gerald. Who knows what he might be ready to spill? "I mean, yes, thank you. A drink would be lovely. I'll have a glass of dry white wine, please."

"Come on now. You look like you need something stronger than that." His grey eyes seemed anxious as he peered at me. "You really are looking quite peaky, you know. Here, try this. It's my favourite single malt whisky. Definitely not for the customers." He poured generous measures of the peaty brown liquid into two glasses and handed one to me.

I shrugged and took the glass. I raised it to my lips and coughed as the fumes hit the back of my throat before I'd even tasted it. "Strong stuff," I murmured, my eyes watering.

"Sip it slowly," he said with a smile. "You're supposed to savour it to get its full benefit, not knock it back like it was medicine."

I took a tentative sip and smiled back. Donald wasn't such a bad chap. And maybe, if he was relaxed a bit after a glass of his special malt, who knows what he might tell me? Obviously there was something about Gerald Crabshaw that was bothering him.

"You were saying about Gerald Crabshaw, before Will phoned," I prompted. "That you had your suspicions about him. What sort of suspicions?"

He rubbed the back of his neck, his face troubled. "The worst. He really is a nasty piece of work, you know, and if you have evidence against him that will help put him away, then that's all to the good. I'll give you all the help I can."

I wished I had a notebook and pen with me but reckoned if I had, Donald wouldn't have been so willing to speak freely.

He raised his glass to me then took a long, deep swallow that almost emptied the glass in one. Obviously, his advice to sip it slowly only applied to novices like me. He was certainly more practised at drinking the stuff than I was, because his eyes showed no sign of watering. Instead, they were clear and steady.

"You were absolutely right about that so-called alibi I gave him as being false, you know," he said. "Luckily, the police didn't ask me for one, else I'd be in all sorts of trouble now, wouldn't I? Goodness only knows what Joyce would say if she came back from her cruise, to find I was in trouble with the law. Publicans have to be very careful, you know. I could lose my licence just like that." He snapped his fingers.

"I suppose you could. Then why did you do it?"

He topped his glass up, cradled it between his hands and gently swirled the amber liquid. "It was just as you thought. He was blackmailing me," he said in a low voice that had me straining to hear him. "I'd got in a muddle with my VAT returns – just a straightforward series of bookkeeping errors, and certainly no attempt at fraud on my part. But the Revenue and Customs didn't see it like that and were making all sorts of threats. Demanding money that I simply didn't have. I was at my wits' end. Joyce was going to go ballistic when she found out."

"Why didn't you go to the bank, if you needed a loan?" I asked gently.

"They'd already turned me down. I was frantic. Then one afternoon, Gerald and I were sitting here, like we are now, sharing a couple of glasses. And, well, I suppose like an idiot, I'd had a couple more than I should have and was foolish enough to tell him about the mess I was in. He was very sympathetic and lent me some money to clear the debt. And, like an even bigger fool, I accepted. As soon as I did that, I was in trouble. Big, big trouble. You see, he has this scam going with Shane Freeman. You know, the lorry driver who does all those runs to Europe?"

I nodded. Excitement surged through me. So Jules had been right about that. Suddenly it all began to make sense. "I've seen them together, on several occasions. They looked as if they were up to no good." I thought about Amy's mum saying she'd overheard Marjorie having a go at Shane about something. Telling him it had to stop and that she was going to tell the police. And Shane calling at her cottage on the day of the murder. It sounded like he was in it up to his tattooed neck.

"So what was this scam?" I asked. "Or can I guess? Duty free alcohol and cigarettes?"

Donald gave a weak smile. "Got it in one. I always said you were a bright girl, Katie, didn't I? Goodness knows where the stuff came from, I didn't like to ask. From Shane's regular trips to the continent, I imagine. Anyway, Gerald 'persuaded' me to sell some of it in the pub in return for a small percentage of the profit. Like a fool, I agreed and that was it. He had me by the ears, as he so delicately put it. He said he'd made sure there was evidence against me and not him, that the paper trail ended with me, and threatened to report me if I didn't back up his story about being with him the day Marjorie Hampton was killed. Well, I'll be honest, I thought I was just covering up for one of these sordid little affairs he's always having, and so I went along with it. I know what I did was wrong. But he can be a very persuasive man – and a dangerous enemy."

"The guy's a first class rat." My mind was racing. If Donald could just keep his nerve and repeat what he'd said to the police, then we had Gerald Crabshaw 'by the ears'. I raised my glass towards him and smiled encouragingly. "Cheers."

"Cheers," he said, as he glanced down quickly at his watch. "You're looking better now. I always think a good glass of malt is better than any medicine. It should be on prescription."

I agreed wholeheartedly. Particularly when it loosened tongues, the way it had loosened his. "You could be right. I could get a taste for this stuff."

Donald smiled briefly, but then looked his usual anxious self again. "Of course, I realise now it wasn't an affair he was asking me to cover for, as he'd led me to believe, but something much, much worse." It was as if, now he'd started talking about it, he just couldn't stop. I couldn't help feeling sorry for him. The whole thing had obviously been eating him up inside. "I think – I'm afraid – he may have killed Marjorie Hampton, and I don't know what to do about it. I don't mind telling you, Katie, it's been giving me nightmares. I wake up most nights, sweat running down my face, the image of that poor soul, head first in that freezer with her legs stuck up in the air—"

I stopped, the glass half way to my lips. "How did you know?" I asked.

His eyes had the startled look of a rabbit caught in a poacher's flashlight. "How did I know what?"

"How did you know Marjorie was found with her legs up in the air? As far as I know, the police haven't released that bit of information."

"Oh Lord, is that right?" He chewed the back of his thumb, his thin, grey face creased with worry. "You say the police haven't released that information?"

I shook my head.

"Well, I'm afraid that confirms my worst suspicions. Because, you see, Gerald told me about the way she was found. He hated poor Marjorie so much, that he…" he swallowed hard, his Adam's apple bobbing convulsively in his thin throat. "I'm sorry to say he found it quite funny. It made me feel ill, the way he carried on. I thought he must have read it somewhere. But if you say the information isn't in the public

209

domain, then it looks pretty certain that he was actually there, which can only mean one thing, can't it? He killed Marjorie. And Doreen too, probably. The man really is sick, don't you agree?"

Sick? The thought that Gerald Crabshaw found the sight of poor Marjorie's undignified end amusing was beyond sick. It was inhuman. He deserved to go down for a long, long time.

"What do you think we should do?" Donald looked as if what he would like to do was run a mile. He was scared, as, of course, was I. It was one thing to speculate as to who might have committed murder. But it was quite another to be faced with the truth.

"We must tell the police, of course." It was no comfort to me to be proved right, even though I couldn't stand the man. Because there was something seriously unsettling discovering that someone you've known all your life, the man who's opened fetes, judged the flower and produce show and laid the wreath on the war memorial every Remembrance Day, is also a cold-blooded murderer. I shivered as I remembered how he'd gripped the handlebars of my bike and wouldn't let go. How his eyes had blazed with hatred. "Gerald waylaid me when I was on my way here. Goodness knows what he'd have done if Elsie and Olive hadn't come along."

"He threatened you? How? What did he say?"

"It wasn't so much what he said. It was the way he looked at me. And he grabbed the handlebars of my bike and wouldn't let go."

"Why would he do that?"

"He was trying to get me to agree to meet him here in the bar."

Donald looked surprised. "But why on earth did he think you'd agree to that? No disrespect, Katie, but I wouldn't have thought you were his type."

I flushed. "Yuck. Nothing like that," I said quickly as I suppressed a shudder. "He said he had a story to give me that was so big, it would get my by-line on the front pages of the nationals. Said he wanted to make things right after getting the editor of *The Chronicle* to drop me. He seems to be making quite a habit of getting me sacked, don't you think?"

Donald had the grace to look embarrassed. "What could I do?" He took another long swig of his malt. "You know how things were between me and him now. It wasn't my doing, I can promise you. I am sorry about it, though. I mean, if, when this is all over, you want your job back…"

I thought of Jules and Ed and their struggle to make ends meet with a new baby on the way, and shook my head. "Don't worry about it. I've moved on – and I certainly don't need any help from Gerald Creepy Crabshaw. I imagine that, had I fallen for his ridiculous story, there'd have been some sort of 'accident' before I got here." I suppressed a shudder at the thought of how close I'd come to agreeing to meet him.

"But you didn't fall for it?" Donald said.

"What? His scoop of the century story? Of course not." Donald didn't need to know that, just for a second, I'd been tempted to let ambition override common sense. "It was just a ploy to get me to agree to meet him."

He smiled. "Very wise. But I've got an idea – why don't we —?" he stopped and shook his head. "But no, it's too dangerous. We've already established we're dealing with a very ruthless man who would stop at nothing. It wouldn't be fair to ask you."

"Ask me what?"

"It was a stupid idea anyway. I just thought, why don't we play him along? You know, trick him into admitting it? You know how he likes to boast." His grey eyes shone with barely suppressed excitement. "You never know, he might give us something we can take to the police."

"But I've already told him no."

"And you'd rather not. That's ok. I understand. Forget it. You ready for another one, by the way?" He raised the bottle towards me. "One for the road?"

"No. I'm all right, thanks."

"But you've hardly touched it. Don't you like it?"

"Yes. Yes, it's lovely," I lied because, to be honest, it tasted like medicine. But I didn't like to upset him. "I'm just savouring it, like you told me to."

"Very wise," he gave another brief smile, another quick glance at his watch.

"Look, I'm obviously keeping you from something," I said, getting up to go. "I'd best be…"

"You're not keeping me from anything, I promise you. It's just – well, truth to tell, I'm just a little nervous. That's all. Just the thought of Gerald, out there… well, you know what I mean."

I did indeed.

"You wouldn't have to meet him, you know," he went on. "You could hide behind the bar there, and I could egg him on, get him to tell me about Marjorie – and, of course, Doreen. He's such a bragger, he won't be able to resist. All you'd have to do is listen."

"Hey, you could be on to something." My heart was zinging. Who'd have thought Donald would have had it in him? Amazing. It would be one hell of a thing if he and I could show Gerald up for the cold-blooded killer he was. And, from Donald's point of view, it would break the hold that Gerald had on him. As for me, I owed Gerald. For Marjorie and Doreen.

"Look, I'll spin him some story that will bring him here," Donald said. "You stay here and finish your drink while I go and call him. Then we'll get you well hidden behind the counter. You'll be in no danger, I promise. So, are you up for it?"

I didn't like the idea of being in the same room as Gerald Crabshaw, even if I was going to be well hidden. But I very much liked the idea of the net closing in on the monster who murdered those two poor women. I was up for it.

Chapter Twenty-Four

I nodded enthusiastically but as I slipped off the barstool my foot caught in the strap of my bag. I staggered slightly and put my arm out to save myself.

Donald was there in an instant, hovering and anxious like an over-attentive waiter. "Are you all right?"

"Yes," I said, feeling more than a little foolish and trying to make a joke of it. "This stuff must be stronger than I thought."

"But you haven't had more than a thimbleful. Drink up. Just the thing to steady the nerves."

"I'm fine. I just got up a bit quickly, that's all."

"Ok then. I'll just go and phone Gerald. But are you quite sure you're all right about this? Maybe this isn't such a good idea after all." His thin face was pinched with indecision as he chewed his thumb. "Look, why don't we simply forget the whole thing and just call the police? If Gerald squirms his way out of it, so be it. Better that than put yourself in danger. Even though it means everyone will know what a fool I was, and you lose the big 'how I helped bring a vicious killer to justice' story. But you'll still have plenty to write about, won't you? And most people around here think I'm a fool anyway, so nothing would have changed there."

The sleepless nights were, indeed, beginning to catch up on me and I was feeling a bit woolly and desperately in need of some fresh air. I wasn't very good at drinking in the middle of the day at the best of times and, coupled with the fact that I'd had no breakfast this morning, this was a long way from that.

Even so, those headlines were very tempting and Liam's 'amateur' jibe still smarted. "It seems a shame, though, when we're so close," I murmured.

"You're right. It does seem a shame." He frowned and looked deep in thought for a moment. "Look, I'll tell you what

I'll do. I'll lock the front door and tell him to come around the back. That way, he won't catch us unawares because we'll hear him coming. It will give us time to make sure you're well out of the way before he comes in." He crossed the bar and locked the front door. "How about that?"

I swallowed against the wave of nausea that rose in my throat. Was I being stupid? Should I call the whole thing off, as Donald suggested? Or maybe phone Will and ask him to meet me here? But if I did that, he'd insist on knowing why and would tell me not to do it and let the police handle it. And I certainly wasn't going to phone Liam. Ever again.

On the other hand, if I could hold my nerve, I could be in on the ground floor of the biggest story of the century. And wouldn't that put Liam's nose out of joint? He wouldn't be able to accuse me of blundering around like an amateur ever again. "I think your plan could work well," I said with a confidence I was far from feeling, "I just had a bit of a wobble, that's all. Literally and metaphorically speaking, if you see what I mean. Gerald was pretty damn mad just now. I don't mind admitting, he scared me."

"Trust me, Katie, he won't lay a finger on you, I promise." His voice was firm, his eyes steady. If Dippy Donald, the man they all reckoned didn't like going out on sunny days because he was frightened of his own shadow, could find the courage to do this, then so could I.

I took a deep steadying breath. "Better go and make that phone call then, before I lose my nerve."

He smiled. "You're a game girl, I'll give you that." The smile faded and for a moment, he looked very solemn. He glanced down at his watch, frowned, then said in a low mumble, "I'm really very sorry."

"Sorry? What for?"

For a moment, he looked blank, like old Mrs Simmons had that morning in the salon, when she'd lost track of the conversation in mid-sentence. "Sorry – sorry for sacking you, of course,' he said, recovering himself quickly. "You were one of the best barmaids I've ever had."

"That wasn't what you said when you let me go," I pointed

out, then wished I hadn't as his expression darkened.

"I've already explained about that," he said sharply.

"Yeah, you have. Sorry," I passed a hand in front of my eyes. "I guess I'm more strung up than I realised. I must admit, I feel – it's very hot in here, isn't it? Do you think you could open a window?"

"I'm afraid not. They don't open. Haven't done for hundreds of years, I should think. Look, you sit there and relax while I call Gerald. I won't be a minute."

Of course, I didn't relax. How could I? But I felt better knowing Gerald could only get in through the back door, and that he'd have to get past Donald first. But what if he attacked Donald? Gerald was twice his size and desperate. Poor Donald wouldn't stand a chance.

I took my phone from my pocket and placed it on the bar, behind a charity collection tin. Donald had said I was a game girl. A weird expression that made me sound a bit like a pheasant. But my gameness, if there was such a word, was just a front. I felt as wobbly as a kitten on a tightrope. And just about as weak. In fact, at the moment, I doubted if I could have stood up if I'd wanted to. And it was getting hotter in here by the minute.

I thought about ringing Will, as my nerve began to fail me again, and wished I hadn't lied to him about where I was.

But before I could reach for my phone, Donald came back. I slumped back in the chair, as the succession of disturbed nights, coupled with the realisation that I was probably doing the most dangerous – and foolish – thing I'd ever done in my life, left me feeling utterly drained.

"Is he coming?" I asked.

But instead of answering my question, Donald looked down at his watch yet again. "It's taking longer than I thought," he murmured. "Although you're looking pretty sleepy now. I should have given you a larger dose."

"What?" I sat up straight, my heart thumping, my head swimming, my tongue feeling like it was suddenly two sizes too big for my mouth. "What are you talking about? What do you mean by a larger dose? A larger dose of what?"

"I mean a larger dose than the one I gave Doreen," he said, still in the same pleasant, conversational tone of voice that made it almost impossible to take in the full horror of his words. "Of course, you're that much younger than she was, so I suppose that would make a difference. I'm an idiot. I should have taken that into consideration."

"I – I don't understand," I said weakly. "What are you talking about?"

"The dose of sleeping draught I gave you was the same as the one I gave Doreen before I killed her. But never mind, it looks as if it's working now. There's no rush. I can wait."

As he was speaking, his usually bland, expressionless face was transformed by a hideous smile.

Chapter Twenty-Five

I stared up at him in horror. Donald? Dippy Donald, the dull as ditchwater landlord who always faded into the background, was a murderer? Maybe even a double murderer? Surely not. It was far more likely that he was one of those sad people who confessed to crimes they hadn't committed in a bid to get attention. He couldn't even kill a spider and only last week had spent ages trying to persuade one that had been lurking in the bar to climb on to a piece of paper, before carrying it safely outside.

"I don't believe you," I said. "You wouldn't—"

"Have the nerve? Is that what you think?" There was an edge to his voice that hadn't been there before. Wild. A little manic. It sent a shiver down my spine. "Which politician was it who said 'never underestimate the determination of a quiet man'? Well, whoever it was, that's me. The quiet man who is very, very determined."

"You're saying you killed Doreen? What about Marjorie? Was that down to you as well?" I asked. "But you said – you said it was Gerald. So how? Why?"

He still had the same scary smile on his face. "I suppose I may as well tell you. It's not like you're going anywhere. So you might as well listen to a nice bedtime story while you're falling asleep. Are you sitting comfortably? Then I'll begin. Once upon a time, there was a nosy old witch, who went around the village making trouble for everyone she met. But one day, she went too far and made trouble for the wrong person. Because that person was very clever and he had a cunning plan."

"You're mad," I whispered. How stupid was I? Naive, gullible and stupid, stupid, stupid. I glanced across at my phone, just out of my reach.

"Damn right I was mad," he said. "Hopping mad. Time was critical, you see. I had just ten weeks, that's how long Joyce's cruise was, to put my plan in hand. And it would have worked, too, if it hadn't been for that nosy old bat. And if Gerald had held his nerve. But never mind. A good plan allows for the unexpected. It can still work."

"Gerald? Then he wasn't the murderer?"

Donald's laugh was no less manic the second time. "He's a lily-livered fool who loses his nerve at the first sign of trouble."

"Whereas you...?"

"Whereas I am clever and resourceful and take my chances when they present themselves. Marjorie Hampton was about to ruin everything I'd worked for. Interfering old baggage. She'd found out Gerald was getting inside information from his contact in the planning department—"

"Doreen Spetchley," I said before I could stop myself. So, Liam had been right about that. "His contact was Doreen Spetchley, wasn't it? So they weren't having an affair?"

Donald grinned. "Well, let's put it this way. She thought they were. The silly creature actually believed him when he said that the money was for their new life together. Pathetic." He tossed back the last of his drink. "Anyway, she'd given Gerald the nod a few times. People in the planning office get to hear about upcoming deals long before they get as far as making a formal application for planning permission, and Gerald has had some nice little earners from that source over the years, I can tell you. And I'd just persuaded him to let me in on it, when Marjorie got wind of it and was threatening to ruin everything. So I got Gerald to arrange a meeting with her up at Pendle Knoll that afternoon."

I didn't want to hear any more. But, on the other hand, I didn't want him to stop talking either. Because I didn't want to think about what was going to happen when he did.

"So it was Gerald who Marjorie was going to meet, after she'd seen John Manning," I said. "Gerald who'd got her dander up, as she'd put it?"

"Exactly. Only, of course, I was going to keep the

appointment instead of him. He'd never have had the nerve to do what had to be done, even though he was more than happy to take his cut of the proceeds. Whereas I not only had the nerve, but the resourcefulness too. I'd taken this," he leant down by the fireplace and picked up a large, heavy iron poker. I shrank away as he waved it at me, "And planned for her to have a little accident. But when I passed the Manning farm, and heard her and John Manning going at it hammer and tongs, I couldn't believe my luck. I'd been wondering what to do with her body and suddenly, John Manning had handed me the solution on a plate – or, to be strictly accurate, a freezer."

"Poor, poor Marjorie." I gave a little whimper as the ever-present image of Marjorie, face down in that freezer, flashed into my mind. "But how did you get her body to the farm shop? Surely someone would have seen you?"

"Stupid, interfering Majorie, more like," he snorted. "John Manning had run up a pretty big bar bill and, a couple of weeks earlier, had given me a spare key to the farm shop and told me to go in any time I was passing and help myself to anything I could find in the freezers up there in lieu of payment. I'd been steadily emptying that freezer of its contents for weeks."

I remembered Will wondering how, when there was scarcely enough money to pay for feed for the livestock, his father had a seemingly endless supply of whisky. Now, of course, I knew.

"Win, win," Donald chuckled. "I got unlimited free meat for the restaurant and he got a supply of whisky. Of course, it was only some cheap, duty free rubbish that I wouldn't dare sell over the bar, but John wasn't bothered what he drank. That was yet another little scam of Gerald's, you know. Only this time with Shane Freeman."

"Duty free alcohol and cigarettes. That, according to you, Gerald blackmailed you into selling in the pub for a cut in the profits."

He laughed. "It makes for a convincing story, doesn't it? That was something else Marjorie was kicking up about, you know. Frightened Gerald to death when she said she was going to the police. As for Shane Freeman, the pathetic idiot was going frantic. According to Gerald, he actually went to her house to beg her not to say anything. But luckily, I got to her first."

That would have been when Amy's mum saw Shane, I supposed. He never was the brightest button in the box. But he was no murderer. Unlike the man standing in front of me.

"I was in Pendle Drove, which as you know goes past the Manning farm," he went on. "We'd been going to meet at the old stone barn to 'discuss' the proposed new development that Gerald and I were involved in. Somehow Marjorie had found out about it and was threatening to make a fuss. As you know, the drove leads directly to the site and Gerald was pretty sure Planning would agree to it being made into an access road for the new development."

"But that's a public bridle way," I protested. "They can't do that. Besides, that would bring all the traffic for the site past the school. The council would never pass it."

"You reckon?" He gave a short laugh. "You'd be surprised what can be achieved with a bit of judicious palm-greasing. Besides, nobody used the drove any more, particularly since Gerald drove his 4x4 up and down there a few times and turned it into a quagmire. It's totally impassable in places now. I have to give him due credit there. It was quite a clever move. Keeps the nosy parkers away. Apart from one, of course. She wanted to meet Gerald in the drove, intending to have a go at him about the terrible state John Manning had got it into, and insisting that the council force him to restore it. She was still ranting on about it when I met up with her after she'd finished lecturing Manning."

"You met her there, intending to kill her?' I shuddered. How cold-blooded could you get?

He nodded. "That was my original plan. But when I heard them rowing, I had a better idea. I told her that Gerald was involved in the plan to turn the drove into an access road, that it was Gerald who had trashed the drove and that John Manning had found out about it. She swallowed it hook, line and sinker. I went on to say that Manning had agreed to meet us at the farm shop, where he'd give us evidence that would implicate Gerald. I was able to show her the key that Manning had given me and of course, she agreed to come to the farm shop with me like a shot."

"Poor, poor Marjorie," I murmured again. My brain had frozen. It was the only thing I could think of. Poor, poor Marjorie.

"Poor Marjorie, my eye," he snorted. "Interfering old cow, more like it. I'd used every penny I had to buy that land. When it goes through, which will be any day now they've got the access sorted, I'll be away from this miserable place and my miserable wife faster than you can say knife. Have you any idea what it's like to be married to someone like Joyce? She's the one with the money, you know, and there isn't a day goes by where she doesn't remind me of that fact."

"But you could have just left her. There's no need to—" I looked at him, my eyes full of horror. "Oh God, you haven't killed her as well, have you?"

He shook his head. "Not yet. But it may well come to that. Now I'm getting the hang of it, as it were. Drugs are wonderful, don't you agree? Doreen just went to sleep and didn't know a thing about it. It was all very humane."

I shifted uncomfortably in my chair. There was no doubt the man was as mad as a box of frogs, but he was clever with it. He'd played the part of an unremarkable, grey man to perfection. While all the time, inside, he was a cold, calculating monster who'd stop at nothing to get what he wanted.

"Marjorie walked into that farm shop like a lamb to the slaughter," he chortled. "Get it? Lamb to the slaughter? And you'll never guess what I hit her with?"

"The poker?" I said, unable to take my eyes off it.

"Wrong. It made me laugh when I heard about the amount of time the police spent looking for the murder weapon. Do you remember that brilliant Roald Dahl story where this woman murdered her husband by hitting him over the head with a frozen leg of lamb, which she then cooked and served up to the policemen who came to investigate? It would have been perfect," Donald went on. "I'd planned to tip her into one of the freezers and, chances are, it would have been months, maybe even years before she was found. But, unfortunately, someone came along and tried the door, just at the wrong time."

"That would have been John," I said, but he wasn't listening.

"I had to leave her there, half in, half out, and leg it." He laughed again, like he was having the time of his life. "Do you get it, Katie? I said 'leg it'. And I did just that. Legged it with the leg of lamb I'd bashed her over the head with, and cooked it, here in the pub. Just like in that story. Went down a treat as the next day's special, if you remember. The pub was heaving."

I felt sick as I remembered the night after Marjorie's body had been found. How busy the bar and restaurant had been. How the lovely smell of roast lamb had filled the entire pub.

I didn't want to think about roast lamb any more. In fact, I didn't think I'd ever be able to eat it again, even if I got out of here alive. Time, I reckoned, for a change of subject.

"But why did you kill Doreen? What did she ever do to you?"

"That was Gerald's fault. I told you he was a lily-livered fool, didn't I? He'd been keeping her sweet for years and, over that time, she'd come up with some pretty good stuff for him, including that supermarket development in Dintscombe. He made a right killing there. I overheard him boasting about it one night and told him that I wanted in on the next one, or else. Well, he caved in, of course, and this one, that I was telling you about behind the old barn, that's going to be huge and earn us both enough shedloads of money. Enough to take me a long, long way away from here. Trouble was, Doreen was getting cold feet and told Gerald she wanted out. Gerald lost his head and tried to break things off with her, stupid idiot. Because that just made her more determined than ever to blow the whistle." He broke off and looked at me closely. "How come you're still awake? Maybe you should have another glass of malt. One for the road, as it were."

"N-not really awake," I slurred, my words stumbling over each other. "V-very s-sleepy."

"Thank God for that. Because I'm afraid, my dear, story time is almost over. The wicked witch is dead. So, too, the ugly old stepsister. And, any day now, I shall be living happily ever after. While you, I'm afraid…"

"Wh-what are you going to do with me?" I managed to ask. "Not… farm shop freezers. Still… still c-crawling with police."

"Didn't I say I had it all planned? This pub has a very old cellar with a nice old-fashioned dirt floor. How convenient is that? And no one will come looking for you here. Particularly as you told the boyfriend you were never here."

"D – don't like s-spiders," I managed to say, my leaden eyelids closing, as I slid down in the chair.

Chapter Twenty-Six

"That's it." He lunged forward, grabbed my arm and peered closely at me. "You're looking nice and sleepy now. Don't fight it, Katie. It'll be easier—"

He didn't get any further. That's because it's a bit difficult to talk when you're suddenly face down on the floor, with one arm twisted behind you and a knee in the small of your back.

"What a pity you didn't want to see my CV when I came to work for you," I said, a little breathlessly. "You'd have seen that I learnt judo at college. In fact, I was actually quite good at it and competed at county level. Of course, I'm a bit of of practice now, but can still do the moves when I have to."

Another thing I forgot to mention was that my Media Studies course had included a drama module, and one of the things we'd been taught was how to make it look like you're drinking when you're not. Useful when you're on stage and don't want to splutter cold tea over your fellow actors.

I'd used the trick to pretend I was drinking the malt whisky Donald poured for me, although I didn't think Sparky, the dusty old spider plant on the counter behind me, would ever recover from being drowned in Donald's finest malt whisky. That first sip had tasted so awful I couldn't bear to drink any more, but hadn't wanted to hurt Donald's feelings by saying so.

Weird to think that small politeness may well have saved my life. He must have put enough in to knock out a horse, as the tiny amount I'd drunk had begun to affect me, although I had, of course, exaggerated my symptoms when I began to suspect what he was up to, in the hope that it would put him off guard.

And it had worked beautifully. Except for one small thing. What the hell did I do now? Ok, Donald couldn't move. But neither could I.

My phone was on the counter, tucked away behind the spider plant. I'd like to have said I'd had my suspicions about Donald right from the start and had put it there, left on record, in the hope that he would incriminate himself. Nothing so perceptive, I'm afraid. I left it there when I thought he was going to spill the beans on Gerald. After the trouble I'd had trying to remember who'd said what at the Parish Council meeting the other night, I hadn't wanted to trust to my memory. Hence the recording, which was still going.

It was a good plan. The only problem was that the phone was now way out of my reach. So to summon help, I'd have to release my hold on his arm.

The front door was locked and the back door looked miles away. If I made a dash for it, he'd get me before I reached it. And – this was the bit that terrified me – he was a whole lot closer to that lethal-looking poker than I was, and I knew for certain he wouldn't hesitate to use it.

What I needed now, I thought desperately, as he wriggled, squirmed and cursed beneath me, was a minor miracle. Correction: what I needed now was a major miracle. John Wayne swooping over the horizon with the cavalry would be good.

Then, as if someone up there had been listening, there came a loud banging on the front door.

"'Help me!" I yelled. "Come round the back! Quickly."

After what seemed a lifetime, the back door crashed open. It wasn't John Wayne who stood there, but Gerald Crabshaw. I groaned and slackened my hold on Donald's arm, as I realised it was all over for me. A numbness swept over me, which was the only thing that stopped me breaking down and sobbing for my mum.

I didn't resist as Gerald pulled me away. All the fight had left me and I slumped to the floor.

"I'm so sorry, Katie," he said. "I tried to warn you—"

"Keep her there, Crabshaw," Donald panted as he scrabbled towards the poker. "While I…"

His words ended in a yell of pain as Will's boot came down

hard on Donald's outstretched arm. Thank God. Not the cavalry after all, but something much, much better. Will.

Where had he come from? I could only think he'd come in behind Gerald. And thank goodness he had. Talk about perfect timing. If I'd been the sort to swoon, I would surely have swooned then. Instead, I pushed Gerald away and snatched up the poker.

"Ok, you. Get over there and don't move,' I said. "I'm calling the police."

"There's no need," Gerald said. "They're on their way. I'd already called them when I saw Will. Please, Katie, put that thing down. I'm on your side. Ask Will."

"Well, I would," I said, never letting the poker drop for one second. "But he's a bit busy with your partner in crime at the moment. So stay back."

"Will. Tell her please," Gerald said. "Tell her how I drove up to your farm and asked you to come down to the pub with me because she was in danger."

Will had, by now, got Donald face down on the floor again. But this time, Donald must have known he was well beaten for he made no attempt to struggle free, probably because to do so would result in a dislocated shoulder. Or worse.

"He's telling the truth," Will said. "I must admit, I thought he'd flipped or something. Couldn't make head nor tail of what he was saying. But when he said you were in danger, I thought I'd better come along and check it out. Just in case. Even though you'd told me you were going to see Elsie Flintlock, which I didn't believe for a moment. I always could tell when you were lying."

"No you couldn't, because I never lie," I said.

"Oh really? What about the time…"

"Ok. Ok. Let's leave it at that. And thank goodness you came." I had, by this time, started to shake as the reaction set in. "Oh God, Will," I managed as my teeth started to chatter. "He – he was going to kill me, you know."

Donald screamed as Will gave his arm an extra-hard tug.

"Please, Will. Don't," I begged. "There's been more than enough violence around here and I really don't think I can stand any more. If, as you say, the police are on the way…"

"I called them," Gerald said, his voice shrill with barely controlled hysteria. "I want you to know that. I never meant things to get this far, and when you told me just now that Doreen's death hadn't been an accident, I knew I had to put a stop to it."

I rounded on him, chattering teeth forgotten as I raised the poker once again. "You didn't try very hard," I hissed. "Just shouted something after me, then drove off. And you were part of the plan to get me here in the first place, weren't you? All that talk about giving me a story of the century? That was just a ploy to get me here so that Donald here could…"

"I thought he was just going to frighten you into leaving things alone," Gerald said. "That's what he said. But after you told me about Doreen, I tried to stop you coming in here, Katie. Just you remember that. So I drove off to get help," he glanced at his watch. "I told the police it was urgent. I – I had nothing to do with those women's deaths, you know. I didn't know what he'd done. He just said he was going to sort Marjorie out. I – I thought he meant he had some dirt on her and was going to blackmail her into backing off. That's how he got to me, you know. Blackmail."

"Shut up, you fool," Donald snarled.

"You've called me a fool for the last time," Gerald said, turning on him. "When the police get here I'm going to tell them everything. You see, at first, I really believed John Manning had killed Marjorie – I'm sorry about that, Will – but when Katie told me they'd let him go, I started thinking about how Donald had gone up to Pendle Drove that afternoon to meet her, although he said she never turned up. So I came to the pub to challenge him."

"That would be when Elsie Flintlock overheard you," I said. "Donald told her that you'd been running up a bar bill. And that was what you'd had words about."

"Which is nothing but the truth," Donald said, although his voice was a bit muffled. "Look, Will, let me up, will you, so that I can explain? It's not fair that this crook should be allowed to push the blame on to me. And after all, I'm not going anywhere, am I?"

"Too right you're not," Will said, as he let Donald move into a sitting position.

"Thanks." He glared up at Gerald. "Let's face it, Crabshaw, you're the one who's been breaking the law here, with your dodgy land deals. What was it? Did Doreen Spetchley threaten to blow the whistle on you? The way that Marjorie Hampton did?"

"How dare you try and pin it on me?" Gerald protested, his face scarlet. "I'll own up to the property scams, yes. And the duty free stuff. But as for the rest of it—"

"As for the rest of it, it's my word against yours," Donald said smoothly.

"Hardly," I said. "There's the small matter of you trying to drug me. I'm sure the police will find traces of whatever it was you slipped into my drink in that poor plant over there, which is where, luckily for me, most of it ended up. And then, of course, there's this. I recorded every word you said."

I reached behind the plant and took out my phone.

"I always said you were a bright girl, Katie Latcham," Gerald said, but I ignored him and focussed on Donald, who was staring at me with such venom, I felt like something cold and slimy had just crept down my spine.

"It's all here." I forced myself not to flinch under that malevolent gaze. "About how you killed Marjorie. And, of course, your little bedtime story about the frozen leg of lamb. Remember? Not to mention what you did to poor Doreen. Do you want to listen to it while we wait for the police?"

As it turned out, there wasn't time, as I was interrupted by the sound of approaching sirens.

Will, still holding Donald, turned to me and smiled. Big, solid dependable Will, with his rugby player shoulders and gloriously sexy blue eyes. Why had I never noticed them in that way before? And what on earth was I doing thinking about it now, of all times?

***

Will and I stood, side by side, and watched as the police cars drove away, Donald, stony-faced and silent in one and Gerald, talking his head off in the other.

"The policeman was quite right, you know," he said.

"Do you mean Ben Newton?"

"I mean the one who said you were all sorts of an idiot for getting yourself in this situation in the first place." He glared at me and shook his head. "Honestly, Katie, I could…"

"It's Kat. And he didn't call me an idiot. In fact, if you remember, he said it was very resourceful of me to record Donald the way I did."

"He was only saying that because he fancies you," Will said. "And I do remember him from school now. Geeky kid with glasses. I think he fancied you back then, and all."

"Don't be ridiculous, Will." I wasn't in the mood for his teasing.

"Anyway, if he didn't call you an idiot, that's what he meant," he growled. Then he took my hand and turned to face me, his gorgeous sexy blue eyes unusually serious. "When I think what could have happened. If I hadn't been in the yard when Gerald arrived. If we'd been a few minutes later getting here. If…"

Gently, I took my hand from his and placed it on his lips to stop him. I didn't want to think about what might have happened. Didn't want to go any further down that particular road. Not now. Not ever.

"But you were there," I said, my voice husky. "You were there for me, just like you've always been."

"Just like I always will be."

My breath caught in my throat, my fingers where they rested on his mouth, felt as if they were melting. What was going on here? This was Will, remember? My almost brother. The guy who moaned at me, teased me and used to call me Scaredy Cat, who'd tied my plaits to the back of my chair. The guy with the sexy blue eyes and the most kissable mouth I'd ever seen.

Why had I not noticed that before? If I took my hand away and lifted my head just a fraction...

It was the sweetest, the gentlest, the most un-brotherly kiss, that turned my knees to water and left me clinging to him, scarcely able to breathe. I murmured a protest as he pulled away, his eyes questioning. Was I sure? I'd never been more sure about anything in my life. All that rubbish, about how weird it would be to kiss the man I'd grown up thinking of as my brother, was just that. Rubbish.

Certainly there was nothing remotely sisterly about the way I answered his unspoken question by wrapping both arms around the back of his neck and kissing him back. Only this time, the kiss was deeper, more urgent, and wiped everything else from my mind.

I forgot about Donald and his murderous ways, about Gerald and his dodgy land deals. Shane with his iffy duty frees. Even about my mum and dad and what they'd say when they found out about my part in Donald's arrest. With Will's arms around me, I felt safe and comforted. Like I'd come home. And it felt so, so good.

Until I remembered what Jules had told me.

"The vet," I said, as I pulled away.

"What?" He looked dazed, like I'd just roused him from a deep sleep.

"Your sexy Swedish vet. Jules told me that you and she…"

He laughed. "Anneka is in her mid-forties and happily married to Sven. I think Jules may have been winding you up. Why do you ask? Were you jealous?"

"What, me? No, of course not. It was just that I—" I broke off, looked up at that very kissable mouth again, and decided it was time for the truth – even though it had taken me for ever to realise it was the truth. "Of course I was jealous, you oaf."

"Good," he said and rewarded my honesty by bending down to kiss me again. "Now you know how I felt when I saw you with that smooth Irishman. And as for…"

"Well, and here was me thinking I'd missed all the excitement," Elsie Flintlock's voice made us both whirl round. "About time, too. I must say, Will Manning I was beginning to despair of you."

"Oh God," I groaned as I watched Elsie bustle off, cackling

away to herself, no doubt in a hurry to be the first with the story. "That'll be all round the village in a nanosecond."

"Do you mind?" Will asked, his arms still around me.

I shook her head. Why would I? Everything was more than all right with my world now. Donald and Gerald were helping the police with their enquiries. Shane Freeman was going to have to answer some awkward questions. I had a brilliant story to take to the editor tomorrow. And I'd lost an 'almost' brother and gained gorgeous, sexy Will, who was without doubt the best kisser on the planet.

The only tiny cloud on my horizon was how to convince my mum that I never, ever wanted to eat roast lamb ever again.

THE END

Fantastic Books
Great Authors

darkstroke is
an imprint of
Crooked Cat Books

- Gripping Thrillers
- Cosy Mysteries
- Romantic Chick-Lit
- Fascinating Historicals
- Exciting Fantasy
- Young Adult and Children's
  Adventures
- Non-Fiction

Made in the USA
Coppell, TX
29 August 2021

61430604R00139